Praise for the authors of
SNOWFLAKES AND STETSONS

JILLIAN HART

"A lovely Americana romance, this book's intense emotions reach
out to touch readers. Betsy's unwavering belief in Duncan and
willingness to fight to save him from himself is so moving you'll
want to cry with happiness as Hart plays on your heartstrings."
—*RT Book Reviews* on *Rocky Mountain Man*

"Ms. Hart creates a world of tantalizing warmth and tenderness, a
toasty haven in which the reader will find pure enjoyment."
—*RT Book Reviews* on *Montana Man*

CAROL FINCH

"Finch has made her reputation on wonderfully realistic
and humorous westerns filled with biting repartee
and nonstop action. She's at her finest with this
action-packed tale of a lawman and a spitfire."
—*RT Book Reviews* on *Bandit Lawman, Texas Bride*

"Finch offers another heartwarming western romance
full of suspense, humor and strong characters."
—*RT Book Reviews* on *Texas Ranger, Runaway Heiress*

CHERYL ST.JOHN

"St.John's strong yet sweet romance is peopled by characters
readers will care about…the lesson St.John teaches in the subplot
about abuse…touches the heart."
—*RT Book Reviews* on *Her Colorado Man*

"Ms. St.John knows what the readers want and keeps on giving it."
—*Rendezvous*

JILLIAN HART

grew up on her family's homestead, where she raised cattle, rode horses and scribbled stories in her spare time. After earning an English degree from Whitman College, she worked in advertizing before selling her first novel to Harlequin® Historical. When she's not hard at work on her next story, Jillian can be found chatting over lunch with a friend, stopping for a café mocha with a book in hand and spending quiet evenings at home with her family. Visit her website, www.jillianhart.net.

CAROL FINCH

who also writes as Gina Robins, Debra Falcon, Connie Drake and Connie Feddersen has penned more than seventy novels in the historical romance, contemporary, mystery and romance suspense genres. A former tennis pro and high school biology instructor, Ms. Finch devotes herself full-time to writing and working on the family's cattle ranch in Oklahoma.

CHERYL ST.JOHN

remembers writing and illustrating her own books as a child. She received her first rejection at age fourteen, and at fifteen wrote her first romance. A married mother of four, and a grandmother several times over, Cheryl enjoys her family. In her spare time, she corresponds with dozens of writer friends, from Canada to Texas, and treasures their letters. You can visit her at www.cherylstjohn.net.

SNOWFLAKES AND STETSONS

Western Christmas Wishes

JILLIAN HART

CAROL FINCH

CHERYL ST.JOHN

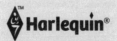

TORONTO NEW YORK LONDON
AMSTERDAM PARIS SYDNEY HAMBURG
STOCKHOLM ATHENS TOKYO MILAN MADRID
PRAGUE WARSAW BUDAPEST AUCKLAND

ISBN-13: 978-0-373-29659-0

SNOWFLAKES AND STETSONS
Copyright © 2011 by Harlequin Books S.A.

The publisher acknowledges the copyright holders of the individual works as follows:

THE COWBOY'S CHRISTMAS MIRACLE
Copyright © 2011 by Jill Strickler

CHRISTMAS AT CAHILL CROSSING
Copyright © 2011 by Connie Feddersen

A MAGICAL GIFT AT CHRISTMAS
Copyright © 2011 by Cheryl Ludwigs

Recycling programs
for this product may
not exist in your area.

www.Harlequin.com

Printed in U.S.A.

CONTENTS

THE COWBOY'S CHRISTMAS MIRACLE

Jillian Hart

Dear Reader,

The Cowboy's Christmas Miracle is a story that has been in my heart for many years, longing to be told. Caroline, a young widow who is grieving the deaths of her husband and child, takes in her best friend's illegitimate son, Thomas. Which means both she and Thomas are grieving different loves lost when a stranger bursts into their lives.

Caleb McGraw is a man full of secrets, marked by injustice and has newly discovered he has a son—little Thomas. All he wants is to see the boy, but he is pulled in by Caroline's kindness.

Is her love enough to heal his wounded heart? Or will his secrets destroy any chance of them becoming a family?

I hope you enjoy this Christmas tale of the redeeming power of love. Thank you so much for choosing Caroline and Caleb's story.

Wishing you a loving and beautiful Christmas,

Jillian Hart

Chapter One

Montana Territory, December 16, 1883

Cold rain fell from a steel-gray sky as Caleb McGraw swept off his battered, wide-brimmed hat. A symphony of raindrops pattered on decaying leaves and plopped on fallow grasses, his only company as he approached the simple wooden cross at the head of the grave. Someone had etched the name Alma Kent into the wood. His knees buckled but he kept on walking until his boots reached the faint line that marked where the ground had once been disturbed. Sadness chilled him like the gust of the icy wind.

Hard to believe she was gone. Truth was, he'd forgotten what she looked like. The detail of the woman's face he'd once loved had faded, leaving only a dim memory of a woman with apple cheeks and brown curls. Alma had recently died but he'd been dead to her the moment a territorial marshal had dragged him off to prison. Rage still burned in his chest at the old injustice but he'd learned the hard way fury did a man no good. Life was full of unfairness and betrayal and loss. Especially loss. He bowed his head, wishing he had flowers to put on her grave.

"Alma don't get visitors." A grizzled, rough voice rang

above the rhythmic raindrops and the whir of the December wind. "As far as I know, you'd be the first."

"How long exactly has she been gone?" He rose from his knees with solemn resignation. Best to brace himself for whatever attitude or judgment would be coming his way. He'd gotten used to it the past ten days since he'd been released from prison. He never should have come home.

But he didn't know the old man who limped over. Gnarled by arthritis, the cemetery caretaker swiped rain off his brow with his patched coat sleeve. "It's been nigh on four months, maybe more."

No one had written him. No one had told him. His only cousin had disowned him, slamming the door in his face when he'd knocked. Old friends had turned from him on the street, so they hadn't been inclined to give him the latest news. But Alma's grandmother could have told him. When he'd walked into her parlor, the woman could have said more than the simple fact her granddaughter had passed away. The lash of the grandmother's anger still stung like a whip mark.

It's your fault, Caleb McGraw, you lowlife. Your fault and none other's. You sentenced my girl to shame.

He didn't know what that meant. Perhaps Alma had felt humiliated for having once accepted a convict's marriage proposal.

"Such a pity. She was young. Barely twenty-four years old." The man limped closer, eager to talk. "How did you know the young lady?"

"We grew up together. I'm back home visiting." That was true enough. His hopes of finding remnants of his old life had died one by one. He couldn't stay in Blue Grass. He would be moving on before nightfall. He had no notion where.

"Then you musta jest heard the news of her passing. I'm awful sorry." The old man's mouth and unkempt white beard wobbled as if with sorrow. "It's a shame what happened to her. I hear some fella proposed to her but got her into trouble afore the wedding rolled around."

"Into trouble?" He clamped his back molars down hard. That wasn't right, that wasn't the way events had unfolded. He had been arrested, not Alma.

"The fella got hisself thrown in jail, the lowlife. Left her in a family way." The man shook his head as if it were the worst shame he'd heard of.

A family way? The air whooshed out of his lungs and his heart stalled in his chest. Ice spilled into his veins as he took in those words. A family way. She'd been pregnant? Just one time and she'd conceived their child?

"Cute little young'un, too." Sadness softened the judgment in the old man's words. "Jest a true shame."

He died a little as he glanced at the neighboring graves. "Did the child pass away of diphtheria, too?"

The rain drummed harder, driven by a merciless wind. He saw a cross, a miniature version of the one bearing Alma's name. He broke inside, wondering if that was their child. Why hadn't Alma written to tell him? It would have taken one letter, one sentence, just a few words to let him know. The shock brought him to his knees. He hit the ground hard enough to rattle his bones.

"Was a near thing, but the little one made it." The caretaker squinted with an expression that was half worry, half dread. "You ain't havin' some sort of spell, are you, young man? I kin fetch the doc."

"No, I just didn't know." A little one. A child who still lived. He felt hollowed out, empty. Whatever softness lived within him had died years ago. His heart, his soul, that essence that had made him who he was had been stripped away during seven long years of hard labor and harder treatment. "Where is the child now?"

"He's off with some friend of the family."

"He?"

"The wife might know. She's a gossipy sort." The old man smiled and grabbed hold of Caleb's elbow. "My cottage is over yonder. A shot of whiskey ought to put the starch back in yer knees."

It would take an entire bottle but Caleb bit his lip, climbed to his feet and took one last look at Alma's grave. Had she been too ashamed of him to tell him about their baby? Or too angry? He would never know.

You ruined your life for good, Caleb. Worse, he'd tarnished Alma's. Her grandmother's words made sense. She would have been unmarriageable and in a small town like this, she would have been all but shunned. He felt sick and broken to the core. Nothing he could ever do would erase the harm caused by one impulsive act. As cold inside as the winter rain, he followed the caretaker around graves and crumbling crosses. He thought of the harm he'd done, intentionally or not.

The heartless beat of the rain intensified, striking the earth with a vengeance, striking him. He had a child. A son. Caleb digested that, swallowing hard past the painful lump bunching in his throat. A child, come hell or high water, he intended to see.

Caroline Dreyer cracked an egg on the bowl's rim and carefully broke the shell. Yoke and whites cascaded onto the flour mixture with a plop. Her attention wasn't on her baking on this last Sunday afternoon before Christmas but on the boy standing at the front window. His hands gripped the sill, dark hair tousled, cowlick sticking straight up. Sorrow radiated from the child with the same strength of grief alive in her heart. Both her and the boy were mourning different loves and different lives lost.

The image of a spacious kitchen with two large windows, a laughing husband and a bubbly baby flashed unbidden into her mind, a picture too painful to look at. Sorrow lashed her and she pressed the images down until they were nothing but darkness. Best to stay in the here and now. Looking back or ahead was unbearable, but she'd been able to survive four years now by taking one moment at a time.

"It's starting to snow." Fat white flakes fell in a straight descent in front of the windows where a few moments ago it had been the dreary gray streaks of rain. "Did you want to bundle up and play outside?"

No answer. Thomas shrugged his shoulders. Was the child remembering the way his life used to be? Knowing how it felt to wish for the past, she wiped her fingers on a towel, abandoned her bowl on the table and circled around the sofa. Heat from the stone fireplace chased away the chill in the air.

The flames crackled merrily in the hearth, serenading her as she knelt down beside the boy. At this lower vantage, the snow looked magical tumbling from sky to earth like promises in a fairy tale. She wished a little of that magic could touch the sad little boy she'd tried so hard to reach, although it was hard not to look at the child and remember her son. Had Mathias lived, he would have been six years old, too.

"When I was a girl, we would try to catch snowflakes on our tongues. The first snowfall of the year always tasted best." She smiled at the memory of three dozen girls laughing and rushing to slip into their wraps and squeeze out the doorway into the yard. Growing up in an orphanage had been hard, but they had been a family of sorts and Alma Kent had been her sister not by any blood tie but by bonds too powerful to break. That was why she'd honored the wishes in Alma's letter and taken the child.

Thomas, so still, so small, hadn't moved a muscle. She could feel him straining to listen, perhaps hoping for a story of his mother. She knew what it was like to yearn after those who were lost, so she gave him what comfort she could.

"Your mama had a bright red knit hat and scarf and she used to put her arms straight out, tilt her head back and twirl round and round in the falling snow. Pure white flakes would shower all over her and she would try to catch them with her tongue. She caught the most of any of us." Almost twenty years ago, the image came as bright and clear as if it had happened yesterday. The long ago love she felt for her honorary sister burned in memory. "I suppose boys don't do things like that, but judging by the rate the snow is falling there's enough to make snowballs to throw. Soon, there will be enough for a snowman."

"Okay." The boy remained statue still, wrapped in sadness. Was he remembering last Christmas season with his ma and his great-grandmother? There was nothing like the cozy feeing of being loved and wanted. She wished with every fiber of her being she could give him the same security. She wanted to reach out but she could not cross the void her heart had become.

The biscuit batter needed mixing, so she left the boy to watch the magical white flakes swish and swirl as a light wind blew in. Her shoes made an echo through the small log cabin.

"Aunt Caroline?" Thomas's solemn voice drew her back. "What is that man doing with our horse?"

"What man?" She squinted through the snow, following the direction of Thomas's finger. A man's shadow broke out of the haze near her small stable, leading a horse by the reins. Her horse! Kringle shook his head, trying to break free and stomped a front hoof. The gelding didn't like strangers.

Alarm shot through her. She grabbed a chair, leaped onto it and seized the old rifle from the pegs above the door.

"Stay inside. Do you understand me?" She slid a cartridge into the chamber and threw the bolt. "I need your promise, Thomas."

Owl-eyed, the boy nodded as he trembled slightly. "Will you come back?"

"It will be all right." She whipped open the sagging door and stalked out into the bitter cold. Her breath rose in great puffs as she raised the gun and lined up the notch in the barrel with the man wrestling her disgruntled gelding.

"You had best walk away from that horse, mister." Fear made her voice shivery, betraying her. Had the ruffian heard it?

"I don't take orders from a woman." The horse thief spit out a stream of tobacco juice.

"I'm an *armed* woman," she corrected. "I'll shoot if I have to." She squared her shoulders. "Back away from my gelding."

"Fat chance. You won't do it, lady. A frilly thing like you don't have what it takes to kill a man." Disdain curled his upper lip as he mounted up. "Put the gun down. Just go back to your baking."

How had he known what she'd been doing? A shiver quaked through her. It radiated outward until her teeth chattered. The gun began to shake, too. He'd been spying on them? What if he'd wanted more than the horse?

Just do it, Caroline. Stop him. Take a breath and pull the trigger. She willed her arms to stop shaking, planted her feet. But the storm closed in like a veil between her and her target. He became a shadow that faded away, lost in the white.

"I'd do what the lady says." A different voice boomed like winter thunder through the snow. Threat rang in that deep baritone along with a power that made Caroline shake again. Her gun slipped down, nose first, to rest on the snowy porch.

What was happening? She couldn't see anything. Footsteps crunched in the snow. She heard a faint scuffle. Kringle's neigh. Something fell to the ground in front of the steps, a man's shadowed form. It was the horse thief trussed up like a captured pig.

"Go on inside, ma'am. I'll stable your horse."

The white-out conditions stole her rescuer from view. Who was he and where had he come from? She thought of her neighbors, soft spoken men and middle aged. This stranger's voice rang with the force of a man in his prime. She batted snowflakes from her face and eyelashes. "Excuse me, but do I know you?"

"No. I'm just someone passing through."

"Then I'm doubly grateful. It's not every stranger who will help another stranger in need."

"It was the decent thing to do. That's all." He knocked snow off his hat, fighting the instinct to step away from the woman. Was this the right house?

It had to be. When he'd asked a clerk when he'd first ridden into the little town of Moose if she knew Caroline Dreyer, the kindly lady had given him detailed directions. This was the fifth home south of town, but this woman wore no wedding band. No sign of a husband anywhere. Alma wouldn't have given their son to an unmarried woman, would she?

"I don't know how to thank you for what you've done. You saved Kringle. He could have been long gone with that thief and I never would have seen him again." She edged closer to the crooked rail. A loose board squeaked beneath her shoe.

Definitely a dainty slip of a female. Willowy, feminine, innocent-looking. Not at all what he'd expected. He holstered his old Colt .45. "Next time, don't hesitate. I know it's a hard thing to pull that trigger, but horse stealing is a hanging offense in this territory. There's no telling what a man that desperate might do, as well."

"I always thought I could fire this rifle if I had to." She shrugged, apologetic, grateful, and the door opened wider. Light tumbled onto her, turning her from a shadowy impression into living color. Gold hair, pink calico and a perfect heart-shaped face. She was the prettiest sight he'd ever seen.

A movement in the doorway behind her grabbed his attention. A child crept into the threshold, beheld by lamplight. Big blue eyes stared up at him. Round button face, vulnerable, the boy broke his heart into pieces.

His son.

A rush of love hit him harder than the leading edge of a Montana blizzard. His legs buckled and he grabbed the rickety rail for support, breathing hard. His son, alive and well, stared at him with a hint of fear.

"Aunt Caroline?" he asked with a tremble. "Who is that?"

"I don't know," the woman answered. "But he just saved Kringle for us."

"I saw. That other man tried to steal him."

"Yes. Just when I'd come to believe there wasn't a chivalrous man left in the world, you came along." She gazed at him with kindness. "I'm Caroline and this is Thomas. And you are?"

"Caleb McGraw." His throat closed up. That was all he could get out. It had been so long since anyone had looked at him kindly. Not like a criminal, not like a convict. He took a step back already knowing he didn't belong here, but he could not take his gaze from the boy, from his child.

Chapter Two

"It's good to meet you, Mr. McGraw." Caroline squinted as the storm tried to steal him in gusts of swirling white, wanting a better look. Their rescuer paced closer into the wind shadow of the house and the faint glow of light behind her illuminated him enough. The tall, powerful man placed one boot on the bottom step, holding Kringle's reins in one large hand.

Beside her Thomas gasped and took a step behind her, hiding behind her skirts. She didn't blame him. Her pulse lurched at the intimidating sight of the mountain of a man. Dark hair flecked with snow, granite face and square jaw set, he emanated a power that not even the fierce Montana wind could diminish. A giant of a man.

Yet when her gaze met his, she saw someone familiar in eyes as blue as sapphires. Familiar? That was completely odd, because she didn't know him. She'd never set sight on him before. Or had she? "Are you sure you aren't from around here?"

"No, ma'am." His attention shifted to Thomas. "Like I said. I'm just passing through."

Kringle shook snow off his face, jangling his bridle bits. Interesting, how the gelding stood calmly with this stranger. The horse nibbled the brim of the man's hat. If she needed any confirmation as to Mr. McGraw's character, then this would be it. Kringle didn't like just anybody. He was clearly one of the good guys.

"Maybe we grew up in the same town. I lived in Shelby all my life, until recently."

"Never been there, ma'am."

"Caroline." Such a polite man. She smiled at him fully, all guards down.

"Caroline," he agreed with a self-conscious shrug of those iron shoulders. For one brief moment their gazes latched and she felt a spark of connection, something she'd never experienced before. It was as if she looked into her own heart. He tensed, all six feet plus of him. "Then you call me Caleb."

"Caleb." She felt a tug on her skirt as Thomas slipped more safely behind her. She could feel his tension, poor boy, uncertain at every unexpected change. "It's all right, Thomas. Everything is fine now, thanks to Mr. McGraw."

No answer from the child, only the slightest shuffle of his shoes on the porch boards. Her chest coiled up tight with failure. She had to keep trying to reach the child, to help him the way Alma would have wanted her to. "Go inside, sweetheart. It's cold out here. Unless you want to play in the snow?"

No answer. Just the shuffle of shoes, a creak of a board and the boy drifted through the doorway, such a sad little thing. Big saucer eyes glanced back one last time, lighted on the man tied up in front of the step. It was hard to say what the boy was feeling as he disappeared into the warm house.

She shivered, aware of the cold creeping in, now that the adrenaline had worn off.

"That's a nice little boy you have there." Caleb McGraw's words sounded strained as he stared past her into the house, so intent on the child he was unaware of the horse stealing his hat.

I know why he seems familiar. It wasn't the man, but that yearning look in his gaze. He watched Thomas through the window with eyes so full of wretched sorrow and agonized longing it radiated off him. She could feel the force of it like the cold on the wind as it whipped by her.

The poor man. Her stomach fell, lost in sympathy. Even now, whenever she spotted a blond-haired little boy, her heart would stop, her soul would ache and the careful barriers she'd walled her grief in tumbled down. In those moments, all she saw was the past and the lost child she ached for.

"If you are just passing through, do you have a place to stay in town?" The question rolled off her tongue more easily than the question she did not ask.

"No. The hotel in town was too expensive. No way could I afford something like that." He did not lift his eyes from the child who stood at the window, staring out at the snow. "I didn't look around much. I'll find a boardinghouse when I get back to town."

"I shouldn't be offering you this. You can see the type of men there are in the world." She gestured toward the horse thief, struggling against his bindings and cursing at the feet of the invincible man. Caleb McGraw disregarded him, unmoved by the man's threats. She tried to do the same. "You could stay the night in the stable. It's snug and warm, and I'm a fair cook."

"Don't know if I should accept your kind offer. What about your reputation?" A muscle jumped along the square line of his jaw, betraying his tension. His gaze didn't stray from the window.

She'd never seen such sad, beautiful eyes. Had he lost a little boy, too?

"My reputation will be just fine." She wrapped her arms around her middle, trying to keep warmth in and her teeth from chattering. "You helped us, now we help you. That's a fair trade, isn't it?"

"I don't know if it's fair, as I did nothing much."

"Are kidding? I wouldn't have fired the rifle. I know that now. And you're right. What if he'd decided since he could have taken the horse so easily, he could help himself to more? No, I owe you, Mr. McGraw—Caleb."

"You don't owe me anything. Not one thing. But I'll think on it." Muscles bunched in his neck as if it took all his mighty strength to tear his gaze from the child. When he turned his attention to her, the impact of his sad blue eyes hit her like a punch. Sorrow lived in him so sore and deep he could not hide it, although he tried. His capable hands fisted, his impressive frame tensed. He looked ready to face any fight and win it.

It was sorrow she saw in him. Deep understanding made her want to reassure him in some way, but he was a stranger to her. Still, she would do what she could. "I'm already freezing and I've only been standing on this porch for a few minutes. If you've been traveling, you've been out in this cold all day. I'll bring a hot cup of coffee to the stable for you."

"I would appreciate that, ma'am. Caroline."

"Good. Because no good deed should go unrewarded."

"Isn't the phrase unpunished?" A tiny quirk in the corner of his mouth. "No good deed goes unpunished?"

"You haven't tasted my coffee. Maybe it's terrible."

"Maybe." He shifted his weight on his feet, kneeling to haul the trussed up prisoner onto his feet. He ignored the spitting venom and curses, his interest shifting back to the window. To Thomas. He couldn't help sighing. The boy had Alma's nut-brown hair and apple cheeks. Love seized him so fiercely he could not breathe.

His son. He couldn't look at him enough. He'd never seen anything as wonderful.

"I'll bring some quilts, too." Caroline's sweet alto captured his attention, drawing his gaze back to her lovely heart-shaped face and the caring that rang like music in her voice. "The stable is snug, but this storm blowing in has me worried. I think it will be a fierce one."

"Don't worry about me." He could get lost in the shine of concern. "I'm used to the cold. I'm tough."

"No doubt." Two bashful dimples flashed alongside her

shy smile. "But you're my guest. I'm going to make sure you are comfortable."

It had been a long time since anyone had cared about his comfort. His throat closed, making it impossible to answer. He gave his prisoner a slight shove, just enough to get him moving in the right direction.

"Aunt Caroline?" Thomas padded into the doorway, framed by light. "Can I have a cookie?"

"Okay. How about a glass of milk to go with it?"

A single nod. That was the boy's only response as he hung back, safely inside the house. Small for his age. Fear rounded his eyes as he looked out at the thief and at him.

At him. An arrow to his heart, and Caleb hung his head. Pain ratcheted through him, but it wasn't strong enough to overpower the devotion consuming him.

"There's nothing to be afraid of." He wanted the boy to know. "I'm big but I'm not scary."

Thomas said nothing. Not one thing.

The whirling snow closed in, coming down like a wall of white between him and the porch, hiding the woman and child. The need to see his Thomas plunged him forward until the winds shifted, allowing a glimpse of the house. Of the woman as she reached a loving hand to the boy's chin. Her gentleness drew his attention. Her loving gentleness.

Her words were lost in the howling wind but there was no mistaking her kindness. Gratitude filled him as he drank in one last sight of his son. Thomas wore good sturdy shoes, newish denims and a blue flannel shirt, a compliment to his blue eyes.

Eyes the same shade of blue as his own. Caleb stumbled, realizing he'd forgotten about the horse thief, his own mustang and Kringle, who nickered low in protest. The wind cut like blades, sharp and brutal. Time to get the horse inside and whistle for his mustang, Ghost, who stood somewhere in the yard, lost in the storm. He'd gotten a good look at the boy. That's what he'd come for.

Now it wasn't enough.

The storm closed in again, dropping like an impenetrable wall between him and the cabin like a sign of what could never be. With a heavy heart, he put one foot in front of the other and did not look back.

The sight of the man in her stable sent a ripple through her. Caroline peered through the doorway, ajar enough to see the muscled line of his back as he worked the curry over Kringle's shoulder.

"That's right," Caleb crooned in a low, easy tone. "You just relax. You're safe now, big fella."

A giant of a man, he dwarfed the small barn, although no one could have been gentler. A tingle settled behind her sternum. Admiration, nothing more.

She nudged the door wider with her foot. A very old white gelding standing in the aisle nickered a curious hello as she stepped into the fall of lantern light.

"Caroline. Making good on your promise?" A hint of kindness layered his words as he put the curry comb back on its hook. "That coffee smells good."

"You sound surprised."

"You led me to believe it might not be." He shook out Kringle's blanket and smoothed it over the horse's back. "Not that I wouldn't have still been grateful. I've learned beggars can't be choosers."

"I also made a sandwich. I feared you might not have had the time for lunch."

"That was thoughtful of you."

"It was the least I could do. I have a feeling after you leave here we won't be seeing you. You're the kind of man who just keeps moving on, aren't you?"

"Why would you say that?" His movements rippled with a confident, masculine grace like a man at home in his skin. He buckled the blanket beneath Kringle's belly like someone who'd been around horses all this life. He glanced over his shoulder at her as a challenge sparkled in his friendly eyes. "I must look like a drifter."

"You aren't forthcoming with information, that's for sure. I have to admit I am trying to figure you out."

"There's not much to puzzle. I'm not complicated."

"You're humble. You're unassuming. I can think of any number of men in town who would boast about their good deed, ready to accept as much thanks as they could get. They certainly wouldn't be in my stable doing my work." She laid the food bundle on the lantern shelf. The cup of coffee steamed, heat seeped through the wool of her gloves and she set it down, too. "You don't have the look of someone settled."

"You wouldn't be wrong." He rubbed Kringle's nose before stepping out of the stall and latching the gate. "Truth is I don't know where I'm headed. Reckon I'll find out when I get there. If I do."

"I'm glad you drifted this way."

"I am, too."

She felt awkward. When was the last time she'd been alone with a man? She couldn't remember. Perhaps with the reverend after her baby's and husband's double funeral. She'd forgotten how much bigger a man could be than a woman, how much stronger. But she wasn't afraid, just shy. When his gaze found hers and held, she saw again the grief veiled within him. She again felt as if he were someone she'd befriended long ago.

Definitely strange.

"Where's Thomas?" His voice grew tender over the child's name.

"In the yard playing. Finally. He's such a sad little boy. His mother died four months ago and he had nobody but his disabled great-grandmother. No one else in the world." Her voice broke because she knew that feeling. She knew when she saw Caleb's rugged face pinch that he'd experienced grief, too.

Maybe that's why he was drifting.

"That was noble of you to take him in." He watched her

carefully as he swept snow off his saddle. His horse stood patiently, jangling his bits.

"Noble? Not at all. I couldn't leave him alone."

"How did he come to be with you? Did you know his mother?"

"Alma wrote a letter to me on her death bed." Snowflakes clung to her, bits of melting white sifting across her pink cap, gold hair, slender shoulders. "We grew up together in the orphanage, until her grandparents recovered from their financial losses and could take her home with them again."

"So you were childhood friends?" That explained why Alma had never mentioned this to him during their courting years. Her years in the orphanage had been something she'd refused to talk about.

"Friends? Alma was like a sister to me."

"Wasn't that a long time ago?" He reached for another towel.

"What does time matter? When I had no one else, I had her. How could I let her down? I couldn't, regardless of my circumstances." She bobbed her head to brush a lock of gold out of her light blue eyes. "Besides, Thomas needed me. He's such a good boy."

"So I see." His throat closed up. The love in her voice amazed him. He'd been without it for so long. His empty heart tugged. Heat swept through his blood, sweeter than desire and more pure than physical need. Dizzy, he patted the saddle dry.

A brutal wind slammed into the north side of the stable, sending snow swirling between cracks in the wood. Lantern light thrashed, falling over Caroline in one bright arcing swoop, as if to cradle her in gold. The heat in his blood kicked up a degree.

What's wrong with you, McGraw? He had no business noticing a fine woman like that. Ashamed, he willed his eyes to stay on the horse as he swiped melting snow from Ghost's coat. If she knew what he was, she would not be looking at him trustingly. She wouldn't feel safe standing alone with him, offering him coffee and lunch.

"What about the boy's father?" He folded the towel. He took his time, not daring to face her again.

"No idea. Alma hadn't married him, although I shouldn't say that. I don't want word to get around. It could change the way folks in town treat Thomas. He doesn't deserve that."

"No, being a bastard is a hard thing to overcome I'd guess." He swallowed hard, unable to stand that he'd done that to his son. A child like that would be taunted by the other kids in school. Mothers would warn their children to keep away. "I won't say a word. I would never hurt a child that way."

"You lost one, too, didn't you? A little boy?" The raw pain lurking in the quiet notes of her voice arrowed through him, piercing deep.

That pain made his throat tighten and strangled his words. "You lost a son? You were married?"

"For two wonderful years. When little Mathias was born, life became incredibly good. It was like touching a dream. But it was one that didn't last. Michael and Mathias died within days of each other."

"I'm sorry." He set aside the towel, his movements slow. He couldn't imagine someone having to go through that. His situation as tough as it was paled in comparison. It was the promise of a happy married life he'd lost, the dream of it. Not the reality.

The beautiful, golden woman standing in the aisle looked ready to crumple. He caught her in his arms, not sure he had the right to touch her. She smelled like sugar cookies and lilacs and she felt much smaller than she looked. Tenderness wedged into the hollow of his heart.

"Are you all right?" He worried about her unsteadiness. He worried she might start crying. Heck if he knew what to do with a crying woman. That always made him feel helpless. As far as he knew, there was no way to fix her problems or to make up for her losses. That was life sometimes, a harsh winter without hope.

"I'm fine. It's hard every time I say it aloud." She focused her light blue eyes on him, he'd never seen a truer color. "Maybe I shouldn't have asked you about your loss."

"I did lose a son. I was away when he was born and I never got to see him." It was the truth. Thomas could never be his son. He could never be Thomas's father. "I never thought anything could hurt as much as longing heart and soul to lay eyes on him."

"I know that longing, too." She drew in a shaky breath, took a wobbly step away from him but her hand remained in his. A real, human contact. A touch of comfort and connection.

Years of loneliness faded, as if forgotten, as if they had never been when his gaze collided with hers. He didn't feel the stain of prison in his soul when she smiled at him. He shouldn't be standing here like this, losing himself in her eyes. "I'd better get my prisoner to town."

"Hurry back, Caleb." She drew her scarf more tightly around her throat, took a few steps back and swirled away from him. Snow obscured her when she opened the door. She was only a hint of shadow, a swish of skirts and a remembered scent of cookie dough as he watched her go.

A woman like that could make a man believe in just about anything. That life could be good again, that hardship might be behind him. But he wasn't that man. He couldn't afford to be. He'd found what he'd come for and Caroline's words confirmed he needed to keep on going. If the local lawman recognized him from an old wanted poster, if he came across someone he'd known in prison or from his life in Blue Grass, then Thomas would be branded a convict's bastard.

No, he had to move on. He tucked the sandwich into his coat pocket to eat on the ride to town. The coffee warmed his chilled hands as he downed it. He caught sight of Thomas rolling a snowman in the yard. A serious, silent shadow of a boy. Hard not to want to go to him and draw him into his arms. Just hold him tight.

But he had to do the right thing. He untied the thief from the water trough, mounted up and let the storm wrap around him. He nosed Ghost toward town. Loneliness wrapped around him like the whirling snow. Leaving was like being torn apart but he kept going. He wanted one last glimpse of Thomas and of Caroline, but instead he closed his heart and rode into the bitter wind.

Chapter Three

Caleb hesitated on the boardwalk outside the jail, keeping a good tight hold on his captive and on his courage.

"Lemme go. I'll get you gold. As much as you want. I'm real good at getting my hands on it." The horse thief had been bargaining on his long walk to town behind Ghost. Even half-frozen from the inclement journey, the criminal hadn't given up. "I'll do anything, man. Just don't take me in there."

"Then you shouldn't have been stealing a widow's horse." He didn't like lawmen. A sheriff's mistake had been the reason he'd served hard time but he yanked open the door, gave his prisoner a shove and followed him into the warm office.

"Do we have a problem here?" A marshal looked up from his desk, scattered with paperwork. Sharp, assessing eyes met his. "I'm Mac McKaslin. What's going on?"

It wasn't easy walking into the lion's den but he did it for Thomas and Caroline. "Mrs. Dreyer had some trouble with a horse thief. I caught him in the act. Since you're the law, he's your charge now."

"Is that so?" Marshal McKaslin rose slowly, his gaze probing deep. Authority rang in that voice as he circled his desk, taking his time, taking in the situation. "Just who are you? I know everyone in these parts, but I don't recognize you."

"The name's McGraw." The stain of prison clung like a brand he was sure the marshal could see. Caleb released his hold on the thief. He waited, expecting the worst.

"McGraw? Not a name I hear in these parts. You're not from around here."

"No, just passing through on my way west. To find work." Caleb fought the urge to look down, ashamed of who he was. He'd been innocent of the crime he'd been charged with, but the punishment had branded him. It had forever marked him. All he could do was stand his ground like the man he used to be and meet the marshal's gaze.

"I see." As if satisfied, Mac McKaslin turned his attention to the trussed up man looking over his shoulder for a way out, as if still hoping for escape. "You, son, do look familiar. Your face is on a wanted poster on my office wall. Right over there. Good thing Mr. McGraw caught you before you did something worse."

Relief eked out of his tight chest, one mouthful at a time. Maybe his secret would stay hidden and buried, not visible after all.

The marshal ignored the wanted man's ardent professions of innocence and showed him to the single cell in the corner of the room. The clank of the steel bars hooked deep, drawing up memories. Fragments of misery and hopelessness rushed up to dim the light from the room. Times he didn't want to remember, so he headed to the door. His duty was done. He was a free man. To leave or to stay. It was his to decide.

"Where you going, McGraw?" Mac McKaslin's tone boomed across the sparse room. "You might want to stay around for a moment or two. You've got a reward coming."

"A what?" His hand froze on the doorknob. Surely he hadn't heard that right.

"There's a bounty on Carter's head." The lawman managed a smile, friendly. "It's yours."

"Mine? That doesn't seem right. I didn't do much."

"You did what was right. The money is yours fair and

square." Mac took a cup from a shelf and filled it from a coffee pot rumbling on the potbellied stove. "I'll put in for the funds. I'm sorry to say it may take more than a few days to get here. You might want to stick around town long enough to claim it."

"Will do." A reward. How about that. He shifted his weight, thinking this turn of events over. Now he had a reason to be in town and see more of Thomas. The fact that also meant seeing more of Caroline sent tingles through him.

"How well do you know Caroline?" the marshal asked.

"I only just met her. It can't be easy for a woman raising a child alone." His throat knotted, aching in ways he couldn't explain. Her lovely face flashed into his mind, porcelain daintiness and goodness. He would never forget the way she'd looked at him, as if he were a real man, whole, untarnished.

"No, you're right. I think she is struggling hard to make ends meet."

"Struggling?" He'd been so absorbed by the sight of his son and the woman's effect on him to notice.

"I keep an eye on things in my town. It's my job to know who needs help. When she moved in three months ago with that little boy in tow, I'd never seen a sadder sight. I hear she's a hard worker, but a woman can't make what a man can in this world. It's a plain fact. One I don't much like, but there it is." The lawman shrugged. "It's good to meet you, McGraw. I hope you stick around for a while."

"I'm considering it." The moment his boots hit the boardwalk it was settled. He needed more time with Thomas—just one more day. It would give him the chance to assess Caroline's situation, make sure she was all right and to help where he could. Then he would be on his way. He didn't lie to himself. Riding away was the best thing he could ever do for his son.

It's starting to look like Christmas, Caroline thought as she set the last loaf on the table to cool. The fresh doughy smell of baked bread filled the main room with a cozy feeling. Content, she surveyed her afternoon's work. She'd been surprisingly productive after Caleb left. She ignored the little sputter in her heartbeat whenever she thought of him. No, she wasn't about to become attracted to the man. It was sympathy she felt—nothing more.

The sagging door creaked opened and a snow-covered little boy trudged inside. Apology shone in his gaze, all she could see of his face as she circled the table and came to his rescue.

"Goodness, Mr. Snowman. What are you doing in my house? Have you seen Thomas anywhere? I expect he's getting mighty cold. He's been outside a mighty long time."

"It's me, Aunt Caroline." His words were muffled by his scarf until he tugged it off his face. "I'm Thomas."

"Oh, my. I guess you are. For a minute there I thought a snowman had come to live with us, too." She nudged off his hat, snow tumbling. "What do you think a snowman would eat? Surely not the bread I just baked."

A twinkle of interest flashed in his eyes.

Progress. Satisfied, she dusted off his icy coat. "Maybe snow pies?"

A faint smile curved up the corners of the boy's mouth.

"Snow pies. Maybe snow and dumplings." She worked a snow-caked button through its buttonhole. "I don't have any recipes for those things, so I'm really glad it's you and not a snowman in my kitchen."

"Me, too. It would be cold to be a snowman." Thomas shrugged out of his coat, snow tinkling to the wood floor all around him. "Besides, a snowman *couldn't* come in here 'cuz he'd melt."

"Right. Why didn't I think of that?" She took his coat. "Go warm yourself by the fire. I'll bring you some hot milk."

The boy trotted off. She barred all memories of the past from her heart as she hung up his things. The wool coat she'd made him, the hat, gloves and scarf she'd knitted. Determined to stay in the present, she circled around the table for the small pan on the stove, simmering on a trivet. Steam curled from the milk's surface and scented the air as she poured it into Thomas's tin cup.

The *thud, thud* of boots stomping on the porch step echoed through the house like gunfire. Her pulse lurched. Could it be Caleb? The pan slipped out of her grip and thunked to a rest on the trivet. She didn't remember launching forward and skirting the round oak table. All she knew was the cool glass knob in her hand and the slap of icy air when she opened the door.

"Hope that invitation is still good." He looked like a snowman, too. A snowman with strong, capable shoulders and the promise of a smile on his sculpted lips.

That odd sense of rightness returned, like a key turning in a lock, opening her heart. "Come in out of the cold, Caleb. I can make you a cup of tea."

"Sure, but that looks good, too."

"What? Oh." She still carried Thomas's milk. "There's more where that came from. I can save you a cup."

"I'd appreciate it." He glanced over her shoulder, his expression softening. He'd probably spotted Thomas standing before the hearth. He squared his mighty shoulders. "Looks like you could use some wood. Do you have a supply in the lean-to?"

"Some. You don't need to worry about the wood box." She opened the door wider, hoping he would budge from the icy porch and take shelter in the warm house.

He didn't. "I've got the horses fed, watered and bedded down for the night, stalls clean. Might as well get the rest of the outside work done. Do you need any water from the well?"

"That would save me a trip outside." She whirled around to set Thomas's milk on the edge of the table and fetch two ten gallon buckets. Across the main room, Thomas watched with worried eyes. Caleb's size was intimidating, she decided. The man practically filled the entire doorway as he reached in for the buckets. His large hands closed around the pails, brushing hers.

The contact was brief, but a lightning bolt arrowed through her chest. She stumbled backward, startled. Whatever that was, it certainly could not be a jolt of attraction. And if it was, she couldn't admit it. A woman with debt and a child to raise wasn't high on any man's most wanted list. And certainly not a man without roots and no apparent desire for them.

"Unlock your back door for me, please." He said no more as he shouldered away, merged into the dark embrace of the blizzard and disappeared from her sight.

Realizing the house was a good bit colder, she wrestled the door shut against the wind and retrieved Thomas's cup. Time to put more wood on the fire. She was a sensible woman. Always had been, always would be so she refused to wonder about the man outside doing chores for her. Refused to let him pull at the forgotten places in her heart.

"Why did that man come back?" Thomas took the tin cup with both hands. Worry furrowed his brow.

"I invited him to sleep in the stable. As a thank-you for rescuing Kringle for us." She eased a thick piece of split wood from the box and set it into the grate. Flames leaped. "Are you afraid of him?"

Round eyes blinked once. Thomas shook his head slowly with great determination.

"Good boy." She smoothed a wet shank of his hair, glistening with melting snow. Affection crept into her battered heart. "Mr. McGraw is going to be sharing supper with us."

"And breakfast, too?"

"Yes. Is that all right with you?"

A little gulp of air, another nod.

"Then I had better go check on supper." She stood, wishing there was more she could do to reassure the boy. He turned his attention to his cup and took a halting sip. The roasting chicken's fragrance emanated from the stove as she swept by. First things first. She found her way through the dark, chilly lean-to and unlatched the back door. When she gave it a shove,

the wind caught it and tore it from her hands. It struck like
thunder against the wall.

"Here's your water." A hulking shadow moved in as she
stumbled back. Two big buckets sloshed to a rest against the
floor. "You go back in where it's warm. Don't even think about
carrying those heavy buckets inside. That's my job."

"I'm used to carrying my own water."

"Not when I'm around. I do the heavy lifting. Got it?"
Tenderness softened his tone. He'd meant to sound tough,
invincible, in charge, but the respect he felt for her shone
through, raw and naked in his voice. It embarrassed him. Hell,
he didn't know what she might think of him. She was too kind
of a lady to laugh in his face at the preposterous notion that
he liked her.

What wasn't there to like? Her beauty, her generosity, the
fact that she didn't look down her nose at a roughneck like
him.

"I suppose I can allow it this once, since it seems to make
you happy." She tipped her head back to get a good look at him.
Humor danced in those deep blue depths, the most mesmer-
izing sight. "I'm not used to having a man around. It's nice."

"We'll see if you still say that after I mess up your clean
floor with my boots." The quip came easier than the truth.
Laughter chased away the fondness wedging its way between
his ribs. He liked the sound of her laughter, light and lilting,
almost musical as it joined with his, like melody to harmony.
The hollows in his heart ached with loneliness.

He'd spent many long nights in prison before he'd fallen
asleep picturing the life he'd lost and the one he was determined to find. Year by year the dream faded and reality set
in.

A lady like Caroline can't be in your life, he reminded
himself as he abruptly turned away. Ice pellets scrubbed his
face, blinding him and yet he preferred the bitter cold to the
bleakness of his life. No decent woman would have him. A
sheriff and a judge hadn't believed him. After a conviction

and a sentence served, no one would. He simply had to deal with that and not to start wanting things he couldn't have.

He hadn't taken two steps and he could still feel her watching after him. What a pretty picture she made framed in the doorway with the lamplight at her back, a swirl of pink calico and golden compassion. He took a moment to smile at her in reassurance. "I won't be much longer."

"I'll have supper on the table in a few minutes." Her smile could make him forget the man he was—and that must not happen. He steeled his spine, shored up his resolve and watched her spin away in a sweep of skirts. The wind felt colder without her.

Foolish, that's what he was being. He tromped to the snow-covered woodpile marching along the back wall of the cabin. Fortitude and discipline had gotten him through his incarceration. Surely he could show a little bit of that now. He swept off the snow, peeled aside the tarp protecting the split chunks of pine and filled his arms to his chin. The blizzard fought him hard on his return trip, harder on the trip after that.

It took four loads until he was satisfied with the stack in the lean-to. He shouldered the fourth load through doorway into the kitchen, snow and all. The bright lamplight burned his eyes, making them hurt. At least that was the reason he told himself as crossed the cozy cabin that felt like a home. Like no home he'd had in a long, long while. The scents of boiling potatoes, baked bread and roasted chicken made his stomach grumble.

"Look, Thomas, we have another snowman." Caroline laid gleaming flatware on the table in neat, precise place settings.

The boy in the corner didn't answer. Uncertainty pinched his eyes as he set down his tin cup. Not one word, just silence.

"He must be a snowman because he's melting all over my floor." Lightly, she didn't appear to let the boy's silence dim her cheer as she set down the last fork and plucked a towel off the small counter.

"Sorry about that." He felt bad about the snow on the polished floor. "No way around it with a storm like that."

"He speaks. I guess he isn't a snowman after all." She sailed toward him. "Don't worry. I'm prepared. A little snow doesn't bother me."

"Glad to hear it, because I shook off all I could, but there's still a fair amount."

"You're carrying one load of wood that I won't have to. It's a nice change. Thank you."

"Just earning my keep."

Gratitude shone in her soft blue gaze. Good thing he had his barriers up and a good hold on his resolve or he would fall right into that gaze and just keep tumbling.

Maybe agreeing to spend the night here hadn't been such a good idea.

His boots struck the polished floorboards, his knelling gait echoing in the small room like hammer blows. Thomas stiffened with every step he took nearer to the boy. How did he reassure the little fellow? There was no one in the world he thought dearer than this child. He dumped his load into the wood box with a clatter, noticed water dripping down the stone chimney and tried to figure out what to say to his son.

His son. He knees went weak. It was the closest he'd ever been to Thomas. Just a few feet, maybe three, separated them. He drank in every detail he could. The expression of trepidation. The worried purse of Cupid's-bow lips. The tiny cleft in his chin.

He had one, too. As he peeled off his gloves, he found more of himself in the boy's face. A sprinkle of light freckles across his nose. Funny, how he'd had those too when he'd been young. They shared the same set and slant of eyes, sloping nose, long curling lashes, and the exact shape of their ears. Remarkable. Caleb swept off his snowy hat, not knowing what to say.

Never had he felt a more powerful force than love for his child. Not just love, but commitment, devotion and duty.

"Supper is on the table." Caroline's dulcet alto touched his soul, spinning him around, luring him to look at her. This had to be a dream. Home and hearth, comfort and kindness. Things he'd forgotten existed, but they were real. Right here. Right now. He thirsted for these things and craved them with the whole of his being.

The little boy put down a chunk of wood with a rough cut etching of a horse on it and dashed to the table.

Caleb couldn't move, watching his son go. A cowlick stuck straight up at the back of his head. Like the one he smoothed down on the back of his own head with trembling fingers.

"You may as well take off your coat and sit a spell." Caroline pulled out a chair for Thomas. "I hope you like chicken."

"I do." The words sounded torn from him. Feelings welled up as out of control as a flash flood. It took all his willpower to wrestle them down.

He hardly noticed crossing the room or pulling out the extra chair she'd brought to the table. Best to focus on why he was here. On making sure Thomas had what he needed and finding a way to help Caroline. The marshal wasn't wrong. He could see the details that had passed him by before. The simple, secondhand furnishings, the patch on Caroline's dress sleeve, the hearth in need of repair. But the food on the table spread out before him, plentiful and aromatic. His mouth watered.

"Guests first." Caroline gave the chipped serving dish a nudge in his direction, giving him first choice of the chicken pieces.

First choice. The lady had no notion what kind of man she dined with. He wanted nothing more in this world than to feel whole and released from the stain on his reputation. He wanted her to gaze at him forever with that look of kind acceptance.

It was wrong of him. He knew that. But it had been so long since he had felt his own worth. It was almost as if his past could stay hidden. He could be free. Cleared. Renewed.

If only.

"Give Thomas first choice." He noticed the boy staring with hope at one of the chicken legs. Love left him helpless.

He gave the platter a shove in Thomas's direction and earned Caroline's smile.

Yep, he figured he'd do just about anything to earn such a pretty smile. He grabbed hold of his tin cup and took a sip. Warm, steamed milk sluiced across his tongue, true to her word.

How about that.

Chapter Four

Caroline closed the book, smoothed the covers under Thomas's chin and rose. The bed ropes squeaked in protest. "Sleep well, little one. Have sugar-spun dreams."

The child sighed, a forlorn sound in the dark room. As he did every night since he'd come to stay with her, he curled up on his side and hugged his pillow for comfort. The bedtime ritual was hard on them both, with him remembering his mother and she thinking of her child. The remembered sweetness of tucking Mathias in and watching sleep tug down his heavy eyelids lodged deep in her heart, aching. Wishing she could take that same pain away from Thomas, she smoothed a hand over his wayward cowlick and smiled into his blue, blue gaze.

The two of them were definitely a pair.

She set the book on its shelf and lifted the lantern by its brass handle. The flame danced on its wick as she whirled toward the door, giving her a perfect view of Caleb seated in the extra wooden captain's chair, watching with his familiar-seeming eyes.

There was something about him, something she couldn't quite place her finger on. She closed Thomas's door behind her, shivering. The main room felt chilly. The temperatures must be plummeting outside. When she breezed by the fireplace the heat seemed to disappear the instant it left the hearth. Would Caleb be safe in the stable? Worry gnawed at her.

Now that they were alone, she had some questions for him. "How did it go when you showed up at the marshal's office?"

"Fine enough. Your horse thief is behind bars where he belongs." His blue eyes darkened. "I was right. Turns out he was a seasoned outlaw with a five-hundred-dollar bounty on his head."

"Five hundred dollars." She couldn't imagine that kind of money. What kind of an outlaw had that much of a reward on his head? Another kind of chill shot through her. "I'm doubly grateful you came along when you did. To think a man like that had been close enough to spy inside this house. He'd known I was baking."

"It's over now. With any luck, no more trouble will come your way again." He leaned in, gaze intent, that shade of blue stirring her memories.

"Do I need to stop by the marshal's office?" she asked. "Did Mac say I would need to fill out any paperwork?"

"No. I reckon he knows where to find you if he does." Caleb grabbed Thomas's piece of wood from the floor. "I noticed the boy playing with this. It's his pretend horse?"

"It was one of the few toys he had." Inadequacy filled her, pinching her with shame. Maybe a man like Caleb couldn't understand what it took to put down roots and provide for a child. She certainly wished she could do more for him financially. Thomas deserved it. "He calls it Bingo. It's supposed to be a wild mustang."

"I see." He tumbled the chunk of wood in his large, capable hands. "It can't be easy supporting the two of you on a woman's wages."

"No, but we get by. It's not easy, but it's not difficult, either. I have a good job. It's the best one I've ever had. I'm lucky." She didn't get the sense he was judging her, but life mostly fell far short of the ideal. "I'm patching the patches. He keeps wearing out the knees."

"That's a boy for you. He spent a great deal of the evening on his knees galloping this piece of wood around the braid rug."

"The rug is the meadow where the mustang lives."

"Oh, I see." He looked down. "Well, the rug is green. That makes sense."

"Yes, in the spring and summer. But not in the winter." She couldn't help it. Humor slipped out of her whenever Caleb was around. She felt light as air, in spite of her worries and her troubles.

"You need a white rug, I guess. Although I dropped my fair share of snow on this rug earlier. Say, do you think he would mind if I whittled this? I'm a fair carver. It might even look like a horse when I'm done."

"Seriously?" Her needle stilled. "I'm sure he would love it, but wouldn't that take a lot of time?"

"I've got time now." He pulled a knife from his trouser pocket and snapped open the blade. "It's been a long while since I've whittled. I'm out of practice."

"Where did you come from, Caleb McGraw? You rescue stolen horses, deliver thieves to the marshal, haul in enough wood to see me through the storm and make a toy for a child you don't know." Her breath caught at the sight of emotion etched into his rugged features. He truly was striking.

Not that she ought to be noticing. It was best to ignore the skitters of attraction beating like butterflies behind her ribs. She pulled the needle through the fabric and fussed with the stitch until it edged the patch just right. "I've never met a man like you."

"You ought to count yourself lucky on that." The humble half-smile looked good on him.

Too good. Blushing, she peeled her gaze away and concentrated on her next stitch.

"I'm from a small town on the Montana prairie." His confession resonated warmly in the night air, all trace of lightness had gone. His features set into a mask of stone, making it hard to believe in the gentle, kind side of him she'd seen so much of during the day.

What hardship had done that to him? He rose from the chair, straight and powerfully tall, a hulking brawn of a man as he paced through the darkness into the kitchen. Without his hat on, his dark hair fell in thick tufts past his collar. Except for a curl of a cowlick at the back of his head, sticking nearly straight up remarkably similar to Thomas's.

Probably a lot of people in the world had exactly the same cowlick.

"My parents were farmers." His baritone rumbled deep and rich. "I grew up helping my father in the wheat fields, helping raise cattle and take care of the horses. It was a nice way to grow up."

His broad shoulders dipped as he swiped the dishpan leaning against the wall. The shadows swallowed him, stealing him from her sight but the warmth remained in his words, the obvious love in his tone. "My parents were good people. They had me late in life. I was their middle-life surprise. The good thing about being an only child was that I had them all to myself for so many years. I had that comfort when they passed away, first my mother and my father soon after. He couldn't live without her."

"It was true love. My parents were the same way." The memories of her early years swirled back to her, bringing with them the first year of her marriage. Newlyweds besotted with their love for one another and then happily awaiting the birth of their baby. "When my pa started a sentence, Ma would finish it. They could look at one another and instantly know without words what the other thought. They died way too young. I always assumed that given more time together, Michael and I would have been the same way."

"I'm sorry you didn't get that chance. I don't believe a person only gets one shot at true love." His gaze deepened, so intensely blue they were hard to resist. "There still may be hope for you. One day you might find a man who can finish your sentences."

"It's a nice thought, but I can't imagine it happening." His gaze mesmerized her.

Blueberry-blue, just like Thomas's.

Exactly like Thomas's. So was his cowlick and, now that she thought about it, the shape of his ears. A chill snaked down her spine. Her needle stilled as she looked into those familiar eyes and saw the layers of regret and remorse. Caleb bowed his head to slide his knife across the block of wood and a thick chunk tumbled into the dishpan.

She carefully retrieved her needle and slid it through the edge of the patch. The sharp tip clinked against her thimble. "I'm not sure any man would be interested in taking on a widow and a young boy. I'm not sure I have the heart to love like that again. Being with Michael gave my world color. Without it, everything seems like shades of gray."

"I know that feeling." His knife dug into another corner of the block. "I've seen a lot of gray."

"Thomas helps put a little color back into my days." She pulled the thread through and made another stitch.

"I'm glad to hear that." Shavings of wood curled at the tip of his knife.

"I wasn't sure I could handle taking him in at first. When Alma's letter arrived, written in the final days of her illness, I wanted to turn her down. Tell her I couldn't have a child in my life to remind me of what I'd lost. I was afraid that in remembering my Mathias all the pain of losing him would come rushing back."

"Did it?"

"Yes. But so did the good memories, ones I'd let myself forget because they hurt too much." Firelight caressed her in soft waves, polishing her with a loving radiance that drew the air from his lungs and the wishes up from his soul. She fussed with the thread, smoothing it unnecessarily. "I'm grateful to

Thomas for that. There are so many beautiful things I do not want to forget. I wish I could do the same for him. Maybe one day."

"I'm certain you do more for the boy than you know." His chest might implode from the strain of wanting what he could not have. More time with his son. More time with Caroline. He ran the blade of his knife along the curve that would be the horse's flank, concentrating on his work, but where was his gaze? On her sitting there so luminous, his bone marrow ached with longing. "He has a lot of grieving yet to do. I can't think of anyone better for him than you."

"That's kind. Alma trusted me to raise her child. I don't want to let her or Thomas down." Emotion traced across her face, so poignant it made her even lovelier. She gathered her needle, straightened the thread and returned to her mending. "How long has it been since you lost your son?"

"It's been many years."

"Six?" She made another stitch as if she'd said nothing of importance, nothing that made his pulse stall in his chest.

Why six? Why had she guessed at that number? His knife stilled on the slight curve of the horse's back. She had to know the truth, she had to have put the pieces together. His hands shook too hard to trust using the blade so he sat there like a fool struck mute, his secrets about to be exposed. He'd grown hard enough in prison he ought to be able to get up and walk away without a word. To not give one hoot what she thought of him. To not care about what he was leaving behind.

Truth was, he'd never been that hard. Not even close. He'd never been cut from the same cloth as those men in that place, where ruthlessness and heartlessness were first nature. His hands kept trembling while he waited for her next words.

What had Alma said in that letter about him? Had she said anything about his prison sentence? He could not endure lifting his eyes to see the expression on Caroline's dear face. He did not want to witness the moment when her kindness turned to suspicion and fear.

"Your son didn't die, did he? You're Thomas's father."
Instead of accusing, her words wrapped around him like a
sympathetic hug, the only true comfort he'd felt in years. "Why
didn't you tell me?"

"I feared you would think I'd come to take him from you.
I haven't. I don't want to disrupt his life." His throat worked.
He stared at the knife blade so hard it blurred. "I wanted to
see him, that's all. Make sure he was okay. That he didn't need
anything."

"I see." Her slender fingers stilled. She set aside her mending, her skirts rustling with her movements. Her hands, at the
top edge of his field of vision, folded together. Such gentle
hands.

He felt horrible. "I deceived you and I'm sorry. It was true
that I lost him. When I came back to Blue Grass to check on
Alma, I was told of her passing. It took a bit more to find out
about the son she had. That was my fault. My doing. You don't
know how I regret it. I had to leave town suddenly and I just
didn't know." The words bunched in his throat, heavy with
guilt and shame. "She knew where I was. If she'd written, I
would have married her. Somehow or another, I would have
done everything I could have to make it right."

"I believe you." Her words were magic. Unexpected. The
most remarkable gift he could imagine. "I don't know you
well, but I see enough in you to know that you do the right
thing."

"I try." Emotion gnarled his words, choked and strained.
Grateful to her for seeing this in him and for understanding,
he didn't know how to say it. "I only just learned I had a son."

"So that's why you happened to be in my driveway to rescue
Kringle. You were coming to see Thomas."

"In truth, I wasn't sure if I would have knocked on your
door. I didn't know the right thing to do." He put aside the
block of wood and knife before he dropped them. "I had to
set eyes on him, that was all."

"Alma didn't tell me about you. If I'd known, I would have

tried to contact you." The tenderness in her alto lured him with a strength he could not fight.

When he dared to lift his chin and meet her gaze, he read more than tenderness in those compassionate depths. Understanding flowed from her heart to his, a silent acceptance that made his eyes sting. She rose from the chair, willowy grace and soft splendor. His pulse stilled as she crossed the green braid rug to sit on the wood-frame sofa next to his chair, so close he swore he could feel her heart beat in synchrony with his.

What was it about this woman? He couldn't explain how she'd torn down the defenses he'd carefully built in lockup, determined never to trust anyone again. Yet she could bridge that barrier with a single look. She would lay claim to his heart if he let her.

"Every son should know his father." Her hand covered his, an intimacy he did not pull away from. She meant to be comforting and sympathetic.

What would she think if she knew he wanted more than her sympathy? Desire sluiced through his veins. He had never yearned for any one thing the way he wanted her. He cleared his throat, wrestling with emotions he could no longer hold back.

"Do you want to be the one who tells him?" Her hand squeezed his. Caring telegraphed from her skin to his, spilled into his veins and touched his heart. Did she know what she did to him? Disarming him with her goodness, leveling him with her empathy, leaving him defenseless?

"No, I don't want him to know." The truth wedged like a rock in his throat. The shame within ached like an open sore. "Not ever. It's best for him if I move on. He has you. After meeting you, I'm good with that. I couldn't have picked anyone better."

"You want him. I can see it in your eyes."

"You want to keep him. I can see it in yours." His fingers

tightened around hers. "He's been uprooted enough. I will help out. Send money when I find a job."

"Oh, I didn't expect that." Her eyes burned, realizing what this must be costing him. How could he stand to see his child and never claim him, never hold him or watch him grow? He sat straight and tall as if invincible, as if nothing could tear him apart.

She didn't believe it for a moment. His agony showed in the small things—the set of his bottom lip, the pain pinched in the corners of his eyes, the strain corded in his neck. The poor man. Was he all alone in the world?

"Is there no one who can help you?" She couldn't keep from caring. The heat of his hand in hers trickled through skin and bone and spilled into her blood, a sweet syrupy feeling of connection. "You must have family and friends somewhere."

"No." A muscle jumped along his jaw. "I have no one."

"Yes, you do." Affection whispered through her, more loudly with each heartbeat. "You have me."

His face twisted and he looked away as if he had more to say and feelings to hide.

So did she.

"It's fortunate for Thomas." His baritone sounded strangled. "It's fortunate for me."

Somehow she felt wide-open, as if her feelings were on the outside instead of in where they were safe. No man ever had affected her like this. Caleb was a stranger to her, someone she hadn't known twenty-four hours before and yet she knew what mattered. His heart was big. Hardship had drawn creases into his handsome face. Hard times were evident in his old scuffed boots and well-worn clothes. His palm hot against hers was rough with thick calluses, proof the man had once worked very hard.

An uncommon wanting rose within her, part emotion, part respect, part desire. Minutes passed in silence but when his gaze captured hers no words were necessary. She could feel his emotions as if they were her own. His regret over years spent not knowing about his son. His determination to do right by him. His relief not to be alone.

Could he feel her emotions, too? As he searched her eyes, could he sense the tide of her feelings, her regard of him and the quiet flutter of longing? Maybe she had been a widow for too long, but she had come across many men in her work, especially at the bakery where the townsmen stopped by for breakfast and lunch. No one, not one, had ever roped her heart like this.

"The temperature has fallen so far, even the house is chilly here by the hearth." She withdrew her hand, hating to do so, wishing she could hold on awhile more. It took all her will-power to stand. "I fear the barn will be too cold for you."

"Don't worry about me, Caroline. I've slept in far worse conditions than this. Your stable will be more than fine."

"I'm sure, but I will hardly be able to sleep in my warm bed imagining you freezing out there in the spare stall." She crossed to a tall wardrobe standing near to her bedroom door. Her skirts swirled around her feminine form, drawing his admiration. She was a fine-looking woman. The more he saw of her, the more beauty there was to see. She flung open the doors and pulled out an armful of quilts. "I even have an extra pillow somewhere, too. Oh, here it is."

"I could use the quilts, thanks, but I'm heading outside." He folded the blade and tucked his knife into his shirt pocket. The chunk of partly whittled wood followed. "I'll work on this out there."

"Don't think of crossing me on this." She breezed around him, commanding him with a smile. The quilts tumbled to the couch cushion with the pillow on top. "You will sleep right here by the fire, end of argument."

"I wasn't aware we were arguing."

"Not yet we aren't. I won't budge on this, so I'm warning you. Do as I wish." She swirled toward him, chin set, eyes sparkling, mischievous. Everything a man like him could wish for.

No way could he say no to her. He stood his ground, or at least he wanted to look as if he did. "What happens if I don't?"

"Picture this." She tilted her head back to peer up at him. Flyaway tendrils gleamed in the lamplight, making her golden, making her irresistible. "Light, fluffy pancakes stacked high with butter melting down the sides, dripping with maple syrup. Eggs sunny side up, crisp bacon, coffee steaming. Does that sound good to you?"

"My mouth is watering."

"Now instead picture yesterday's hard boiled egg on your plate, a piece of dry toast. A cup of hot water, not even with tea leaves steeping. That's what you get if you go against my wishes." Amusement twinkled in her, resplendent.

"Is that so?" This wasn't about her getting her way, or him doing as she asked. Emotion struck him hard enough to buckle his knees and drive pain through the center of him. She cared about him. Fondness gleamed in those amazing blue depths. Genuine affection telegraphed from her heart to his as she caught hold of his hand and gave one gentle squeeze.

Please, she asked silently with that touch. She didn't want him getting cold tonight. Her sincere caring meant so much to him the force of it blew like an avalanche barreling down a mountainside, obliterating everything in its path. Gone were his doubts and every reason why he had to hold on tight to his feelings. All that remained was the surge of his affection for her, blindingly strong and pure, the truest thing he'd ever known.

He nodded, just once, all he could manage. Spellbound, his gaze slid to her mouth. Rosebud red, satin smooth, flawless. He'd never wanted to kiss anyone more. He didn't dare search her eyes to see if she felt the same. He could not turn down a plea for a kiss, if it was there. He could love her, if he let himself.

Love her? What do you think you're doing, McGraw? He had no business getting close to her. None at all. Best to wrestle down his attraction because nothing could come of it.

"It's getting late." The words sounded torn out of him.

"Yes. I should leave you." Her words came as equally ragged, full of want and regret. Her shoes knelled against the floorboards like the blows of destiny keeping them apart. "Good night, Caleb."

"Good night." He watched her open her bedroom door, step into the darkness and disappear from his sight. But from this night forth never from his dreams.

Chapter Five

W hy couldn't she stop thinking about him? Caroline braided her hair in the lantern light, her bedroom curtains closed tight against the predawn darkness. The sun hadn't yet risen, but it was Monday morning and she had a job to keep. She ought to be thinking about her responsibilities and getting both her and Thomas out of the house on time. But where did her thoughts go?

Right back to last night. To Caleb. Even thinking his name made the flutters of longing strengthen within her. His hold on her heart remained. He'd been the last thing on her mind before falling asleep and the first thing upon awakening. Images had haunted her dreams—of him sitting in the firelight, masculine and easy on the eyes, carving away on Thomas's toy.

I've lost far too much to ever risk romance again. She stared in the mirror, tying the end of her braid with a string. Her reflection revealed dark shadows beneath her eyes, evidence she'd been more troubled by her dreams than she wanted to admit. The truth was, Caleb may have thought about kissing her, but he hadn't. She kept going over the moment, which meant she wished he had.

What was wrong with her? She shook her head, pinned up her braid and blew out her lamp. A thin ray of light snuck around the door frame, guiding her through the small room and reminding her of the man she couldn't get out of her mind.

She opened the door and there he was, flesh and blood and all man crouched in her kitchen adding wood to the cook stove. The quilts were stacked neatly on the couch, the pillow on top.

"Good morning. The stove's ready and the kitchen is warm." He unfolded his muscled frame, rising to his six foot plus height, dominating the room with his impressive force. The kind regard gleaming in his blue irises added spark to the longing inside her.

I'm just lonely, she told herself, determined to deny the truth of her attraction to him. It would be sensible to ignore it. "Looks like you've been busy. It's a luxury to come out here in the warmth. Usually my teeth are chattering about now as I'm lighting the fire."

"I wanted to be sure and earn those pancakes you promised." Humor transformed the craggy planes of his rugged face into stunning magnificence.

It was hard to turn away but she did it and tapped her knuckles on Thomas's door. She kept her back firmly to the man as if last night hadn't happened, as if she wasn't affected. That's the way it had to be. "Rise and shine, sweet boy. Good morning."

"Mornin'." Thomas blinked. A yawn stretched his mouth. "I dreamed it was snowin' too hard so I didn't hafta go to school."

"Sounds like a good dream to me, but even if school is canceled you still have to get up and come with me. I have to work." She chose the warmest pair of wool trousers from his chest of drawers. "Do you feel the chill coming through the walls? Hurry up and get dressed and come warm up by the stove."

The boy nodded, cowlick flapping adorably. She laid his clean clothes on the foot of his bed, woolen socks, long johns, blue flannel shirt. Through the frame of the doorway, she spotted Caleb watching his son from a distance.

Here she'd been so worried about her own feelings she hadn't stopped to consider his. What must he be going through? The anguish he tried to disguise on his honest face tormented her. He loved his son. Deeply, undeniably, he stood with feet braced, shoulders squared, hands fisted. A steadfast man yearning after what he did not have.

"I got the coffee started and brought some things up from the cellar." He looked uncomfortable as he shifted his weight from one foot to the other. "Eggs, milk, bacon. Anything else you need?"

"No." She focused on the morning's work, made easier because of him. "I'll whip up those pancakes as promised. Were you warm enough last night?"

"I slept better than I have in years."

"I'm glad. That must mean you feel at home with us." She skirted by him, watching the toes of her shoes with determined interest. "That's how you should feel. Because of Thomas."

She wanted to make that clear. He would always be welcome in her home, for the boy's sake. That's all it could ever be.

The yearning remained on his face as Thomas's bedroom door swung open and he trooped into sight. Hair tousled, collar twisted and sticking straight up, sleepy-eyed. She ached simply watching the man and the wish stark on his face. She lifted the fry pans from their shelf.

Thomas stopped in front of the captain's chair next to the hearth. His droopy eyes snapped open.

"It's your horse." Caleb cleared his throat, watching the boy's reaction. "Your aunt Caroline said you wouldn't mind if I whittled it down to make a real horse shape."

"Oh!" He snatched up the piece of wood. Smoothly cut, mane and tail flying, fast hooves prancing. "Bingo looks like a real mustang now."

"That was the idea. I guess you don't mind?"

"Oh, thank you, Mr. McGraw." The boy clutched the horse to his heart. A full smile marched across his button face.

Fatherly devotion hobbled him more completely than any ball and chain. "Glad you like him, Thomas."

"I sure do!" The boy ran his fingers over the horse's carved nose and etched lips. Delight shone off him, chasing away the darkness, changing everything.

His son no longer stared at him with fear.

"Aunt Caroline, can I bring Bingo to the table?"

"No, but you can play with him until we eat. After you wash up." Her lighthearted manner made Thomas grin as she measured flour into a mixing bowl. "The faster you wash, the more time you'll have to play with your new and improved Bingo."

"Okay." The boy set the mustang on the arm of the chair and dashed over to splash in the washstand in the corner of the kitchen. In the small mirror hanging above the basin, Caleb could see Thomas's face. Apple cheeks, blue eyes, nut-brown hair standing up at all angles.

It was going to be hard to leave today. Could be the hardest thing he'd ever done.

"What exactly are you doing, Mr. McGraw?" Caroline gave him a schoolmarm look that she couldn't quite pull off. Good humor curved up the corners of her lush, kissable mouth.

Far too kissable. Blood thumped through his veins as he finished dealing out three plates on the crisp gingham cloth. "I'm setting the table."

"Yes, I see that." She gave the batter a good churn with a wooden spoon. "What I'm wondering is why."

"Maybe I just really want those pancakes you're making." He pulled open the sideboard drawer and counted out flatware. "Besides, I can't stand around doing nothing while you work."

"What about your horse? He might like breakfast."

"Already fed him and Kringle, too." He liked the arch of surprise and the look of approval she gave him. He doled out place settings of knives, forks and spoons. "I'm used to getting up early."

"This is early."

"Earlier than this." The past lurked unspoken, something he could not escape. Morning came quick in a hard labor prison, the call to rise sounded at 4:00 a.m. Remembering pulled the brightness from the lamp and the warmth from the room. He breathed in the aroma of bacon sizzling and coffee boiling. Things he'd missed on the inside, things he was grateful for now.

"I'm all done." Thomas hung up the hand towel, hair brushed, face scrubbed, smile shining. "What's your horse like? Is he a mustang like Bingo?"

"He sure is, but he's white instead of brown." He knelt down so he wasn't towering over the boy. Nearly eye-level, he gave his friendliest grin. "You can see him after breakfast. I may as well ride to town with you and your aunt. Make sure you get there in this storm."

"Okay." Thomas considered that. "Mustangs are my favorite."

"Mine, too." His throat closed up as the boy bounded away. Caleb soaked in every detail he could. The cowlick sticking up, the cut of those little-boy shoulders, the loping gait, all so dear to him.

"How are you going to ride away from him?" Caroline asked as she spooned batter into a pan.

"I don't know." He couldn't look away from the child. Down on all fours, Thomas galloped Bingo across the green rug meadow, making horses sounds that echoed against the bare walls. "Just like anything else I don't want to do, I suppose. Grit my teeth and do it."

"I couldn't." She forked bacon slices onto a platter. How could she admit the thought of him leaving was beginning to really hurt? "I can't imagine how you must be feeling."

"Me? I'm not what matters here." He straightened his spine,

drawing up to his full height, shrinking the walls and stealing all the oxygen from the air.

Honestly, she wasn't ready to let go of him. She wasn't sure he would be better off somewhere else. She flipped the pancakes onto a plate and spooned out more batter. "I know how hard it can be to find a job. It took me months to find a good situation and I had to move twenty miles."

"I expect it won't be any easier for me." A muscle jumped in his jaw, betraying his deeper feelings.

"If my son were alive and I had to leave him, it would tear me apart." She understood exactly how much Caleb had to be suffering. "What will you do, keep drifting from town to town?"

"If that's what it takes to find a job. I meant what I said last night. I'll do my part for him. I can see that you're struggling, and that isn't right. I don't mind hard work, especially when it's for someone I love."

Her heart twisted. She'd lost more than she could bear already. So why did it feel as if her soul secretly yearned to be the one he loved? It made no sense. She cracked an egg on the rim of the fry pan. "Christmas is coming up fast."

"I know. Just, what, a week away? I've lost count."

"Three days."

"Then it's almost here. I haven't celebrated it in a lot of years. I had no cause to."

"Why?"

"I was alone." Despair wreathed his face in harsh, unhappy lines, digging crevices into the corners of his eyes and brackets around his mouth. It kept her from asking why.

"You're not alone now. Why don't you stay for Christmas?"

"That's not in my plans." He might be shaking his head slowly from side to side, determined to stick to his decision, but she saw the ache in him, the need to be near his son a little longer.

"Plans can change. Maybe he needs you to stay."

"No, he doesn't need me." His throat worked. His jaw tensed. His hand curled over a chair back, his knuckles white.

"See how happy you made him with the horse?" She flipped something sizzling in the fry pan, a lovely sight. Blue wool, hair done up like a coronet on her head, ivory sweetness. Heat ebbed through him in slow measured beats.

If he stayed, then he could see her, too.

"It's his first Christmas without his mother. His great-grandmother is too frail to travel." She added more pancakes to the growing stack beside the stove. "I had worried it would be a sad holiday. With you, it would be better."

What he wanted and what he ought to do were different things. Sure, he wanted to stay for good. The territorial prison was a stop on the train line, not more than a hundred miles from here. Anyone released from jail—someone who might know him—could hop aboard a freight car and go anywhere. Even here. This wasn't far enough away to keep his past buried.

"It's just a few days." Caroline reached out, closing the distance between them with a touch. Warm fingers, caring heart, and the click he felt in his soul could only mean one thing. It would be a disaster to stay.

"For Thomas. Just for a few days." He was powerless to say no to her. The hint of dimples and the allure of her unspoken affection made him want a lot more from her than he could ever accept.

"Wonderful." The way she looked at him with respect and happiness left him speechless. His gaze drifted to her rosebud lips. What would it be like to kiss her?

"Oh, the pancakes!" Laughing at her forgetfulness, she pulled away to grab up her spatula.

Little did she know she still had hold of his soul.

"Who was that fine specimen of a man I saw ride up with you? Is he single?" Selma McKaslin asked in the back entrance hall of the town's bakery. "That wouldn't be the stranger who nabbed that terrible horse thief, the one who is tucked away in our jail?"

"His name is Caleb McGraw and you would be wrong to jump to conclusions." Caroline hung up her coat and knelt to help Thomas with his. Leave it to her employer, the optimist, to see romance where there could be none. "He's staying a few days with us. He has no place to go for Christmas."

"He made me this." Thomas thrust up his treasured toy. "Bingo is a real mustang now."

"Why, he certainly is." Selma beamed. "What a fine job that is. Your Mr. McGraw has many talents it seems."

"He's not my Mr. anything." Four years it had been since she'd lost her family. It would never stop hurting. She couldn't open her heart like that again. Not to Caleb. Not to anyone. She helped Thomas out of his coat. "Go play quietly, Thomas."

"Bingo wants to gallop along the canyons." Thomas took off, eager to discover what great thrills and perils Bingo might find on the tables in the front of the bakery. It would keep him busy until it was time to leave for school.

"Such a sweet little guy. He's gold, that's for sure. Reminds me of my boys when they were that age." Selma handed over a steaming cup of tea. "You must be cold. Come in and warm up. I need your fingers nimble. I was in the mood to make cinnamon rolls and that's a lot of rolling."

"I don't mind one bit. I'm happy to roll all the dough you want." She wrapped her cold fingertips around the cup and followed her employer down the hall and into the kitchen. Now, if only she could forget Caleb. Just the thought of him, attractive and manly, made her blood skitter.

She didn't want to be attracted to the man. How did she stop her reaction to him?

"Excellent. So, tell me more about this Mr. McGraw." With a merry wink, Selma adjusted the oven's damper. "Is it handy having him around?"

"Why are you determined to marry me off?" She took a bracing sip of tea and let its warmth sluice across her tongue.

Over the long counter she spotted Thomas racing Bingo along the edge of a table. Caleb had already made his son happy. She set down her cup next to the basin, poured water from the pitcher and washed her hands. "I'm content as I am."

"Yes, but I'm holding out hope for you. You deserve more than a lonely existence." Selma plunged a measuring cup into a flour bag. White powder puffed into the air like a cloud.

"Lonely? I'm not lonely." She soaped up and rinsed. "I have Thomas."

"I won't argue there, but you are young. Don't you want more from life?"

"No comment." She dried her hands. "I've buried my husband. I don't know if I can ever feel that way again."

"I can see your point." Selma sifted, turning the handle crank. Fine white flour rained onto the breadboard. "Mac came in late yesterday. He was on duty when your Mr. McGraw brought in that wanted man. Said it took a lot of skill and courage to face an outlaw like that. Mac thought highly of him."

"I'm not surprised." She couldn't imagine who wouldn't hold Caleb in high esteem. She did. At least she could take comfort in the fact that respect wasn't love; it was a matter of admiration. As long as she could keep control of her feelings and her attraction to the man, then her heart would be safe.

Chapter Six

"Aunt Caroline?" Thomas scooted forward on the sled seat to get a better look through the twilight of winter's early sunset. Blizzarding snow hampered his efforts. "What's he doin' up on our roof?"

"I don't know." She drew Kringle to a stop. The storm raged so fiercely she could barely see the porch. "Where is he?"

"There. By the chimney."

She recognized that silhouette. A wide-shouldered shadow with his Stetson bowed against the wind raised a hammer and drove it downward. Perhaps hearing Kringle's hooves on the hard-packed ice, he stopped, turned, rose slowly. A spectacular silhouette, unconquerable against the background of the storm. Her blood stilled. Why couldn't she control her reaction to him?

"Hello, there." Caleb swung down from the roof and dropped to the ground. Athletic, self-assured, glorious with every step he took. From her seated position in the sled, he seemed to rise up over her, a Goliath of a man. "Hope you two had a good day."

"I could say the most S words of anybody in my whole grade." Thomas spoke up. "What to hear 'em?"

"Sure I do." Caleb's gaze swung to meet hers and the great

heart shining there made her blood feel like slow-heated molasses.

"There's snow. Snowflakes. Sugar. Sugarplums." Thomas's pure voice rose and fell earnestly. "Sleigh. Santa Claus."

"That's a mighty fine list." Caleb took hold of Kringle's bridle bits. "I couldn't think of that many words."

"I've got more. There's sugar cookies. Sweets. Stockings, the kind you hang from the fireplace. Socks, the kind you wear on your feet."

"No wonder you came in first." Caleb offered her his hand. "Let me help you. You've had a long day."

"So have you by the looks of things." Her palm met his and her legs felt weak as she rose from the seat. She lost her balance, lost her center and she knew why. Caleb. Her feet sank into the snow and found solid ground, but he did not release her hand. "You fixed our leaking chimney?"

"With any luck I did. We'll have to go inside and see if it's stopped leaking." He brushed a curl of hair from her eyes with the lightest brush of his gloved thumb. "I had to make myself useful and pay back your hospitality."

"You didn't need to."

"I wanted to do it for you." His gaze found hers for a long moment, jarring her to the soul. Snow ceased falling, the icy wind stopped blowing and Caleb dominated her view. Uncertainty crossed his face. "I never want you to regret letting me into your life."

"Regret it? I could never."

"Never say never. That word has a way of coming around to bite you good and hard." He had to close his eyes to keep them from drifting down to her lips. The need to kiss her, to know the sensation of her hammered at him, so he spun on his heels. Arctic winds battered him as he knelt to lift Thomas from the sled. "Hang on tight to Bingo."

"He's not afraid of blizzards." Thomas reached out with both little arms and wrapped them around Caleb's neck.

Nothing—not one thing—had ever felt as precious. He

cradled his son tight for one priceless moment as he carried him to the porch. As much as he treasured Thomas, it was Caroline he noticed. He didn't know why she drew him. There was some magic connection that bound them. A mystery he could not solve, because if he did then he would have to accept his deepening feelings for her.

Feelings he could never admit or acknowledge, much less reveal.

"I thought of more words that start with *S* and one that doesn't." Thomas released his arms the instant his shoes touched the porch. "Stormy. Strong. Friend."

Hard not to fall in love even more with the boy. He saw himself in Thomas's eyes, the child he'd once been. Innocent and open and infinitely good. He never thought anything could touch him this deep, not after what he'd been through. All the hardship, the abuse, even torture in that prison had worn the softness right out of him.

Thomas had given it back.

"I can think of a few words, too." He gave the boy's cap a gentle tug so it covered his ears completely. "Good. Smart. Friend."

Thomas's grin split his face, chasing away the shadows. Clutching Bingo, he dashed past Caroline, turned the doorknob and tromped inside, where it was warm. Caleb had lit and built the fires earlier so the house would be welcoming to him and Caroline, a refuge, the way home should be.

"I can't believe you." She breathed up at him, appreciation shimmering like a rare gem. When she looked at him like that, he felt ten feet tall. His past vanished, a tarnish that could not touch him as her smile grew. "How did you do all this?"

"I stopped by the jail and talked to the marshal. Learned who your landlord was and knocked on his door. He agreed to provide the supplies if I did the work."

"And you've been busy all day." She didn't need his slow nod of confirmation to know it was true. She could see the evidence of his hard labor. The porch eaves no longer drooped, the porch boards didn't squeak and the door no longer sagged. Not to mention the chimney. "What other kinds of trouble did you get into while I was at work?"

"Lots. When you go inside, you'll see. I'm off to the stable next. If you want to write down a list of what else you need repaired, I'll get to it tomorrow."

"I don't know what to say."

"Consider it an early Christmas gift." He shrugged, a bit bashful, and it looked good to her, a contrast to his breath-stealing masculinity. Her heart beat a little faster as he swept off his hat to brush away the snow clinging to it. "I said I would do what I could. I aim to take care of you and Thomas."

"Just Thomas. Me?" She had to ignore the affection sweeping through her, strong enough to knock her off her feet. "You shouldn't have to worry about me."

"Sure I do. You and Thomas are a package deal. You take care of him, and I'll take care of you." As if unaware of what he'd said, of the commitment that rang like a promise made to be kept, he donned his hat, adjusted the brim. "Go on inside. I have a surprise in there."

"A surprise?" Curiosity didn't have a chance against the rising tide of pure emotion threatening to engulf her. Undiluted affection overpowered any thought about what awaited her inside the cabin. All she could see—all she could ever see—was him.

I vowed I wasn't going to get carried away. She set her chin, straightened her shoulders and dug down deep for a way to stop it. But the emotion remained, refusing to end. Against her will it strengthened as he caught Kringle by the bits. The gelding nickered a friendly greeting, offering his nose for petting. The man obliged, stroking the old horse's nose, a caring gesture.

This was Caleb's fault. His alone. If he wasn't so gentle, then she wouldn't be hurting. If he wasn't so kind, then she wouldn't be struggling. His integrity was the reason she could not stop the wave of affection from rising higher, threatening to drown her.

I cannot love him. She planted her feet and fisted her hands. *I must not.* It took all the effort she had, every last scrap of strength to force her gaze away from the man, to resist the current of her emotions and break away. She stumbled through the doorway as if blind, pulling it closed behind her.

Warmth greeted her. Toasty air chased the chill from her clothes and the sting from her skin. She unwound her scarf in one frustrated tug.

"Aunt Caroline, look!" Thomas stood stock-still in the center of the sitting area, arms dangling, Bingo forgotten in one hand. "Is that a Christmas tree?"

"Yes, it is." The pine tree stood tucked in the corner near the window, green boughs proudly high. Tears lodged in her chest, knotting tight, as memories of Christmases past rose up, happy ones as a newlywed and as a new mother. She hadn't celebrated the holiday properly since the double funeral.

"I've never had one before. Granny didn't approve of 'em." Thomas hugged Bingo tight. "It's like Christmas is already here."

"There's still more to come." Her emotions tangled up, making it impossible to speak. She unbuttoned her coat, warring with her feelings for Caleb, with her warm memories of what was past and of her hope for what could be.

Hope. That was new.

She knelt down beside the boy and brushed his wayward dark locks out of his eyes, exactly like Caleb's. Affection rushed higher and she found her voice. "Trust me, we haven't started our celebrating yet."

"But how's it gonna get even better when it's already so good?" Uncertainty etched across his button face as he stared at Bingo and then at the tree.

"Sometimes life just gets better and better. Usually about the time you think it never will." She couldn't help brushing a stray lock of hair out of his eyes. Impossible not to love this boy. "Tonight we'll decorate the tree. That will be fun. Right?"

Thomas nodded, just once, turning to perhaps imagine those branches decorated with strings of popcorn.

"Tomorrow after work I start baking all our Christmas treats."

"Does that mean cookies?"

"Cookies and fudge and popcorn balls."

"I've never had popcorn balls."

"See? And that's just tomorrow. Caleb will be here the whole time. He can help hang your Christmas stocking. Does that sound good?"

"Santa Claus has never been to my house before. But now that I live here, do you think he might come?"

"You can count on it." Her arms moved of their own accord to draw Thomas against her. The little boy stumbled against her, his small arms encircling her neck, holding on tight for the first time since he'd come to live with her. Bingo, clutched in one hand, bumped into her back but she didn't mind. She gave Thomas a good squeeze so he felt secure, so he knew she was there for him.

When he released her, he kept hold of her heart. His boyish smile lit up the night.

"That was a mighty fine supper." Caleb pushed back his chair, pleasantly full. He was hard-pressed to remember a tastier meal. Caroline's roast beef, mashed potatoes and baked beans had spoiled him for the plainer fare he was used to—that he would be having once he was on the road again.

"I'm glad you think so." Across the table, she set down her fork. Lamplight polished her with a lustrous glow. Porcelain complexion, ice-blue eyes, gold hair gleaming. She was more than beauty. Grace defined her as she cradled a teacup in her slender hands, long fingers curled around the mug.

Better get out of this chair. He'd be wise not to linger here, making more conversation, letting the domestic scene pull at him. He was in too much danger already; in danger of wanting to stay.

"Haven't you done enough today?" She peered at him over her steaming tea. "Do you actually think I will let you do the dishes, too?"

"It was worth a try." He liked Caroline. She sure knew how to hold her ground. He envied the man who would win her heart one day, who would have the right to marry her. He stacked his plate on Thomas's—the boy was already playing with Bingo under the tree. "Don't you even consider getting up. Sit and enjoy your tea. You deserve a moment off your feet."

"And you don't?"

"No, I do not." He liked the shake of her head, the esteem and something more he didn't know how to describe that shone from within her, emotions he could feel as he hefted the dishpan from its shelf and carried it to the stove's reservoir.

"You've worked hard all day, Caleb. I don't think three men could have done the amount of work as one of you." She sipped slowly, watching him over the rim. "You are our guest. You didn't need to do a thing."

"Yes, I did, and there's still more to do." That something more he felt from her tugged at him, reeling him in like a fish on a hook, giving him no choice. He could fight it, he could give in but the end would be the same. "I intend to do right by you, Caroline, and you can't stop me."

"If that's the case, then I don't want to try." It wasn't appreciation ringing in her voice, but more.

It wasn't gratitude he felt but more as he slid the pan on the edge of the table and began shaving curls off the soap bar.

"Tell me something about you. Something no one else knows." She set down her cup with a faint clink, captivating him with a tilt of her head and a bob of her chin.

"When I was a boy, probably Thomas's age, I wanted to grow up to be my father." He set the bar of soap aside and dropped flatware into the steam and bubbles. "I couldn't imagine anyone better. My father was a great man."

"Tell me." She rose from her chair with a whisper of petticoats. "What was he like?"

"Steadfast. Trustworthy. Honorable. He was like a mountain. Unshakable." His granite features transformed, as if hopelessness no longer dogged him, as if he had come out of the cold, no longer drifting. "He was as tough as a Montana winter, but unbelievably kind."

"Sounds like someone I know." Her affections layered her words, impossible to hide because they were so big. Embarrassed, she grabbed the second pan to fill it for rinsing.

"No, not me." His arm brushed her shoulder, sending a spark of lightning zipping from flesh to soul. He didn't seem to notice, he didn't jerk away as she did, but took the pan from her. Always capable and steady, dependable Caleb. He cleared his throat, emotion troubling him, too. "I couldn't have had a better pa. I followed him everywhere, the barn, the fields—where he was, I was. He taught me how to care for horses, how to grow wheat, how to stack hay."

"Mending chimneys and sagging front doors?"

"Yes, those, too." He slipped the pan onto the table beside its twin, so tall he took her breath away, so good he captured her.

How he captured her.

"All I wanted to be was him. I was seventeen when I lost him." He bowed his head, as if determined to gloss over sad memories.

"Seventeen? You were still a boy."

"I had to step up and be a man when ma fell ill. She went first. Pa lived for her. He couldn't bring himself to leave her bedside." A few splashes and he dropped a trio of forks into the rinse water. "The care of the crops and the cattle fell to me."

"That was a lot of responsibility." She plucked the forks

from the water and swiped them with a towel. "I'm sure you were a great comfort to your parents."

"I loved them so much, I refused to let them down. It was harvest, our entire income for the year, so I threshed the wheat, cut the corn and hay. We had a good yield that summer, but it wasn't enough. Ma lingered, her doctor's bills grew. After we lost her, Pa became ill. His care fell to me."

"He was fortunate to have you."

"I did my best for him. I gave him all I had. I mortgaged the farm to get him the medical treatment he needed, but nothing could stop the inevitable. When he was gone, I was alone. I was able to hold on to the land but it's gone now. I lost everything. I have nothing left of them. Not one thing."

"You have what's important." She laid her hand on his arm, felt the manly steel of his flesh and bone and his male-hot skin. "Their love. Memories to treasure. You are what is left of their lives. You."

"If they are looking down on me from heaven, I don't know if they would be proud of me. I fear they would be sorely disappointed."

"How could that be? You always do what's right, don't you?"

"I try. I've learned firsthand the importance of truth and justice. Of the consequences when you know what is right but you don't do it." Regret carved across his features shadowing him, drawing him in stark relief. He submerged the plates and the cups with careful deliberation. "There are things in my life I would rather forget."

"Like the reason you left Alma?"

"Yes." His face twisted. Never had she seen such remorse or the determination to stand tall. "I did not take a situation I found myself in serious enough and I lost everything. My job, my friends, my good name. It was too late to get them back."

"It's never too late. Your name is good here." Beneath her fingertips, she could feel the texture of his skin and the uneven leap of his pulse. Her heartbeat leaped to match. "What mistake could you have made? I see you, Caleb. You are more transparent than you think."

"I made the mistake of choosing to see the good in someone and ignore the bad. I was too trusting. I get that from my ma." He dropped the dishcloth with a splash and turned to her. Damp fingertips caught the underside of her chin. "I see the good in you, Caroline. So much good."

"Me? No. I'm just me. Just doing my best to get by."

"You have given me hope. Belief that there is more good than bad in this world, more light than darkness." He could forget everything, lost in her eyes. He was tumbling, falling into her, into dreams of ice-blue and sweetness. "Everyone makes mistakes, but coming here was the best thing I've ever done."

"Because of your son?" She whispered the words. "He's part of your parents, too."

"That is part of it, yes, but I mean because of you. You make me long for things I have stopped believing in."

"Me? Impossible. What could I have done?"

"You welcomed me into your home. You cared. You made me feel like the man I used to be." He ignored the warning blaring in his head, the one telling him to step away, to put distance between them, to remember what he was. But hope spoke louder, drowning out the doubt and the darkness. Like Christmas come early, he listened it. He opened the bars on his heart, opened the doors wide and let the light in.

Love surged through him with the power of a new dawn. He finally gave in to his need, into his most honest desire. He stared into her lustrous eyes and lowered his mouth to hers.

Sugar-spun sweetness, that kiss, it was a dream come true.

Chapter Seven

Stay in control of your feelings, Caroline. That was her last rational thought before Caleb's kiss claimed her. Oh, that kiss. It melted her resistance with the brush of his velvet lips. It scattered her mind until all she could think about was the tingle of sensation as his mouth stroked over hers in tender butterfly caresses. It enraptured her, the most exquisite kiss she'd ever known.

His lips nibbled hers, sensational little nips of affection. Heavenly bliss. She clung to him, her fingers curling into his flannel shirt, holding on, desperate. What if he stopped? She didn't think she could endure it, but he was already moving away, his lips left hers and he stared into her, breathless. Eternity passed while they stood there, breathing hard, both wanting more and knowing it could not be.

Or could it? What if he could find work in town? Was it foolish to hope? In his true blue depths she saw the promise of a future.

A future. Her chest spasmed with pain and fear, but those things were not as strong as the emotions lifting her up. Hope had a power all its own, a power that did not release as Caleb brushed his lips over hers briefly, gently, finally.

"That was a mistake." The low notes of his baritone rumbled, laden with feeling, rich with love. So tender, the sound of it shattered her every last defense. What was she going to do now?

"That was definitely a mistake," she agreed. "Huge. Gigantic. Colossal."

"But one I will never regret."

"Nor will I."

"I'm surprised you aren't mad at me." His thumb stroked the tender skin beneath her chin, his affection unmistakable. An answering affection whispered through her with a single impossible wish. Maybe he could stay. His eyes, so deep, so blue, held no guile, just genuine unveiled adoration. "You hardly know me and you let me kiss you."

"I know what's important." She laid one hand across the middle of his chest when she should step away. "I know what matters about you. That's enough."

"You are too good to me." He brushed his hand along her jaw, a tender caress. "Which is why I'm finishing the dishes by myself. No argument allowed."

"What if I want to argue?" she protested sweetly.

"I'm the guest and this is what I want." He didn't deserve this moment with her. She wouldn't want him if she knew about his prison record. But he wanted to spend time with her more than anything. "Go show Thomas how to decorate your tree. I'll get some popcorn going, I noticed it in the pantry. You two can string while I clean up the kitchen."

"I've never known a man to do a woman's work." She tilted her head, curious, searching his face for the answer.

"Work is work, and besides, Thomas needs you to make this Christmas special for him. Let me help you do that."

"As long as you are a part of it. Thomas needs you, too."

"I'd like that." Although she removed her hand, the warmth of her touch remained, emblazed upon his soul.

What if he could forget the past, what then? Would he want to stay? Be a husband to Caroline and a father to Thomas?

Yes. Unequivocally. Beyond all doubt.

"Let me help you get the popcorn started." She spun away with a swirl of calico.

"What did I just say?" Chuckling, he pulled her back into his arms. He breathed in lilacs as her soft, feminine form snuggled against his. If only he could hold her forever. "I'll do the kitchen work."

"I know, I heard you." She rocked back into his arms, so dear there was no way to stop the love overtaking him. Unaware, she broke away and scooped a kettle off its shelf. "At the very least, I can show you what pot to use. I'm assuming you have plenty of experience with this?"

"I'm a master. Popcorn is my specialty."

"Really? Well, you are full surprises, Caleb." She plopped kettle and lid on the stove. "I'll go fetch plenty of needles and thread. Don't think you're going to get out of stringing popcorn."

"I have no experience whatsoever with a needle and thread."

"Then you are about to learn." She sailed away, taking the light with her. Thomas and Bingo emerged from beneath the spreading boughs of the tree as she approached. "Guess what? It's time to start decorating. Want to help?"

"Boy, do I!" The boy squared his little shoulders and raced across the room, holding tight to his toy. "Is it gonna look like the tree in the mercantile window?"

"Ours will be more special because it will be homemade. Here's some paper." She carried the precious stack of parchment to the couch. As the boy trotted ahead of her, her attention strayed to the kitchen. Caleb standing in the lamplight could make her dream.

"Here are your scissors." She waited until Thomas was seated on the sofa before handing over her sewing scissors, handle first. "Have you ever made paper snowflakes before?"

A solemn shake of his head.

"It's easy. Let me show you." She settled next to him and began. She ought to be concentrating on her work, but as she cut the sheet into quarters where did her mind go to?

To Caleb and the rattle of corn kernels in the kettle. The imprint of his kiss still burned on her lips. The power of what she felt for him…

Stop. Don't complete that thought. Don't allow one more word. She sighed and kept cutting. What she felt for Caleb made her feel as if there were more room in her heart than before. Enough room to try to love again. That frightened her to the quick because when her gaze locked with his, time stilled. In the space between one heartbeat and the next, she saw his truth. His deepest wish was written across the handsome planes of his face. His feelings shone sincere in the blue richness of his eyes. She shivered, realizing she wasn't alone with her feelings.

"There's something missing," Caleb called out as he held the lid over the kettle and gave it a shake. "Caroline, I'm surprised you haven't noticed it by now."

"Hmm, I'm not sure what you mean. We have popcorn. We're making snowflakes. Thomas, can you think what might be missing?"

"Candles?" The boy scrunched up his forehead.

"That's a good guess," Caleb drawled over the pop, pop, pop of the corn. "We need to find some candles for the tree, that's for sure, but I was thinking of something else. It's awful quiet in here."

"Except for the popping."

"Except for the popping. When I was a boy decorating the tree with my folks, we always sang Christmas carols."

"Singing was a part of my Christmases, too." When she'd been married, she had often hummed carols while she'd gone about her housework, entertaining Mathias who wiggled in his crib. Knowing how Thomas must be thinking of the past too, she recalled a different time in her life. "When I young, the whole orphanage would sing in celebration on Christmas Eve. Alma would sit next to me, right where you are now. She had the prettiest soprano. She was like an angel singing. Do you know what her favorite carol was?"

Thomas shook his head, eyes hungry for the answer.

"'Jingle Bells.' Because it always reminded her of her family, before her parents died. She said her pa always strung bells on his horses during the winter so wherever they went, they made music."

"I sure would like some of those bells." Thomas's sadness was tempered by a smile. Happy memories must be returning to him, too. "So Kringle can have music like my ma had."

"Maybe Santa can manage that." Caleb lumbered over, moving through the shadows and toward them. "We'll see what he can do. In the meantime, should we start with 'Jingle Bells'?"

Thomas nodded, taking charge of the giant bread mixing bowl full of white fluffy corn, which Caleb handed him.

"Dashing through the snow," the big man belted out in perfect pitch. He knelt to brush a kiss against her cheek. "On a one horse open sleigh."

"O'er the fields we go," she chimed in with her imperfect alto.

"Laughing all the way," Thomas added, his voice high and sweet.

Music and laughter filled the air, making the fire warmer and the lamplight brighter.

Happiness lingered in the air of the cabin, centering around the tree decked in popcorn strings, small paper snowflakes and a dozen ribbons Caroline had borrowed from her sewing basket. Caleb knelt in the silent room, alone with the tree. This was his favorite Christmas so far. Never had he needed the spirit of the season more.

Thomas's voice rose faintly from his bed, where Caroline tucked him in. Caleb could see the outside line of her arm, the curve of her shoulder, one loose tendril of gold hair. Her laughter clung to him, a treasured memory never to forget. He'd helped his son hang his first ornament. He'd had the privilege of holding the boy up so he could decorate the highest branches. Because of tonight, he felt full up, no longer empty.

"He fell asleep the instant his head hit the pillow." Caroline closed the bedroom door. Her cheeks pink, her smile merry, she radiated a quiet joy that looked good on her. Very good. His heart twisted, wringing with love for her.

"I'm not surprised. I've never seen anyone run around so much. Back and forth, back and forth, to and from the tree." His voice cracked with emotion.

"He was excited. You were so good with him, Caleb."

"He's easy to be good to." He shrugged one shoulder. She was wrong. She was the wonder. "Do you suppose I can find a string of bells in town?"

"Who knows? I sure hope so. Did you see Thomas's face?"

"I did. There's no way I can let him down." He set the final chunk of wood into the fire, nudged it into place with the poker and set the metal tool aside. When he stood Caroline came to him, sliding into his arms. He held her while the fire crackled and breathed in the amazing sensation of having her tucked against his chest.

"How about you?" She tilted her head to peer up at him, delicate brows arched, her adorable mouth pursed with the question. "What do you want for Christmas?"

To stay here with you. The words stuck on his tongue, refusing to be spoken. He longed for her. He never wanted to leave. When he gazed into her ice-blue depths, he saw her love for him. He saw where he belonged. He dreamed improbable dreams of a family and a future right here.

"I want your happiness," he said. That was what he desired most.

"I am happy. You did that." She wrapped her arms around his neck, holding on when he should be pushing her away.

"What do you want for Christmas?" His turn to ask, and since he had two more shopping days before Christmas, he counted it as an important question.

"Your happiness." Her sincerity rang true, pure and selfless, capturing him more. She rose up on tiptoe to brush her lips across his in a shy, brief kiss.

Too brief. He circled his hand around her nape. He fought the images sifting into his mind of her wearing his wedding ring, of her welcoming him home after a hard day's work, of her cradling their child in her arms with Thomas at her side.

He wanted so much for Christmas. More than he could have. But was there a way? He knew there wasn't. But did that keep him from hoping? No. The wish built within him that maybe, just maybe, he could stay. She made him feel as if the injustices of the past were truly gone. That maybe his luck was coming back around and good things were in store.

You know better, McGraw, so stop wishing for it. He drew her against him, kissing her deep. No, he couldn't stop wishing. Infinite affection spiraled through him, more pure and powerful than he'd ever believed could be. She was his one true love and he never wanted to let her go.

"It sounds like a wonderful family night." Selma McKaslin had that knowing look of delight as she strong-armed the pan of morning rolls out of the bakery's oven. "When my boys were little, oh, the time we had trying to keep them out of trouble when we decorated the tree. One was trying to climb it, a pair of them would suddenly start wrestling, heavens! Those were merry times and gone too fast."

"Yes, but now you have grandchildren." Caroline glanced over her shoulder—Thomas was playing with Bingo on the floor—and spread a thick layer of strawberry jelly over the kneaded dough on the worktable in front of her. "Have you finished all your sewing and shopping for them?"

"Just barely. I've got baking to do and cooking. Which reminds me, dear. I expect you to bring our new beau to my Christmas Eve dinner party. I don't want to hear a single excuse."

"What makes you think Caleb is my beau?"

"Oh, a few reasons. The look on your face. The glint in your eye. You've come alive, Caroline. You are a woman falling in love." Selma slid the baking sheet onto the table with expert flair. "Don't even think about trying to deny it."

"Fine, I won't. I can see trying to change your mind is a hopeless cause." She set aside the spatula and crimped the edges of the dough together. "I'll ask Caleb and see if he will come along. It's good of you to include us."

"Why wouldn't I? You're practically family. The moment you stepped off the train with little Thomas in tow, I just lost my heart to you." Selma didn't add that she lost her heart to everyone. "Which is why I should be the first to know about you and your little romance. Why aren't you giving me the details? I need details."

"Romance." Caroline repeated the word, smiling, remembering last night's kisses. Oh, dear, was there no way she could keep control of her feelings?

"Ah, just as I thought." Selma plucked the rolls off the sheet and onto cooling racks. The bell rang above the door. "Oops! It sounds like we have another customer."

"I'll see to it." She wiped her fingers on a clean cloth. The back of her neck tingled. Caleb's familiar gait echoed in the quiet shop and affection spiraled through her. She'd been at work only a matter of hours and already she sorely missed seeing him.

"Is it school time?" Thomas asked, gazing up with adoration at the man.

She knew just how he felt. Caleb, so good and strong he made her feel safe and protected, as if hardship and cruelty could never touch her. Last night in front of the fire, being sheltered in his arms had been the most wonderful thing. Remembering their loving kisses, her face blushed. When his deep gaze fastened on hers, she knew he was remembering that intimacy, too.

"It's time. Go get your things, cowboy, and I'll take you to school." Caleb ruffled the boy's hair, tender. Love so pure scrawled across him unmistakably as he watched his son trot off in search of his winter coat.

She loved the man. Totally, completely, beyond all reason loved him, even when she'd thought it could never be possible again. Joy filtered through her like the morning's sunlight, illuminating everything. She was no longer left with the ashes of her past. She wanted to love again, to live again. She wanted to spend her days at Caleb's side and her nights in his arms.

"You look cold. Would you like a cup of coffee?" She skirted the front counter.

"No, I'm fine. You look busy back there." He spotted a grandmotherly looking woman in the back setting dough on a baking sheet. Her gaze sparkled merrily at him, as if she were already hearing wedding bells for him and Caroline.

What if there was a way? That question kept chasing him. He knew there was no way, but the wish haunted his dreams. It whispered to him when he'd opened his eyes first thing this morning and it shouted at him now. His entire being ached for it, his soul longed for it.

"We have dozens of Christmas orders." Caroline's skirts swished around her slim ankles as she waltzed closer. How did she become more beautiful with every passing day? She filled his senses—musical alto, red calico, vibrant loveliness. "It will be a busy day of baking."

"And I'll be busy working on your fix-it list." Not a bad list, considering the old rental had seen better days. The closeness of last night lingered, the texture of her lips, the taste of her kiss and the sensation of being lost to her for those close, intimate moments. He wanted more. He wanted her for his wife. "I can pick Thomas up after school, too."

"He would like that. Here he comes." Unmistakable pride filled her as she bent to tuck his scarf more securely around his chin and to tug down the brim of his knit cap.

He loved her more for it. He would love this woman for the rest of his days, infinitely and forever. It wasn't easy parting from her, but they would be together tonight. He already looked forward to the evening ahead. Going about the chores with her. Talking over Thomas's day at school. Settling down to whittle another horse out of a spare scrap of lumber. That was what he wanted, as impossible as it was. His most cherished Christmas wish.

"Goodbye, Bingo." Thomas handed over his toy with great reluctance, for no toys were allowed at school. "Aunt Caroline will take good care of you."

"I'll make sure he's warm and safe while you're gone." Satisfied the child was well wrapped against the bitter cold, she let him go. "He'll take a long nap and be rested up and ready to gallop when school is over."

The bell jangled over the door, announcing another customer. He didn't pay it any heed. He held out his hand to Thomas, waiting for the boy. "If you did *S* words in school yesterday, will you do *T* words today?"

"M-maybe." A single stutter.

"Then let's think of a few *T* words on the way. I got one. Want to hear it?" He heard the outside door swing open. Boots knelled on the floor, accompanied by the metal jingle of spurs. The hair stood up on the back of his neck, a warning sign he ignored. "Turnip."

"Thomas."

"Terrific." He cherished the moment when his son's mittened hand crept into his, so small, so precious.

"McGraw? Is that really you?" A strange tenor shattered the moment. Boots and spurs came to a stop behind him.

Caleb blinked, spun around and stared at the newcomer. The stranger wore a marshal's black shirt and silver badge. Strange, he didn't know the man but something familiar sparked at the back of his mind, something he couldn't put his finger on.

"I can't believe my eyes. It sure is you," the marshal drawled.

The drawl triggered a memory, flashing him back to seven years ago when he'd been sentenced for rape. The ring of spurs, the chime of the cell door key and the cold sour taste of fear on his tongue. Recognition rocked through him. Marshal Douglass had taken him from Blue Grass's small jail cell following his brief trial to the territorial prison. He stared, too stunned to move, overwhelmed as panic surged through him like a flashflood.

"I'll be. I'm just flummoxed." The marshal planted his beefy fists on his hips. "After what you did to that woman, what are you doing out of jail?"

Not like this. Caleb withered. Not in front of Thomas. And Caroline— He squeezed his eyes shut for one brief second. The shock was too much. It shot through his veins like ice water, washing away all he'd gained here and everything he had.

It's over. All of it. He swallowed hard and opened his eyes. Thomas gazed from one face to another, confused. Caroline stared at him, mouth open in a surprised O, hurt stark on her face. Silence reigned, settling in around him.

He should have known this would happen. It was inevitable. He'd feared it all along. He felt like a lowlife, like scum on a pond. Humiliated in front of the people he loved.

"Answer me." The marshal's tenor thundered with authority and a hint of menace.

"I was released early for good behavior." The words tumbled out, numb and disconnected. The only thing that mattered was the hurt leaving Caroline's face and the horror settling in. She was going to hate him. She would never believe the truth. He felt his last hope die as his dreams crashed to the ground.

Chapter Eight

She couldn't hear anything over the rush in her ears. Caleb had been in jail? For rape? She didn't want to believe it. She couldn't believe it. But part of her must have already accepted. Fear quaked through her in fine, trembling shakes until her teeth rattled.

Caleb was a violent ex-convict. Her Caleb. No, she shook her head, still struggling to deny it.

"Released?" The marshal bellowed, jaw set, fury dark on his harsh round face. "How can that be? Why don't I check on that to make sure it's true? I expect you to come with me quietly, unless you want to make it an official arrest in front of these nice people?"

"No, I'll come quietly." A muscle jumped along Caleb's square jaw, but he didn't look at her. He didn't meet her gaze. He gently let go of Thomas's hand. "You go with your aunt."

Tears pooled in the boy's eyes but did not fall. He was frightened by the strange man and confused by the change of plans. She marched forward to sweep Thomas away, holding him tight. So tight.

"You're lucky I came along, ma'am." The somber truth in the marshal's dark gaze struck her. It was the force that shredded the last bit of her denial. He laid a hand on his holstered

.45. "I came in for some breakfast. You wouldn't be able to make my meal to go?"

"I'll see to it, Marshal." Selma bustled into sight. "I'll bring it over myself. I'm supposing that's why you're in town, since I don't know your face. Come to take away the wanted man in our jail?"

"Yes, that's right. I'd appreciate a cup of coffee, too. Thank you, kindly." The marshal tipped his hat. "C'mon, McGraw. Let's go."

Caleb's gaze found hers. He stood tall and strong, invincible the way any good man should be. Shadows darkened his eyes and a poignant plea shone there, one she could sense as clearly as if he'd said the words aloud. *Forgive me.*

He wasn't denying it. He wasn't discounting the marshal's claim. Her knees buckled as she watched him walk away with his shoulders wide and back straight, as if only pride held him up. He'd as good as lied to her. She'd trusted him. She'd believed in him.

She'd loved him.

Pain cracked through her, the first sign of her heart rending. Sharp, tiny shards broke apart within her, slicing through flesh and bone as they fell.

"Maybe it isn't true." Not even Selma seemed to believe it as she patted Caroline's shoulder. "Get Thomas to school. Take some time for yourself. Come back when you're ready."

"But it's one of your busiest days." Her gaze tracked the tall, dark-haired man and the stern marshal along the length of the front window. Sunshine gleamed so brightly off the white glittering snow, her eyes burned. Her throat closed. She felt as if she were dying.

"Aunt Caroline? Why did Mr. McGraw hafta go with that man?" Fear raised Thomas's voice several notes.

"It will be all right." She kissed his apple cheek. She had to wrestle down her agony. Right now, she had to think about her boy. "Come, we don't want you to be marked tardy."

"Tardy. That's a *T* word." Thomas's shoes pattered across the floor.

She felt the attention of the customers as she took her coat from Selma. "Table."

"Train."

Traitor. He'd betrayed her. He'd made her think he was a wonderful man, that she was safe with him. That Thomas would be safe with him. She yanked open the door. Icy wind wrapped around her, but it wasn't the reason why she felt chilled to the marrow. Across the street, Caleb snared her attention. His gait was slow and steady and his large frame braced as he entered the marshal's office.

He was an ex-convict, just released from prison. That was the reason he'd left Alma. That was the reason he didn't know Thomas. Devastation crashed through her. She felt her heart break piece by piece.

"Why is Mr. McGraw going with that man? Is he in trouble?" Little fingers tightened around her own.

"I'm sure it will be fine." She tucked down her feelings, ignored the jagged pieces of her decimated heart and put all the reassurance she could into her voice. "Trouble is a *T* word. Can you think of another?"

"It's right here." Marshal Douglass moseyed through the doorway, telegram in hand. "Word from the head of the prison himself assuring me you are a free man. Guess you weren't an escapee after all."

"Which is what I told you." Bitterness burned like acid on Caleb's tongue. It was an old anger and a pointless one.

"Can't blame me, though. Once a bad seed, always a bad seed." The marshal crumpled up the telegram and tossed it into the garbage basket.

He could not change the past. He could never escape it. He shoved out of the chair, unsteady on his feet. He would always be looked at twice. What had he been thinking letting himself dream otherwise?

Time to stop listening to his heart. Caroline hated him. Now that word was out, the town's lawmen would likely run him out. He drew in a steadying breath and set his spine, determined to walk out of here like the free man he was.

"That's enough, Douglass." Mac McKaslin stood up from behind his desk. "The last train east comes by in twenty minutes. Chain up your prisoner and get on your way. I want you out of my office for good. McGraw, you're free to go."

"Thanks." He didn't waste time. He grabbed his coat and hat from the wall hooks.

"Your reward money should be here sometime tomorrow." Mac handed over Caleb's confiscated Colt .45.

"I'll be in to get it." He slid the handgun into its holster, unable to meet the marshal's eyes. Disgrace hung over him like a cloud as he shoved open the door. He kept his head down, avoiding eye contact with everyone he came across on the boardwalk.

The small mountain town bustled on the last few days before Christmas. Shops were busy but he kept on walking. No point in putting off what had to be done.

The late-afternoon sun slanted low over the treetops, casting long shadows before him as he walked out of town. Those shadows lengthened, a harbinger of what was to come. Snow crunched beneath his boots as he trudged down the fifth driveway and the snow-bound cabin came into sight. Thomas's snowman stood sentry near the front porch, but the boy wasn't out playing. Not today. No, Caroline would keep the boy safely tucked inside.

Away from him. He swallowed hard, gathered his courage and climbed the porch steps. He didn't dare hope she would understand. That she would look at him and see the truth, see the good inside him and welcome him back into her arms. No, not a chance of that. He wasn't surprised as the door swung open before he could knock.

"Caleb." She blocked the doorway with her slender body, chin up, ice-blue eyes fierce. The ruffled white apron she wore told him she'd been fixing supper. "You are to take your things and go."

"I would like to talk about what happened today." He let down his guard. Let her see his sincerity, the integrity of the man he was and would always be. "Can I please explain?"

"Oh, I don't think that's necessary." Distrust pursed her soft, lovely mouth that had kissed him with great tenderness. The memory slammed through him, mocking him, as if to cruelly remind him of what he'd lost. She slung a thick shawl over her shoulders, shoved his saddlebags at him and slipped onto the snowy porch, closing the door tightly behind her.

Protecting Thomas from him. The realization knifed him to the core. Couldn't she see that he would give his life to keep his son safe? That nothing would ever diminish his true love for her? He slung the pack over one arm. It was heavy with his belongings.

"You won't be staying here tonight. You won't be returning here. You will forget you ever met us." She wrapped the ends of the knit shawl around her like armor. She radiated pure strength and power. An awesome sight.

He loved her more for it. He swallowed hard, cleared his throat and hoped his voice didn't break. "I understand you're frightened. You don't need to be."

"You hid the truth from me. You had to be perfectly aware that had I known what you were, I never would have let you set foot in my home." Tears gleamed in her eyes. Hurt twisted her sweet face, a world of hurt.

He'd done that to her. He hadn't meant to and there was no way for him to fix it. "I'm sorry." It was all he could offer her. "Truly, deeply sorry."

"You should be." She blinked hard. "You have to go, Caleb."

"Can't I tell my side of the story?"

"No." She had to let him go. She lifted her chin another notch, struggling to do what was right. Those kisses in front of the fire, her love for him, it all had to be forgotten. "Goodbye."

"But—"

"Goodbye." Regret, remorse, despair ripped her apart as she grappled for the doorknob. The knob rattled when her fingers found it and she gave it a turn. Just do it, she told herself. Do what has to be done.

Why did she linger? Why didn't her feet move? Her gaze found his one last time. Deep blue brilliance, the sheen of honesty so starkly real she couldn't reconcile the man with Caleb McGraw, ex-convict and rapist. She thought of the thin bedroom door that had separated her from him at night and shivered. Why hadn't she felt afraid? Why hadn't she felt even a hint of a clue about his secret?

Tears stung her eyes and knotted in her throat. She gave the door a push, stumbled through the doorway and turned her back on him. It had to be done. He was a dangerous and violent man.

Agony tore through her as she threw the bolt. Misery cinched up her ribs, making it impossible to breathe. She'd done the right thing, so why did it hurt so much? She rubbed the heel of her hand over her heart, surprised by the agony buried there, refusing to budge.

She waited for the sound of Caleb's boots on the steps. Slow. Reluctant. Sad. The ring of his gait pulled at her because she'd wanted this outcome to be different. She wanted him to be different—to be the man she'd fallen in love with. She'd known nothing true about him at all.

She shrugged out of her shawl, hung it on its peg and sighed out agony. It was over. There was nothing to do but go on from here.

Cold snow fell from an inky-black sky as Caleb dismounted in front of the town's livery stable and led his horse by the reins through the wide double doors. Once inside he swept off his battered, wide-brimmed hat. A symphony of icy snow tapped on the wall as he headed down the main aisle.

"Is that you, McGraw?" The owner, Austin Dermot, stuck his head out of his office. Surely he'd heard the rumors that had to be going around town, but he made no show of it. "Are you sure you want to bed down with your mustang? It's awful cold out there and the temperature is falling."

"I'll be all right." A stall thick with straw and hay was far better accommodations than he'd had for seven years. "I've got my bedroll. I'll be fine."

"If you need more blankets, help yourself. There are horse blankets in the tackroom and a couple quilts in my office." Austin shrugged into a thick wool coat. "I'm heading home. Is there anything else you need?"

"No, but thank you." He cross-tied his horse in the aisle and bent to unbuckle the saddle cinch. Dermot's footsteps faded away. The front doors creaked shut and the cold air whipping down the aisle ceased. A couple of horses nosed over their gates to nicker at him curiously as he stowed the saddle, brushed down Ghost and led him to their assigned stall.

While the mustang crunched on oats, Caleb rolled up in his blankets and dug out the package of beef jerky buried in his packs. Loneliness had never hurt like this. He missed Caroline. He missed Thomas.

Caleb, you knew better. This hurting is your fault. He tore off a chunk of cured meat and popped it in his mouth. A man's past always caught up with him. Once branded, always branded. There was no escape.

Caroline. He grimaced, wretched over the way she'd looked at him. She despised him. As wonderful and renewing as her gazes of love had been, they were gone.

Never again would she peer up at him with affection and respect. Light had vanished from his world. She would never be his wife welcoming him home from work. Thomas would not come running eager to tell of his school day. There would be no cozy family suppers, no evenings spent whittling and chatting by the fire, no Christmas mornings watching Thomas open his presents.

Caleb bowed his head. Hopelessness blinded him. He was nothing without them.

Chapter Nine

∽◯◯◯◯∽

"Whew, I think that's it. What a morning!" Selma turned the sign from Open to Closed. Her apron fluttered as she strained to get a good look out the bakery's front window. "A storm is blowing in. That means snow for Christmas Eve."

"Thomas will be thrilled." Caroline swiped a sudsy cloth along the worktable and tried not to think about Caleb. She shouldn't care where he was and if he was warm and safe.

"I suppose you can't wait for Christmas morning to come around. Those horses and that wonderful barn you made out of fabric and quilt batting." Selma had watched her progress over the earlier month or so during Caroline's lunch breaks. "He is going to love them."

"I hope so." Affection warmed her as she wrung out the dishcloth, soap bubbles popping. She couldn't wait to see Thomas unwrap her gifts. Bingo would finally have friends and a home. "First things first. We are definitely coming over to your party tonight, storm or not. I'm bringing buttermilk dinner rolls—no, don't you even think about arguing. After baking all morning here, you don't need to do it tonight. You have enough to do."

"Then I won't say no, my dear." Selma skirted the counter and plucked the cloth from Caroline's hands. "You came in early and worked hard. It's noon on Christmas Eve. We're closing early. Go fetch Thomas from school and go home."

"But there's dishes to dry and the floor to sweep."

"Those things will wait until after Christmas. I suppose your Mr. McGraw won't be accompanying you tonight?"

"You know he won't." Thinking of him drilled like an arrow through the debris of her heart. "Now that the truth is out, I imagine he's long gone by now. Or he should be."

"Well, I'm not so sure." Selma leaned against the worktable thoughtfully and crossed her arms. "Your Caleb was always gentle and polite. He seemed so strong and good."

"He was a good pretender." Her chest coiled up tight as grief cinched it. That was the truth about Caleb. He'd covered up the real man he was so well, everyone believed it.

"That may be." Selma turned to move a half dozen decorated cupcakes into a small bakery box. "But you know everything you need to about a man by the way he treats others. That Marshal Douglass shorted me five cents on his breakfast when I brought it by the marshal's office. No tip. My son Mac works there, as you know, and he didn't think much of Douglass. He and Mac did think a lot of Caleb McGraw."

"Why? I would have thought they would want a man like that far away from this town."

"Because whatever the man's past, he doesn't look as if he could hurt a fly. The way he is with you and Thomas. And that ancient horse of his he treats like a prized racehorse. I've seen him ride by on the street. And all the work he did on your cabin. When Rush Travers, your landlord, was in this morning he went on about all the free labor. Caleb didn't charge him a penny."

"That doesn't count. He was trying to get on our good sides. To make us believe he was a better man than he truly was."

"What was the point? For what purpose?"

Caroline hung her head, refusing to say. He'd wanted to get

close to his son, that was all. And the love he'd shown her, why, it didn't matter. She could have nothing to do with the man now that she knew his true nature.

"My son sees firsthand the kind of men who commit those horrible crimes. They might seem charming on the outside at first, hiding who they are, but that's all it is. A veneer. Something that peels away to reveal the truth beneath. You know Caleb best. What kind of man did you see?"

Kind. Gentle. Loving. For one brief unstoppable moment the memories washed over her. Caleb's raw strength but not brutality as he tossed the horse thief to the ground, bound and conquered. Caleb full of wretched sorrow and agonized longing when he first set sight on his son. Caleb's undisguised love on his face when he'd swooped Thomas into his brawny arms. His kindness to her horse, standing in the kitchen bathed in lamplight doing the dishes, talking about his love for his parents and for Thomas, and his kisses….

What are you doing, Caroline? She cringed inwardly, fighting hard not to let those beautiful images carry her away. Perhaps he'd tried so hard to be a different man from what he used to be, she reasoned. Maybe that was why he'd been so determined in his kindness. He wanted to make a new start. A good start.

But it didn't make him a safe man, a man she should trust.

"For you and Thomas. A little treat for your Christmas day." Selma closed the lid and held the box of cupcakes out to her. "Oh, my, is that the school bell ringing? You better hurry if you want to fetch Thomas."

"Thank you, Selma." She kissed the dear lady's cheek, seized the bakery box and hurried to fetch her coat. She felt as if she were drowning, as if she could never again draw in air. She hadn't hurt like this since Michael's death. How had a drifter come to mean so much to her?

Regretting the day Caleb McGraw came into her life, she buttoned her coat. She burst outside into the cold, where snow fell like tears.

* * *

Packed to go, Caleb rode Ghost through the downfall. The thick veil of snow wrapped around him as he dismounted in front of the jail. The mustang jangled his bits, glancing right and left, not certain what was to come next. The old boy had been harshly treated somewhere along the way. Caleb patted the gelding's neck in reassurance and tethered him by both reins.

"I won't be long, buddy," he promised.

A mean wind chased him to the door where he hesitated. Yesterday's humiliation clung to him. A man couldn't escape his past, but he could control how he lived each moment. He took a deep breath and opened the door.

"McGraw." Mac glanced up from his desk. A few other marshals crowded in the room, one pouring coffee, one feeding the potbellied stove, another filing paperwork. "Good news."

"The funds came in?"

"I've got them right here." He sorted through folders on his desk. "I was afraid it might not come until after Christmas. Looks like you're in luck."

"I appreciate this, Marshal." He strolled forward, spine straight, pushing aside his humiliation.

"Here you are." Mac stood up to hold out a small envelope. "Five hundred dollars."

"Thank you. This will come in handy." He took the thick bundle and slipped it into his coat pocket. "Merry Christmas."

"Same to you, McGraw." Mac accompanied him to the door. "I suppose you're headed out of town?"

"That's my plan. You don't have to worry about me staying around." He knuckled back his hat, determined to do this right, meet the lawman's gaze and say goodbye.

"That's too bad." Mac turned the doorknob. "The moment you brought in that felon trussed up like a pig, I've kept my eye on you. The way you have looked after the Widow Dreyer and Thomas says something. You're related to the boy, aren't you?"

He nodded, unable to deny it. "How did you know?"

"You look a lot like him. I told you I keep watch on things in this town. It's my job to know what's going on with the people I protect. I also know the look of a hardened man, one violent enough to do anything to get what he wants." The marshal's gaze sharpened. The room silenced.

Snow slapped against Caleb's shoulder as he stood in the threshold, already knowing the lawman was about to condemn him.

"You aren't that kind of man." Mac's stern face cracked, showing a hint of understanding. "I've seen innocent men go to prison and guilty men get off scot-free. Justice isn't perfect. So I say it's a shame you are just passing through. Seems Caroline would have an easier time trying to support that boy if she had someone to stick around and help."

His throat closed up. Not a chance in heck could he get a word out edgewise. He'd never figured anyone would see the truth. It meant so much, he could only nod and stumble out the door. Snow battered his face like fists as he blindly felt his way to the hitching post.

Ghost nickered with concern and lipped the brim of his hat. Still too choked up to speak, he stroked the horse's velvet nose. Good to know he was welcome in this town, in spite of his past. But what good did that do him?

Caroline was afraid of him. She, the woman who owned his heart, couldn't see in him what the marshal, a perfect stranger, had.

No, he had no choice but to go. There was no way to resurrect his dreams, no way to hope for a life loving her and raising Thomas. There was nothing for him here.

He blinked hard, his vision came into focus and he unknotted the reins. He had one more errand left to do before he rode away forever and it wasn't going to be easy.

Caroline Dreyer slipped the last packet of dinner rolls into the picnic basket and surveyed her kitchen. It looked as if she had everything—a pot of baked beans, a crock of butter and three dozen rolls to contribute to Selma's Christmas Eve supper. One last glance at the clock told her she was right on time.

"Thomas? Are you almost ready to go?" She closed the basket's lid tight.

"I guess." His hands gripped the sill. His dark hair was tousled. His cowlick stuck straight up. New sorrow radiated from the child, matching the sadness in her heart. They both missed Caleb with a grief that could not be put into words.

Memories from last night flashed unbidden into her mind, making her grief fresh—of Caleb standing mountain-strong in the lamplight belting out the chorus to "Jingle Bells" in his resonant baritone. Of Caleb at the stove popping corn in the soup kettle, his granite face gentle with happiness. Of Caleb leaning closer and closer to her until their lips met. Her soul sighed at the memory. Nothing on earth had been as tender as his kiss.

How could her gentle Caleb have been convicted of rape? She gripped the basket's woven handle, confused, torn apart, not understanding.

"Come put on your coat. I've got the fire to bank, the lamp to put out and then we're out of here." She hefted the basket off the table and set it beside the front door.

"Aunt Caroline?" His deep blue gaze widened, so pure and sweet and true.

She was reminded of another man when she looked into those eyes.

"I see something." Thomas clung to the sill, struggling to peer through the storm. "There's a man with our horse."

"What man?" She tapped closer to squint through the haze of snow. A shadow briefly appeared, wide shouldered and sure, leading Kringle by the reins. Kringle plodded along obediently, head bowed against the gusting wind, unconcerned.

It could only be one man. Just one.

"It's Mr. McGraw!" Thomas launched from the window.

His shoes knelled with fast, desperate beats as he dashed around her.

"Wait! Thomas!" She tried to stop him but he'd already flung open the door. Thomas stood on the threshold, eagerly searching through the shadows of the storm.

She laid both hands on his shoulders, intending to draw him into the house but Caleb stormed into sight. Swathed in snow, he towered above them like a Western legend come to life, like everything good and marvelous in the world.

She wanted more than anything to believe in that image, but she knew better. She had Thomas to think of. She stepped out onto the porch and into the biting cold, standing between the boy and his father. She hated doing it. She had to.

"Caroline, don't be frightened." The deep notes of Caleb's voice rolled through her, infinitely honorable and wonderfully familiar. Like a sound she'd been longing to hear all her life, a sound she never wanted to forget.

Why couldn't she stay in control of her heart? She steeled her spine, wondering why he was here, why he had come. "I'm not frightened. I just want you to go. It's the right thing to do, Caleb."

"I know." He strode up the steps, slow and easy, brushing snow out of his face with one gloved hand. Power emanated from him, but not brutality. Raw masculinity defined him as he climbed the last step to stand on the porch that no longer squeaked. Under eaves that were no longer loose. "I couldn't go without apologizing."

"It's not necessary." She had to look away. She couldn't bear to see the face of the man she still loved. "It's best if you just get on your horse and keeping going."

"No." Thomas's voice pitched upward in a high tone of pain. He slipped around her and barreled straight into Caleb's arms. "No, no. Mr. McGraw, you hafta stay. You've just got to."

"It's all right, cowboy." The man's words soothed like a deep-noted lullaby as he lifted the boy off the porch, holding him against his broad chest. "Things are going to be just fine. I've got your Christmas present. Do you want it now?"

A solemn nod.

She wanted to charge over and pluck Thomas right out of Caleb's arms, but she couldn't move. Maybe it would be better for the boy to say his goodbyes and end things in a good way.

"It's right here in my coat pocket. Why don't you reach it for me, since I can't?" Caleb's gaze seemed to drink in the boy's features, lingering on his chiseled chin, his eyes, his dark hair with a cowlick sticking up.

The boy leaned in and pulled out a wooden caving, a perfect replica of a mustang. She couldn't imagine the time and the care it must have taken Caleb to get every detail just right—the flying mane, the arched neck, the prancing hooves.

"Oh, wow." Thomas stared transfixed at the horse, unable to say more. Just stare.

"Now Bingo has a friend."

"But Mr. McGraw? I don't got a present for you." Worry crinkled his adorable face.

"Knowing that you like the horse is present enough for me." He swallowed hard. He would always have this moment to remember, holding his son in his arms. He shifted Thomas's weight on one hip so he could pull the envelope out of his other pocket. "This is for you, Caroline."

"No, I can't accept it." For a woman dead set against him, she didn't sound harsh. She didn't sound disgusted. Her dulcet alto held no venom. Just pain.

It struck him like a blow. He wished he could relive the last handful of days and do it differently, so they'd never met and he could have spared her. He drew in a ragged breath. If she'd been angry, it would be easier than facing her quiet pain.

"It's not a gift. It's the reward money on the horse thief." He held out the envelope. "I want you to have it."

"No, that wouldn't be right." She held out both hands.

Such soft hands. He recalled the magic of her touch, the comfort she'd given him, the hope. He wished he could give her those things in return. Heartbreak was killing him. That was his own fault. He'd known from the start not to fall for her. A fine lady like Caroline wouldn't want a man with his record.

"Please, take it for Thomas."

"Oh." She hadn't seemed to expect that. Maybe she figured because he had seven years of hard time under his belt that he didn't have what it took to keep his commitments. To do the right thing.

"There will be more when I find work." He set the envelope into her hand, watching her reluctance. Her top teeth dug into her bottom lip as her fingers closed around the packet. Probably debating the merits of accepting it. Probably hating to admit how much she could use that for Thomas's sake. Maybe buy them a little house in town close to school and the bakery with enough left over to make things real comfortable.

That was all he wanted—well, all he could really have. He steeled his spine, resisted the urge to kiss Thomas's cheek and gazed at the child who'd brought them together one long last time.

"Did you hitch up Kringle to the sled?" She looked at him as if she'd never seen him before, assessing him. "I was going to do that."

"I knew you would be leaving and I wanted to save you a step." He shrugged, feeling foolish now. It was the last thing he could do for her, the last gesture he could make. "It was no trouble."

"Where will you go?"

"West."

"I meant for tonight. It's Christmas Eve." She untucked the envelope's flap and peered inside. So many greenbacks. What had Selma said? *You know everything you need to about a man by the way he treats others.*

"Don't worry about me, Caroline. I've been through worse. I guess this is goodbye." Boots braced, he towered above her, as mighty as ever. Humility rang in his words. Dignity emanated from him as he turned his attention to Thomas. His gaze was so full of wretched sorrow and agonized longing she could feel the force of it deep in her soul.

"Don't say goodbye." Thomas's voice pitched higher, raw with pain. "I don't like goodbyes. Not at all."

"I feel the same way, cowboy." Caleb brushed a kiss to the boy's cheek. Such a sweet gesture.

Her heart crumpled. This was the side of Caleb she adored. Gentle. Loving. Strong. Had he really just been pretending all this time? Did she really believe that? She thought of everything she'd seen him do, every way he'd behaved and every word he'd uttered. Words, acts, deeds of a good man.

Integrity shone from him as he brushed a few flakes of snow from Thomas's hair. Love burned from within him, from the honest places of a man's soul, and the look of it was hard to deny.

She curled her fingers around the thick envelope in her hand. An envelope full of money. He had no home, few possessions, and no security anywhere. Wouldn't a ruthless and dangerous man keep it for himself?

"What happened?" The question rolled off her tongue. She had to know the truth. "Why were you arrested?"

"Because when the town sheriff followed a rapist's tracks from the neighbor's house through the wheat field, he spotted me in the distance cutting my crop." Honesty shone from him, an unmistakable light. "Instead of checking to see if there was any evidence that someone had taken off down the river to hide his tracks, the sheriff crossed the river, broke a path through the uncut wheat and arrested me."

"This was on your family's land?"

"Yes, after my parents were gone. I was out there alone. I had no witness to confirm it. The sheriff ignored the fact that there were no tracks from the river to my land on the other side. I didn't take his accusations too seriously, I mean, I was innocent, I was a farmer, not a rapist. I thought everyone could see how wrong the lawman was, but I was convicted."

"You were innocent." It was plain to see now.

"You don't have to believe it. Trust me, no one else did." A muscle snapped along his jaw, but it wasn't anger that laced his voice. Not bitterness. Just acceptance. "Once I was in jail, I learned why. Everyone there was innocent, too. They would proclaim it all the day long even when they weren't."

He looked weary. He gazed at her with Thomas's eyes, so honest they had nothing to hide. She could really see him.

All of him. Just as she had all along.

He brushed Thomas's cheek with his free hand, devotion stark on his face. A father's protective love that was both as unshakable as the earth and as kind as Christmas. "Maybe I'll whittle up a few more toys now and then, if your Aunt Caroline doesn't mind, send them along with the money. Would that be okay?"

"Y-yes." No. Agony clawed behind her ribs as she watched him lower Thomas to the porch.

"So this isn't really goodbye." He unwound from the boy's grip gently. "We can always remember being friends."

"But you're leaving." Thomas clutched his horse and let out a shaky sigh. "You'll be g-gone."

"Love doesn't end just because people are apart." He knelt to catch a single tear with the pad of his thumb. Heartbreak shadowed his eyes as he laid his hand over Thomas's small chest. "So wherever you are, I'll be right here. All you have to do is remember me."

"O-kay." The boy choked on a sob. It was no comfort.

No comfort at all. She knelt down beside Thomas, surprised when he threw himself into her arms, needing her comfort, needing her love. She held him tight, stroking his hair and the middle of his back.

"For what it's worth, I'm sorry." Caleb pulled her attention, his apology low and anguished. Cords worked in his neck as he wrestled down his own emotion. His sapphire-blue eyes—Thomas's eyes. They were the same, Caleb and his son. Thomas didn't only have his father's eyes, but his heart.

"I'm sorry, too." Tears burned behind her eyes and rose up regardless of how hard she fought them. "I'm sorry, but I have to protest. I won't let you say goodbye."

"What?" Confusion furrowed his forehead. Disbelief twisted his handsome face. "I don't understand."

"Please don't go." She knew him. She'd known all along. How could she have ever doubted him? He could she never have committed such a horrible act. Not Caleb. It was the hardship she saw when she looked into his eyes. The honest suffering of a man who'd had an unfair turn in life and his goodness never wavered.

She saw his soul and every bit of his spirit. Enduring devotion wove through her, powerful enough to last for eternity. He had saved her. He'd given her what she'd never believed she could find again.

"Do you mean it?" Disbelief twisted his face.

"Absolutely." She could not let Caleb go. The chance to be loved by him, by the tender, decent man he was, was all she wanted. Her soul felt bound to his. She was nothing without him. "Please, stay for Christmas. Stay forever."

"Forever? Really. That sounds perfect to me." His arms wrapped about her, drawing her against the safe harbor of his strong chest. She listened to his heart beat, where only kindness lived. This was a man chivalrousness enough to always be what she needed, a man honorable enough to always do what was right. "I'm in love with you, Caroline."

"Thomas and I love you." So, so much. More than words could possibly say. "You wouldn't want to come with us tonight? Selma would be thrilled to have you."

"Sure, I will. It's not every day a man gets his Christmas wish." Happiness lit him up, an amazing sight to see. He scooped Thomas into his arms, father and son, all of her heart.

Love was the best Christmas gift.

Epilogue

Christmas Eve, one year later

"Are you sure you feel up this?" Caleb brushed the snow off his coat as he shouldered through the door. The little home they'd bought in town was cozy and warm, their very own place. It was a good feeling to see the life he and Caroline had made together since their spring wedding. He'd found work at the marshal's office and folks in town accepted him, once they'd gotten to know him. Happiness grabbed hold of him as it always did whenever he saw his Caroline. His beautiful wife looked up from latching the basket's lid to welcome him with a smile.

"Yes, I'm sure. I'm still a bit nauseous, but the worst of the morning sickness is over for the day and it's almost gone entirely." She stroked the small curve of her belly, where their baby grew. Radiant, she smiled, her love for him plain in her eyes. "Besides, Selma would never forgive me if I miss tonight. We're practically family or so she insists, since she was the one who championed you all along."

"She's been good to us, that's for sure." He brushed a kiss to her lips, love and desire filling him up. "Too bad we aren't staying home."

Her amused chuckle made him laugh, too. She flashed a dimpled smiled up at him. "There will be time enough for that later tonight. Supper first."

"Pa!" Thomas came running with Bingo in one hand. "Can I help hitch up the horses?"

"Sorry, son, but I already did. I strung the jingle bells on the harnessing, too. But how about I let you help me drive the horses?"

"Wow. All right!" They had chosen to tell him the truth about his father. Now they were a family bound by love of the strongest kind.

"Put on your wraps. It's time to go." She ran a hand through Thomas's hair, smoothing it, for all the good it would do. He would soon be running and playing with Selma's grandchildren. Her heart filled seeing him so happy.

"Okay." To her surprise, the boy heaved the basket off the table and manhandled it to the door. Perhaps determined to be just like his father, he set it down with a capable air and reached for his coat.

"You look happy, Mrs. McGraw." Caleb leaned in and pulled her close.

"Happy? No, I'm much more than that." She relaxed against his chest, listened to the reliable thump of his heart and thought about the last year.

Caleb was an amazing, attentive husband and a man with a heart of gold. Immeasurable gratitude welled up. She could not believe how lucky she was. She had Caleb to adore, Thomas to love and a child on the way—Caleb's child. Her world was filled with color. Everywhere she looked she saw shades of brightness and beauty and, most of all, love.

"Jingle bells," Caleb began singing as he unhooked her cloak from its peg.

"Jingle bells," Thomas belted out slightly off tune.

"Jingle all the way," she pitched in.

They sang together, a family, as they tumbled out into the December night. Snow sifted over them like a fairy-tale promise as Caleb took her hand.

* * * * *

CHRISTMAS AT
CAHILL CROSSING

Carol Finch

Dear Reader,

Welcome to Cahill Crossing, Texas! The holiday season roars in with a blizzard that leaves boutique owner Rosa Greer stranded in a snowdrift. What she needs is a Yuletide angel to rescue her. What she gets is a snarly wolf dog and a gruff ex-Texas Ranger soured on life. Rosa is determined to repay Lucas Burnett by including him in the community festivities she has planned for Christmas.

Lucas doesn't want to be dragged into society. He wants to be left alone—but Rosa, who is hiding secrets from the world, intrigues him. So…what's a man to do when he is bedazzled by a lively angel? The real question is: Who is saving whom at Christmas?

I hope you enjoy this fast-paced tale as much as I enjoyed writing it. Join me next month for the first book in the continuing series about the founding family of Cahill Crossing. In *The Lonely Rancher,* you'll meet Quin, who clashes with Rosa's cousin from Boston. The woman is too much like his two brothers and sister—who tramped off to chase their dreams—leaving Quin to manage the family ranch alone. Quin has enough problems with his estranged family without adding feisty Adrianna McKnight to his woes. But she's in his face and she is here to stay!

Carol Finch

Chapter One

Texas, December, Early 1880s

Rosalie Greer shivered as a blast of icy wind slapped her in the face while she drove her wagon, filled with precious cargo and supplies, down the road to Cahill Crossing. She had left the train depot at Wolf Grove early enough in the day to drive the ten-mile distance and arrive home before dark. Or so she had thought. Unfortunately, the train carrying her freight had been behind schedule and she had waylaid to grab a bite to eat before heading home.

That had been a gigantic mistake, she mused as she stared uneasily at the bank of low-hanging black and gray clouds rolling toward her. She popped the reins over the horses' rumps, sending them into a trot. Although Rosalie had moved to the fledgling community of Cahill Crossing only two years earlier to open her boutique, she had endured a Blue Norther blizzard the previous winter. She had developed a wary respect for them—and quickly. One look at the threatening sky and the feel of the frigid wind assured her that it was going to be a long, cold ride home.

Another blast of frigid air swooshed past her, bringing

gigantic snowflakes. Rosa set aside the reins to fasten the coat, which, at best, provided only meager warmth.

"Confounded weather," she grumbled to the world at large. "Never know when storms are coming. This is—"

Her voice transformed into a gasp when stinging sleet mingled with the oversize snowflakes. Sweet mercy! One minute it was just beginning to snow and then wham! She was in the middle of a full-blown blizzard. Within a half hour the blowing snow had pelted her so relentlessly that she nearly lost her sense of direction. Visibility decreased to one hundred yards—at best. The farther west she traveled the larger the piles and the thicker the sleet and snowflakes. Shifting snow and drifts made it difficult to tell the trodden path from the ditches bookending it.

Rosa gritted her chattering teeth, huddled inside her flimsy jacket and wished the rented team of horses and wagon could sprout wings and fly back to her cozy rooms above her boutique on Town Square. No such luck. Despite her noble crusade to purchase her cargo in Wolf Grove then unload it under the cover of darkness—so no one would be the wiser—Rosa faced disaster.

She had never contemplated her own demise very seriously, but freezing to death on a deserted road in the middle of nowhere just before Christmas had not been at the top of her list.

The howling wind whipped through a grove of leafless trees that reminded her of bony fingers reaching into the ominous sky. One of the horses, a bay gelding, pranced sideways and slammed into the sorrel, causing the wagon to jerk unexpectedly.

"Confound it!" she muttered in frustration.

When the skittish bay bolted into a gallop, startling the sorrel gelding into a trot, Rosa clamped her fist on the seat of the buckboard to steady herself—and failed. With a startled yelp, she somersaulted backward onto the lumpy wagon bed loaded with supplies. Her shriek startled the jumpy horses and the team thundered off while she rolled around in the wagon bed, trying to regain her balance.

"Whoa, you idiotic horses!" she yelled. To no avail.

With grim determination, Rosa crawled onto her hands and knees to anchor herself against the back of the seat. Despite the hampering skirts, she slithered over the seat to grope for the reins on the floorboard. Right there and then she vowed to give the rent horses a bad recommendation—*if* and when she made it to town to speak to the livery owner.

It was true that one of the reasons Rosa had packed up and moved west was to satisfy her sense of adventure and follow her dream of opening her own business. However, hanging on for dear life in a buckboard attached to two flighty horses was not exactly the adventure she'd had in mind. From the look of things, she wasn't going to live past the age of twenty-six. Worse, she wouldn't survive to follow through with her grand plans for Christmas.

"Heaven help me!" she yelped as the wagon careened then skidded across the layer of sleet-covered snow that she *presumed* was the road. But it was difficult to tell because the ditches were level full of drifts. The raging snowstorm and gathering darkness had combined to make travel treacherous.

Mustering her resolve, Rosa clamped her hands around the reins and clambered to stand upright on the floorboards. "Whoa! And I mean *whoa,* damn it!" She stamped on the brake, simultaneously jerking as hard as she could on the reins.

"Oh, Lord!" she shrieked as the wagon skidded sideways, throwing her off balance again. This time, however, she managed to catch herself before she cartwheeled to the ground and kerplunked into a snowdrift.

The infuriating horses finally stopped then tossed their heads to shake off the snow. Rosa glared good and hard at the troublemakers. "About time," she growled at them. When she tried to proceed at a slow, methodic pace, the distant howls of wolves made the horses uneasy and anxious to run again.

Rosa glanced around warily then pulled up the collar of her

jacket to keep the icy wind off her neck. Chilled to the bone, she twisted around to rummage through her cargo to locate a pair of gloves and a scarf. She glanced this way and that, barely recognizing the canyon that dropped off the bend of the road. It was the site where Earl and Ruby Cahill, the town founders, had suffered the tragic wagon accident that took their lives two years earlier. The locals referred to the site as Ghost Canyon and swore you could hear voices in the wind that swept up the rock-strewn slope. Rosa winced, certain she was hearing voices herself. She was more than anxious to quit the place.

Eventually, she managed to get the horses moving at a slow pace but it was difficult to make out familiar landmarks when visibility dropped another dangerous notch.

"Come along," Rosa demanded when the horses stopped and pricked their ears at the sound of howling wolves. When the horses did no more than shift sideways she climbed down, determined to lead the horses forward. "Lamebrain animals!" she railed in exasperation. "You're supposed to have horse sense—awk!"

The horses bolted forward, jerking the wagon sideways on the slick road. Rosa yelped when the wagon slid into an unseen ditch filled with snow. The bay gelding reared up then fell off balance when the heavily loaded wagon teetered sideways. Rosa groaned in pain when the bay slammed into her then stepped on her leg as they went down together. She held on to the harness for dear life as the downed horse whinnied and struggled to regain its feet. It was made harder by the sorrel gelding who kept shifting in alarm, anxious to run. Rosa groaned in pain and scrambled to move out of the way before the downed horse trampled her while trying to stand up.

And suddenly, all Rosa wanted for Christmas was *not* to be dead!

To her dismay, she noticed the bay came up limping. Worse,

the jostling of both horses had left the wagon tilted to a sharp angle in the ditch.

"This cannot be happening," she grumbled as she balanced on her good leg while the other leg began a cold, steady throb that spread from her ankle to her knee. "People on noble errands should be protected, shouldn't they?" she asked, staring heavenward.

Apparently, the answer to that question was, *not necessarily.*

A chill dribbled down Rosa's spine while she stood on one leg in the darkness, serenaded by an eerie chorus of howls. The tormenting sounds grew louder by the minute. Frantic, she tried to hobble forward to drag the wagon from the ditch, but it was no use. One nervous horse and one lame horse couldn't get the job done.

Rosa's precious cargo was as stuck as it could get.

Desperate, she glanced around the darkness, barely making out the drift in front of the wagon. All she could think to do was scream for help—which she did until she was hoarse. Then she realized if there was any *saving* to be done, she would have to do it herself. If she had any chance of surviving this night when hell seemed to have frozen over, she had to dig into the snow to make an improvised igloo.

Like a dog unearthing a bone, Rosa pawed the snow until she carved a hole large enough to crawl into and gather her skirts around her. Panting for breath, she sent a prayer heavenward then listened to the howls of approaching wolves that carried in the wind like a death knell.

"Blasted horses were no help at all," she muttered.

Rosa figured the pack of furry beasts would get her if she didn't freeze to death first. Her thoughts drifted to the recent letter from her mother in Maryland. Rosa had the depressing feeling the invitation—to come home for the holidays—would be the last correspondence she'd receive from anyone.

Her injured leg throbbed in rhythm with her pulse while the wolves howled and moved in for the kill. *To better days,* if

I have any days left. That was Rosa's last thought before she closed her eyes and shivered uncontrollably. Then the darkness swallowed her up…and she succumbed to the cold silence….

Lucas Burnett pulled on the black hood that protected his head and face before he ventured from his barn to confront the raging blizzard that had descended on his horse ranch. He well remembered from his days of service with the Texas Rangers, and from his youth in Comanche camp, that Texas blizzards were unusually brutal. He had taken the precaution of doubling up on coats and breeches before he exited his cabin to feed and water his livestock. The buffalo-hide coat held in his body heat and the long black canvas duster repelled the sleet and snow.

"This is still better than the bad old days," Lucas reminded his limping dog—named Dog. His faithful companion had saved Lucas's life three years earlier and had taken a bullet in the leg in the process.

Dog stared up at him with dark eyes then shook off the white flakes from his dark coat. They trudged side-by-side through the wind-driven snow toward the welcoming cabin where golden light glowed in the window.

It isn't a night fit for man nor beast, Lucas mused as he stared at the cabin he had built with his own hands. He had received this parcel of land, lying east of Cahill Crossing, in exchange for his service with the Rangers. Never mind that this land had once been part of the Comancheria and he could go where he pleased—until white folks wanted it and did whatever necessary to get it.

After ten years of dedicated service, Lucas had constructed the cabin for himself and Dog. The barn, lined with stalls for his horses, had taken a year to erect. He glanced over his shoulder, noting that his small herd of cattle had had the good sense to cross the pasture to use the barn and sheds for wind blocks. Hopefully all his livestock would survive the winter blast.

With his rifle clamped in one hand—because he had learned the hard way never to go anywhere unarmed—he stopped in his tracks. An unidentified sound drifted in the wind. Lucas couldn't name the source of the sound, but it put Dog on alert, too.

His gaze bounced back and forth between the cabin and the snowy darkness. The thought of tossing another log on the fire and sitting beside the hearth to sip on steaming coffee held tremendous appeal. But the odd sound carrying in the wind had him concerned. Then he heard a distressed whinny—and he was definitely familiar with that sound. He reversed direction to the barn. Once inside, he held up the lantern to see his prize horses all safe and unharmed staring back at him from their stalls.

Whoever or whatever was out there in the howling darkness would have to stay there, he told himself. Hadn't he served humanity long enough? And what thanks had he gotten? He'd been called a *breed* because he was a quarter Comanche, a quarter Spanish and half-white. White and Mexican outlaws had jeered at him and Indian renegades labeled him a traitor because he was often forced to fight against them. His Indian cousins didn't seem to realize that if not for his ability to act as their interpreter there would have been far more bloodshed and misunderstandings among white, Spanish and Indian than there were already.

Well, as far as Lucas was concerned, all of fickle humanity could go hang themselves. If he had his way, he wouldn't have been *forced* to grant right of way to build the railroad and the road that joined Wolf Grove and Cahill Crossing. In fact, that fledgling town called Cahill Crossing—which had sprung up in anticipation of the coming railroad—could shrivel up and die for all he cared. He and Dog got along fine with limited exposure to white society.

Somewhere, a horse screamed in the inky darkness. The howls of wolves drifted on the wind. Lucas glanced down as Dog limped beside him. Dog was half wolf and half shepherd, and he heard the call of the wild. There had been a time—or three—in the past when Lucas thought Dog might answer the call. However, since the injury that had caused a limp, the animal rarely prowled the darkness unless he traveled with Lucas. Yet that didn't mean Dog didn't prick his ears and stare into the blowing snow, as if he, like Lucas, wasn't quite sure where he belonged.

What was left of his conscience, and the smidgeon of good-will toward men that cynicism hadn't burned out of him, raised their noble heads.

"Well, hell," Lucas grumbled sourly. "What if some idiotic traveler is stranded out there, stalked by wolves?"

Dog whined and stared up at him.

Lucas blew out his breath. "Fine, Dog. We'll make the effort if *you* insist."

Lucas lurched around to return to the barn again. When he whistled, every horse lifted its head. "Come here, Drizzle," Lucas commanded the dark gray Appaloosa with a white rump that looked as if someone had dribbled blotches of black paint on it. The well-trained stallion had been through hell with Lucas, just as Dog had. Sturdy, steadfast and experienced, Lucas mused as he set aside the lantern to saddle Drizzle.

With the swiftness that came with endless practice, Lucas readied Drizzle for travel. Then he lit a torch to guide the way through the blowing snow. The smell of kerosene swirled around Lucas as he lifted the burning torch over his head. Dog limped ahead of them, following the sound of frantic whinnies and the distinct howling of wolves.

Lucas stared through the holes of his protective hood. He held the torch in his left hand so he could grasp the reins and his trusty rifle in his right. His senses went on high alert when he spotted the silhouette of a nearly upturned wagon stuck in a snowdrift. A team of horses was hitched to it. One horse whinnied and sidestepped nervously. The other horse hobbled beside it, drawing up its injured leg then lowering it gingerly.

Drizzle whinnied back as the threesome approached the

wagon. When Dog growled, Lucas jerked up his head to search the darkness. He noticed what Dog sensed—a foursome of wolves skulking around the tilted wagon, prepared to attack.

Lucas clamped the rifle against his hip and fired off three quick shots. He dropped two wolves but the others scattered. That was the bad thing about wolves, he reminded himself as he fired off another round for good measure. If you shot and missed, a wolf rarely gave you another chance. Wolves, like coyotes, were smart, elusive predators and they learned all too quickly.

Dismounting, Lucas propped the torch in the snowdrift to shed more light on the bay's swollen front leg. "Not broken, just sprained," was his diagnosis. "Good, I don't favor putting you down, boy."

Lucas glanced at the sorrel that didn't look as if it had suffered injury. Then he scanned the darkness, unsure what had become of the idiotic man who owned the horses and buckboard. Drifting snow obliterated any footprints that might lead Lucas to the missing traveler. For certain the man had written his own death warrant when he ventured off the track.

The tilted wagon was only a few hundred yards away from Lucas's cabin, but visibility was so low you couldn't see the light in the window. Hell, Lucas *knew* where his cabin and barn were but he couldn't see them, either.

Lucas unhitched the two horses then mounted Drizzle. He started off, making slow progress toward the barn, leading the hobbling bay and the skittish sorrel. A moment later he realized Dog wasn't beside him.

"Dog? Double damn, this better not be the night you decide to answer the call," Lucas muttered beneath his protective hood. "Dog! Come!"

Dog didn't come. Lucas expelled an impatient sigh. He was cold, tired and anxious to huddle by the hearth and warm his innards with coffee. "Dog!"

Dog barked loudly twice.

Lucas frowned then lifted the torch to locate Dog. He was

standing in front of a snowdrift near the tilted wagon. Frowning curiously, Lucas rode over to look down at his pet.

"You sensing something I can't, boy?"

Dog whined and pawed at the snowbank.

Befuddled, Lucas dismounted and tethered the horses. He stabbed the torch into the drift then stared wide-eyed at the lady's kid boot Dog had unearthed…and the foot still in it.

"What in the hell—?" Lucas croaked in disbelief. "A damn fool woman tramping around at night? Alone in a blizzard? Lady, you better hope you don't get what you deserve—which is *dead* and *frozen solid* for your foolishness!"

Displacing the wet snow and sleet, Lucas uncovered frilly skirts then noticed the pathetically ineffective jacket covering arms that were half-frozen from exposure to the cold.

"Any man who'd let his wife venture out on a night like this ought to be shot," he said then glanced sideways, wondering if there was an iced-over husband who had walked off to find help…and encountered the wolf pack before the predators surrounded the wagon, looking for dessert.

Lucas didn't have time to tramp around in search of a possible husband. The woman was unconscious and she needed attention. He slid his hand beneath her skirt to check her body temperature and his hand glided over her firm, shapely leg. She was deathly cold. He grabbed her by the hips then gave a mighty heave-ho, dragging her from the makeshift snow cave and onto his lap, falling off balance in the process.

He gasped in amazement when the snow-caked scarf that covered her head and face came free. A pile of frothy silver-blond hair spilled across the snow, glowing in the torch light.

"Rosalie Greer?" he crowed in amazement.

Of course he knew who the attractive boutique owner was. What man in Cahill Crossing didn't? She was considered quite a catch, though it was said that she had discouraged every would-be suitor who came calling. As he'd heard tell, Rosalie cleverly provided each jilted suitor with a good reason why he shouldn't be interested in her. She had sent each one on his way, thinking he had called off the unproductive courtship.

Rosalie had reminded one of her suitors that she was much too old and that he knew he should select a younger woman. She assured another averted suitor that she was much too independent and outspoken. And what man had the patience to deal with such glaring flaws in a woman's personality?

Yet another beau received a lecture on trying to woo her with flowers because, according to Rosalie Greer, they reminded her of funerals and she didn't even plan to attend her own so he shouldn't bother with bouquets.

Lucas wiped the ice from her pale cheek. "What the hell are you doing out here in this blizzard?" he asked the unconscious female who reminded him of a lifeless angel covered in snow. "You might not like funeral flowers but you might get them anyway."

His own comment spurred him into action. If this bewitching boutique owner was going to survive, he couldn't dilly-dally. He had to get her thawed out—and quickly. He scooped her up in his arms then frowned when her head lolled against his shoulder and the glorious mass of silky blond hair cascaded over his arm. She looked hauntingly lovely, and about as close to dead as a woman could get. He would have to push Drizzle hard to clomp through the snowdrifts in haste to reach the cabin.

The team of horses would have to wait, he decided. Time was of the essence. He couldn't hold the torch, Drizzle's reins, plus those of the other two horses, and balance Rosalie in his lap while moving at a swift pace.

Even when Lucas tossed Rosa awkwardly over the saddle so he could climb up behind her she didn't rouse. Neither did she respond when he levered her over his arm. She lay there like a lifeless rag doll. That didn't bode well.

Holding her close, hoping to share his body heat, Lucas urged Drizzle to make haste to reach the cabin. The powerful, surefooted Appaloosa half leaped and half trotted over the drifts, setting an uneven pace.

When Lucas dismounted then pulled Rosalie into his arms, Drizzle whinnied. "I'll be back in a minute," he told his faithful mount. "We'll fetch the sorrel and bay before they freeze to death."

With Dog trotting along on his gimpy leg, Lucas hurried onto the stoop. He shouldered his way through the door then positioned Rosalie's motionless body beside the fire. Hurriedly, he tossed on a few more logs to provide extra heat. Then he stepped back to contemplate Rosalie's snow-covered clothing.

"Those garments need to come off," he told his unconscious houseguest. "Can't say I won't enjoy this, but I've spent thirty-two years doing what has to be done to survive." A faint smile pursed his lips and he tried to recall the last time he'd felt like grinning. Had he ever? His hardscrabble lifestyle of dodging flying bullets, knives and arrows didn't lend itself to amusement.

Lucas squatted down on his haunches to remove her shoes then her stockings. The lacy petticoats came off next. Naturally, a woman who operated the most fashionable boutique this side of Austin would have the softest, most delicate fabric brushing against her skin, he reasoned.

"There's a reminder I don't need," he grumbled to himself. He was already aware that he had been too long between women. Touching this beguiling female was entirely too pleasurable…considering her unresponsive condition.

"What are you looking at?" Lucas asked the dog sitting beside him. "I don't need a four-legged conscience."

Lucas inhaled a steadying breath then peeled off her stylish but thin jacket. He unbuttoned the front of her crimson-colored gown…and lust hit him below the belt buckle with enough force to steal the air he had drawn into his lungs. The garment lay open, exposing the lacy pink chemise and the creamy fullness of her breasts. Lucas involuntarily groaned when unappeased desire bombarded him.

Her breasts rose and fell with each shallow breath she took. At least it signaled that she was still alive—for now. The farther he pulled down the gown, past her rib cage, her waist then her hips, the more difficult it became for *him* to breathe.

"Double damn," he wheezed as he removed the expensive gown that covered silky pantaloons.

Since her undergarments weren't wet—and too bad about that, he thought—he left her in them.

Rising from a crouch, Lucas lurched around to hurry into his bedroom. He returned with a buffalo-skin quilt guaranteed to warm a half-frozen body within a few hours. He tucked the heavy blanket around her then watched the dancing flames cast light and shadows across her lovely face.

Enchanting, he mused as he studied her with masculine appreciation. In his opinion, she was the most alluring woman in town. With her arresting figure, bewitching facial features and those unique amethyst-colored eyes she could captivate a man without even trying.

Of course, she would have no use for the likes of him, he reminded himself realistically. She looked delicate and polished and he knew she possessed polite and sophisticated manners. Which made them polar opposites. Born and raised by the Comanche, trained as a warrior then as a soldier and finally as a Ranger, Lucas had endured everything life had thrown at him. Rosalie Greer, on the other hand, didn't have enough sense not to venture out alone in a blizzard.

He'd tell her so—*if* she ever woke up.

His thoughts flitted off as he watched Dog sniff the pile of feminine clothing then hobble over to sniff Rosalie's curly hair that spilled across the planked floor.

"Don't know what to make of her, do you?" Lucas said to Dog. "That makes two of us."

He scooped up the damp, frilly clothing then draped the

garments over the back of the chairs he positioned by the roaring fire.

"You can help me fetch the team of horses or stay here with her," Lucas told Dog then wheeled toward the door.

Dog sat down, looked at Rosalie then turned his attention to Lucas. After Lucas pulled the hood over his face to protect him from the cold, Dog reluctantly limped over to join him. Even Dog was smart enough to know he should keep his distance from someone who had no place whatsoever in his rough-and-tumble world.

Lucas exited, reminding himself that he didn't fit into Rosalie's world any better than she fit into his. He would do his best to nurse her back to health then send her on her way.

"And you'd better not spend any more time thinking about how good it felt to touch her," Lucas lectured himself sternly.

The cold wind bombarded him the instant he stepped onto the porch, but it didn't cool the lingering warmth of the erotic fantasy dancing in his head while he rode off to fetch the team of stranded horses.

Chapter Two

Dazed, groggy, teeth chattering, Rosa awakened. Her hands and feet tingled and burned. The kind of warmth she never thought she'd feel again pulsed through her. She frowned, trying to orient herself to her dark surroundings. When she glanced left, she was surprised to see a fire raging in a stone hearth. Shadows leaped like specters performing demonic dancing rituals on the walls.

She tensed when she glanced right to note the wolflike creature that lurked close enough to take a bite out of her. She gasped in alarm when her fuzzy gaze landed on the ominous silhouette, wearing a black hood and a long black canvas duster coat. Firelight reflected off the twin holes of the hood, giving the impression that flames burned where eyes should be.

God have mercy! Rosa thought in dismay. She must have frozen to death in the snowdrift—and gone straight to hell. She was about to be roasted over her personal bonfire while the wolf-dog that guarded the gates of Hades kept a watchful eye on her. And here, she mused uneasily while she cowered beneath the quilt, was the devil himself looming over her. He was here to steal her soul before he cremated her in the fire.

"No!" Rosa shrieked then cursed herself for cowering

before the devil. That was not the way she wanted to leave the world—or rather the underworld. She was not a coward.... Or at least she preferred to think she wasn't.... Or maybe that's why she had landed in hell to begin with, because she wasn't as humble as she thought she was. Or maybe it was because she had wished her disgusting stepbrother to hell in a handbasket and had ended up cursing *herself* to the farthest reaches of Hades.

"Calm down, Ms. Greer. You're okay. Are you warmer now?" the towering demon questioned in a deep, resonant voice.

Of course, the devil would have an eerily provocative voice, she reasoned. After all, he was the master of temptation and seduction, wasn't he?

"Not as warm as I'm going to be when you toss me in the fire," she muttered grimly.

The devil chuckled. A deep, rumbling sound filled the empty space between them. The sound was not as wicked and frightening as she had expected it to be. To her bewildered amazement, the devil removed the dark hood that covered his head, revealing thick, collar-length raven hair, midnight-black eyes and a ruggedly handsome face that boasted a five o'clock shadow that looked at least two days old.

"I hadn't planned to roast you over live coals. I was only wondering if you were suffering frostbite," he said.

Rosa collapsed on the planked floor in relief. Her breath gushed out in a whoosh. This wasn't the devil. It was Lucas Burnett, the former Texas Ranger who owned a horse ranch that butted up against the road to Wolf Grove and bordered Cahill's sprawling 4C Ranch on the east and north. Rosa had noticed the tall, brawny horseman on rare occasions when he came to town for supplies. It was hard not to notice a man whose appearance drew her gaze and speculation. She had been fascinated with his powerful physique and the way he moved with such predatory grace.

He was nothing like the swaggering dandies from the East whom she had left far behind—and good riddance to them!

If Rosa hadn't lost faith in men eight years ago—and had yet to meet a man who had changed her opinion of the male gender since—she might have pursued her secret admiration of Lucas Burnett. Not that he had the slightest interest in her, she reminded himself.

He was a recluse who didn't want anything to do with society. But she suspected Lucas made regular visits to the wrong side of the tracks in Cahill Crossing. Although the train had yet to arrive in town, there was already a Wrong Side and there was a freshly painted train depot waiting to greet the locomotive due to arrive within the next few months.

"Let me check your hands and fingers," he said, reaching for the fist she had knotted in the quilt. "I rubbed on a poultice an hour ago. Hopefully, it has helped to restore feeling and circulation in your arms and legs."

That's when she realized her arms were bare—and so was she! Well, except for her pantaloons and chemise. The gratitude she had yet to voice transformed into embarrassment and outrage in the time it took to blink.

"What did you do to me?" she gasped, slapping away his hand.

Her harsh voice brought the demon dog a step closer. It bared its teeth and growled down at her.

"Easy, Dog, she's female. No accounting for her sudden mood swing." Lucas rose to fetch the two cups warming on the stove. "Coffee, Ms. Greer?"

"You undressed me!" she all but yelled at him.

"Yes, I did." He pivoted with the cups in hand. A wry smile pursed his sensuous lips. "I asked you if you wanted to undress yourself but you didn't reply. So I did what had to be done."

"I couldn't reply," she snapped indignantly. "I was unconscious and half-frozen." She clutched the buffalo quilt, held it beneath her chin and glowered accusingly at him.

Lucas felt the makings of another smile tugging at his lips.

Whatever else Rosalie Greer was she was bursting at the seams with spirit and spunk. She'd made him laugh earlier, and now she had him smiling. Odd, he tried to remember the last time he'd smiled—and still couldn't recall.

"Lady, I just saved your life. You're welcome," he added with a sarcastic snort then ambled toward her.

He was unwillingly intrigued by the way her curly silver-blond hair glimmered in the firelight. Her blue-violet eyes were as spellbinding as he remembered. That, combined with her creamy flesh and the alluring body he'd skimmed his hands over while undressing her and applying the poultice was enough to torment any man.

Even Lucas, a man hardened and jaded by the atrocities humankind imposed on one another.

Rosalie was *not* the kind of woman a man could successfully ignore. He could certainly attest to that!

"You had no right to remove my clothes under any pretense!" she sputtered angrily, dragging his thoughts back to the present. "No man has ever seen me in my unmentionables, though there was—" She shut her mouth so quickly she winced when she bit her tongue.

He wasn't sure what she had decided *not* to say but he felt another smile grazing his lips. He leaned down to hand the coffee cup to her. "Then I suppose I should be honored, Ms. Greer."

"You should be ashamed of yourself is what you should be." She accepted the cup and flashed him a blistering glare. "Just because you used to be a Texas Ranger doesn't mean you can go around undressing women in the name of necessity. Now where are my clothes?"

Lucas hitched his thumb toward the chairs serving as an improvised clothesline. "Not quite dry yet. The last thing a frostbite victim needs is wet clothing frozen to her skin. The Comanche liniment I used heats the skin and the buffalo blanket insulates your body to prevent a condition I've heard a doctor in Austin refer to as hypothermia. The Comanche have another name for it, but by any name it can prove deadly if a victim isn't treated in time."

He stared directly at her, his expression turning somber. "You, Ms. Greer, are very lucky to be alive. If not for Dog, I would have unhitched your team of horses and taken them to my barn. Dog is the one that picked up your scent in the snowbank. Digging yourself into the drift to shield yourself from the wind likely saved your life. But you would be frozen solid by now if not for Dog."

Her indignation and embarrassment fizzled out, somewhat at least, when she realized she *was* lucky to be among the living. "Call me Rosa," she mumbled.

She reached out with her free hand to pet the shaggy-haired wolflike dog that looked as if it weighed one hundred thirty pounds. He bolted to his feet and growled at her. She reflexively snatched back her hand before he bit off a few fingers.

"What's his name?" she asked as the oversize dog took his place beside Lucas.

"His name is Dog."

"How very original," she said mockingly. "Not very friendly, is he? Shocking that he belongs to you."

She glanced pointedly at Lucas. She still hadn't forgiven him for undressing her—whether it needed to be done or not. It left her feeling vulnerable and awkward. She hadn't felt that way in eight years, since…

Rosa squelched the thought. Past was past and that was where it would remain. Men were to be regarded with caution and mistrust. Even the ruggedly handsome specimen hunkered down in front of her couldn't be trusted completely. Lucas was even more dangerous than most because she was physically attracted to him—even though it went against her better judgment and learned caution.

"Look, lady—"

"Rosa," she corrected him.

"Look, Rosa, you can hiss and spit at me all you want. I've dealt with insults and sarcasm half my life because of my mixed heritage," he growled, reminding her a lot of Dog. "But the fact remains that you wouldn't have survived to see Christmas if not for Dog and me."

His glare was hard enough to peel paint. "You were *unconscious* and *half-frozen* and the wolves had picked up your scent. Your flimsy jacket and fancy gown were caked with snow and I peeled them off so I could cover you with the warmest blanket I have in the house. Then I applied the ointment, in hopes that it would prevent you from losing your toes and fingers. The very *least* you could do is say 'thank you very much'!" he practically shouted at her.

She watched him rise agilely to his feet. He set aside his cup then shed the long black coat. Against her will, her admiring gaze traveled from the top of his shiny raven head, across his broad shoulders and down to his lean waist. Double holsters hung low on his lips. Slim-fitting breeches encased his horseman thighs and black boots extended from knees to toes.

No question, Lucas Burnett was six-foot-three inches of power-packed masculinity. He reminded her of the wild mustangs he had captured and bred with Appaloosa stallions before establishing the ranch land he'd been granted as a veteran and ex-Ranger who had honorably served his state and country.

Rosa blinked, amazed at how much she knew about Lucas Burnett, though they hadn't been formally introduced. She had also heard that he was deadly with knives, pistols, rifles and hand-to-hand combat. She wondered what his life had been like in the Comanche camp and how much family he had left to share the holiday season with him.

"Now, if you will excuse me, *blondie,*" he said, his voice dripping sarcasm, "I'll change out of my damp clothes. They got wet while I was checking your injured horse and leading the team back to my barn to warm up. I treated the bay's swollen leg and he should be fine in a couple of weeks, *if* you care."

He glanced stonily at her and added, "The poultice is an old Comanche remedy. Because after all, that's what I am at heart. None of your kind wants to spend much time around a mixed breed like me so I'll keep to myself for your benefit. Besides, most of the folks I've dealt with in the past have been murderers, rustlers, rapists and thieves, and so the so-called members of respectable society figure it takes one to catch one…right? That's what they whisper behind my back when they think I'm not listening."

"Lucas, I didn't mean—"

"I'll get you back to town as soon as the storm lets up so none of my bad habits rub off on you," he cut in sharply. "Until then, you'll have to tolerate Dog and me."

Lucas slammed the door with enough force to rattle the hinges. He blew out a frustrated breath and asked himself why he had lost his temper like that. He usually didn't react to taunts because they had lost their zing years back. And why Rosalie Greer's opinion of him mattered, he couldn't imagine. Why should he care what she thought of him?

They obviously came from two contrasting backgrounds and he was sure she would be embarrassed to be seen in public with him. Still, it would have been nice to have one friend on the respectable side of Cahill Crossing. One who didn't veer out of his path and avoid his gaze when he ventured into town to gather supplies.

Muttering to himself, Lucas tossed aside his shirt and grabbed a clean one. His wardrobe consisted of a few practical garments but he would bet the ranch that Rosa had a closet full of fancy dresses and frilly undergarments…

The thought made him gnash his teeth. The last thing he needed was to dwell on the erotic vision of her soft, frilly drawers and the lush feminine body inside them. Not if he planned to keep from driving himself loco before the storm blew over and he could get her out of his house.

Ah, hell! Why couldn't she be someone else's problem?

Rosa mentally kicked herself up one side and down the other for allowing the bad experience from her past to affect her association with the man who had saved her life. She had struck out at Lucas in embarrassment and outrage. He was right. He had done what needed to be done to save her and she should be thanking him, repeatedly, for venturing out in the hellish storm to rescue her. He had placed himself at risk and she had sounded like a peevish, ungrateful shrew. She would still be chilled to the bone if not for him and Dog.

She sat upright and glanced at the furry creature that watched her closely. "Thank you, Dog. I owe you and Lucas my life."

Dog just stared at her. Obviously, he didn't like her any better than Lucas did.

Sparing several cautious glances at the bedroom door Lucas had slammed behind him, Rosa limped over to fetch her gown. It was still wet so she donned the canvas duster coat Lucas had draped over the handmade chair and footstool. The garment swallowed her and dragged on the floor. Lucas's scent—which was extremely tantalizing, she had to admit—clung to the garment.

Rosa squared her shoulders and raked away from her face the wild tangle of hair that had somehow come undone during her ordeal. Then she hobbled to the bedroom door. Anxious to voice her apology, she breezed into the room, and then stopped in her tracks when Lucas whirled toward her—bare-chested and snapping his pistol into firing position with lightning speed.

Rosa's jaw dropped open wide enough for a Christmas goose to nest. She found herself admiring the rippling muscles on his chest, his washboarded belly…while he leveled the business end of his Colt .45 at her.

The stony-faced ex-Ranger surveyed the duster coat she wore then stared her squarely in the eye. "You should have knocked," he said brusquely.

She felt heat rushing to her cheeks but she couldn't drag her admiring gaze away from him. He was sleek, powerful-looking and oozing sexuality. "I'm sorry."

"Something else I can do for you, Ms. Greer?" he asked with stiff politeness.

"Rosa," she corrected him again, and then limped around the brawny obstacle that was Lucas Burnett to survey the rustic bedroom and handmade wooden headboard. Flickering lantern light filled the homey confines of the room and she smiled appreciatively. So…this was the lion's den. It seemed more welcoming than her upstairs apartment that was filled with expensive furnishings imported from the East.

"You're limping," he said, sounding surprised.

She flicked her wrist dismissively, still admiring the walls that were decorated with bead-and-silver mementos that represented his life with the Comanche. They obviously meant a great deal to him, but he kept them hidden from the world. Just like he kept himself hidden from society.

"What happened to your leg?" he demanded to know.

"When the wagon slid into the ditch, the bay reared up, fell off balance and slammed into me while I was trying to lead the brainless creatures through the storm. Both horses had been acting up since the wolves commenced howling—"

Her voice dried up when he abruptly scooped her up in his arms and placed her on his bed. She yelped and raised both arms to fend off the anticipated attack.

Rejection flashed in his onyx eyes as he quickly withdrew. His reaction crumbled one corner of her heart.

"I'm not going to hurt you, Rosa," he assured her as his expression transformed into a carefully blank stare. "I only want to get you off that injured leg so I can see how bad it is."

"I'm sorry," she gushed out. "I'm much too defensive." She clutched the oversize coat around her modestly. "A woman alone has to be careful, you know. Not every man in Cahill Crossing is a respectable gentleman and I'm on constant lookout."

She inhaled a bolstering breath then stared up at Lucas. "I apologize sincerely for sounding ungrateful. You saved me from certain death. In fact, you are my guardian angel and I shall never forget what you have done for me."

He expelled a snort. "If you knew what I've seen and done in the line of duty and in the name of justice you wouldn't call me an angel. Let's get that settled here and now."

"In my eyes you are an angel and a knight all rolled into one," she declared.

She suddenly realized that she meant exactly what she'd said. Lucas Burnett, a man she had secretly admired from afar since the first day she saw him striding past the pane-glass window of her shop, intrigued her. Wary of the fascination though she had been, she had found the nerve to walk into his bedroom—and she had seen him half-naked, which made them even. She had also gained insights about him when she noticed the mementos of his previous life with the Indians and the framed commendations of his heroic service with the military and the Rangers.

He was a loner who had been labeled dangerous and different. He was obviously cynical of a society that had used him for its protection then cast him aside when he decided to resign his position. She couldn't fault him for his pessimism.

After all, she harbored a lingering pessimism of her own.

Rosa didn't know what had come over her. Maybe it was the burst of emotion prompted by her brush with death. Maybe it was that brief flash of rejection she had noticed in Lucas's midnight-black eyes before he masked the hurt she'd unintentionally caused him. Perhaps it was the secret infatuation she had refused to act upon after she'd lost all faith in men eight years earlier. Whatever the cause she had the impulsive, uncontrollable urge to hug the stuffing out of her bare-chested guardian angel.

"Ooofff..." Lucas grunted uncomfortably when, out of the blue, Rosa surged off the bed, injured leg and all, and looped her arms around his neck. Then she kissed him right smack-dab on the lips. The feel of her shapely body meshed familiarly to his turned surprise into instant lust.

Double damn! He had never encountered a woman who could set off so many emotions inside him at once. She inflamed his temper and set his body on fire in the blink of an eye.

His arms closed around her, holding her off the floor to compensate for the noticeable difference in their height. He forgot to apply the self-discipline he'd spent a decade perfecting while he held her close. The feel of her soft lips against his was like a long-awaited feast for a starving man.

Unruly hunger clenched inside him as he made more of her kiss of gratitude than he knew she offered. He plunged his tongue into her mouth to sample the sweetness within, wishing for more intimacy than a devouring kiss. A kiss that left him throbbing with the kind of aching need that only wild reckless passion—or a long walk in the snow—could alleviate.

When Lucas finally broke the kiss Rosa swore her eyes had crossed and she had lost the ability to think rationally. Worse, he had robbed her of breath and made her burn with the kind of desire she hadn't realized existed. Something fragile and unfamiliar burst to life inside her. She tilted her head back to peer into his ruggedly handsome face, wishing he'd kiss her like that again, but he didn't.

She started to curl her arms around his neck and initiate another kiss, but the voice of caution said, *Get ahold of yourself, woman, before you look like a fool!*

Behave yourself or she will think you are a heathen! the noble voice of conscience railed at Lucas. He set Rosa onto her feet and immediately stepped a respectable distance away. When she wobbled unsteadily, he scooped her up and set her on the edge of the bed once again.

He noticed she was breathing as hard as he was. He also noticed Dog standing in the doorway, staring at him as if he had taken leave of the good sense he had spent thirty-two years cultivating.

"Let me take a look at your leg," Lucas said more gruffly than he intended.

She didn't look at him directly but she poked her injured leg from beneath his duster coat. Then she reached down to roll up her lacy pantaloons. Lucas sighed inwardly. He'd really wanted to do that himself.

He noticed the swelling on her shinbone and the puffy bruise the same size as a hoofprint. The injury hadn't shown up until she began to thaw out, he decided, for he hadn't noticed it while applying warming poultice to her extremities while she was unconscious.

"I'm going to use the same healing liniment I used on your bay horse," he said, rising to his feet.

"Those bean-brain creatures aren't mine," she informed him. "I rented the rig and the team from the livery stable…"

He frowned curiously when her voice drifted off and her amethyst-colored eyes widened in alarm.

"The wagon!" she gasped. "Where are my supplies?"

"Stuck in the snowdrift and they'll stay there until I hitch up a team of four horses to pull it out." He watched her closely. "Unless there is something valuable that I need to fetch immediately. Is there?"

She squirmed uneasily then pasted on a smile. "No, I'm sure my cargo will be fine where it is for now."

Her strange behavior made him suspicious but he didn't fire more questions at her, just focused on retrieving the salve and treating her injured leg.

"I really am grateful to you. In fact, I am eternally indebted," she added as he rubbed the ointment on her leg. "I intend to repay you for your heroic deed."

For some reason her eternal gratitude annoyed him. Maybe because what he wanted from this alluring blonde was acceptance, a degree of affection and respect…and something far more intimate. And he shouldn't be thinking any such thing. He was agitated with himself for wanting what he knew he couldn't have and aggravated with her for being so damn tempting and appealing to him. And hell, he was stuck with temptation until the storm blew over. That was bound to test his self-mastery to its very limits.

"I don't want your money," he snapped as he rose to his feet then turned to put away the poultice. "What I want is for you to show some sense next time you venture off alone so late in the day. Where the hell were you going anyway?"

"To Wolf Grove to pick up the…um…supplies I ordered."

He knew that evasive look having seen it dozens of times on the faces of outlaws. It made him wonder what she was hiding.

"And I cannot predict the weather, you know," she said defensively. "The calendar didn't mention *blizzard*."

"The point is you should have hired someone to fetch your supplies," he chastised harshly.

Her back went ramrod stiff and she thrust out her chin. "I am an independent businesswoman and I do not need a man to fetch and heel for me."

"What's in that cargo?" he demanded in a tone he usually reserved for interrogating swindlers and thieves.

"None of your business." She bounded off the bed, favoring her injured leg, looking like five-foot-four inches of feminine defiance. "I thanked you kindly for rescuing me. I offered to pay you and you lectured me for my stupidity. I believe I'll call it a night," she muttered then limped off.

Lucas scowled. "You take my bed. I'll sleep on the floor."

Head held high, her curly blond hair haloing her bewitching face, she pivoted on her good leg to face him. "No, thank you," she said with exaggerated politeness. "I'm the foolish, unwanted houseguest here. *I* will sleep on the floor as punishment for my stupidity!"

On that parting remark, she hobbled into the hall. Not to be outdone, she slammed the door behind her.

Lucas thought he heard her say, "Take that, you infuriating man!" from the other side of the bedroom door before she hobbled away.

Chapter Three

Rosa spent the night tossing and turning, wondering why she was so sensitive to everything Lucas said to her, trying to figure out what flaws in her character had tempted her to grab hold of that surly ex-Ranger and revisiting that same, mind-blowing sensual pleasure she had discovered in his embrace.

Generally, she didn't pay men much mind, just pretended to be oblivious to their attempts to flirt and court her. However, Lucas—the infuriating, prickly man—was another matter entirely.

Clearly, he was anxious to have her gone, for he spent most of the day working outside—*avoiding* her was a more accurate description.

To spite him, she spent most of the day giving Dog treats and cooing at him until he allowed her to pet him and snuggle up beside him. But goodness, if she couldn't win over Lucas, she would at least soften up his dog.

Lucas returned at noon to mumble and grumble over the peace-treaty meal she had prepared. Then, without so much as a by-your-leave or a thank-you, he exited and he didn't invite Dog to go with him.

Well, she decided midafternoon, it was the holiday season and she was going to be kind and charitable to Lucas, even if he treated her as if she had contracted the plague. Furthermore, he wasn't going to remain out here in the middle of nowhere during the holiday festivities. He refused to accept her money and—the contrary rascal—disregarded her effusive gratitude. Nevertheless, she was going to insist that he attend the social function in Town Square that she was hosting. She intended to badger him relentlessly until he agreed.

He wouldn't be rid of her as easily as he thought, she mused wickedly. She was going to include him in the holiday celebrations whether he liked it or not.

At five o'clock Lucas swept into the cabin. A cold draft accompanied him, matching the chilly stare he directed at her. Then he said, "Why the hell didn't you tell me?"

She blinked, feeling as if she had awakened in the middle of a conversation. "Tell you what?"

He whipped out a porcelain doll and shook it in her face. "Who you really are."

Lucas had used a team of four horses to drag the stranded wagon from the snowdrift. Then, because of Rosalie's strange behavior when he'd asked about the cargo, he had fished beneath the tarp to see toy trains, a variety of dolls, colorful scarves, gloves, hats and expensive clothing for children.

He'd stood there for five minutes, freezing cold and stunned to the bone. A breath of wind could have blown him over. Rosalie Greer was the mysterious Saint Nicholas who had delivered gifts to the local children the first Christmas that Cahill Crossing came into existence. No one in town knew who their generous benefactor might be. But now Lucas knew.

Rosa definitely had her work cut out for her this year, because the two-year-old town had increased from a few hundred to two thousand. Another thousand would likely show up with the completed railroad tracks in a few months.

Lucas had jumped down Miss Secret Santa's throat the previous night because…because he liked her, and his survival instinct prompted him to push her away before he became too attached to a woman who wasn't going to be a part of his life.

Besides, a sophisticated woman had no need for a hard-bitten man, soured on life. He never bothered to celebrate Christmas because he wasn't sure whether white or Indian deities ruled the heavenly roost.

His jumbled thoughts scattered like buckshot when Rosa narrowed her gaze on him then limped over to shake her finger in his face. "If you dare to breathe one word of this to anyone, so help me I'll—"

He waved her off after she poked her index finger in his chest like the point of a knife. "Who exactly am I going to tell? Dog? If you want to adopt every kid in town for Christmas that's your business." He took a step closer, looming over her. "What *is* my concern is where you acquired the money for all those gifts." His brows flattened over his eyes. "Are you embezzling from the investors who own your shop to fund your secret charity? Noble though it might be, embezzling is against the law, blondie. I might have resigned as a Ranger but I won't let you—"

She flapped her arm to silence him then made a stabbing gesture toward the chair, silently demanding that he park himself in it and shut up. He sat down and clammed up.

"First off," she said as she stood over him. "I want your word of honor, or whatever your Comanche kin call a solemn vow, that you will *never* tell a living soul who I am."

"Fine. Comanche promise. I'll throw myself on my own spear before I expose your carefully guarded secret." He puffed up and glared at her so she'd know he meant business. "Now…where did you get the money to pay for your cargo?" he demanded slowly and succinctly.

Rosa pulled over a chair from the dining table and took a load off her mending leg. "There are no investors, Lucas. I just let people assume there are. I bought the town lot from the Cahills and I own the shop, free and clear. I paid for it myself."

He eyed her warily. "You have a pot of gold buried somewhere that no one in town knows about, do you?"

She fiddled with the folds of her gown. "Sort of. My family from Boston is in manufacturing. I'm the only child."

A dull throb thudded against his skull. Double damn! Not only was Rosa a sophisticated young businesswoman but she was rich. No doubt his meager savings account at the bank was loose change to her. Why couldn't he have found himself intrigued by someone in his own social class? Oh, no, not the grandson of a Mexican captive and a Comanche war chief. Not the son of a mixed-breed Indian and a white frontiersman who dragged Lucas all over creation after his mother died trying to give birth to another son.

Hell, he had to get Rosa back to town before he did something stupid—like yield to this severe case of flaming lust that he'd tried to cool down by spending most of the day outside, tramping around, doing chores in the snow.

She has to go—pronto—and you have to keep your distance, he lectured himself firmly.

Lucas tried to rise and move away from the tempting beauty but she grabbed the lapels of his shirt with both hands and got right in his face.

"I have no children of my own and I am long past the usual marrying age," she reminded him. "But *my* children have become the children of down-on-their-luck parents who need to believe in hope and dreams and a little Christmas magic.

"After I got over being embarrassed and annoyed with you for undressing me and for chastising me for being reckless and foolish, I realized God had sent you to me," she declared.

Lucas snorted caustically. "I'm not sure the Great Spirit, Indian or white, knows who I am. He sure as hell didn't send me to you, blondie. He sent *Dog.*"

Rosa tossed back her head and laughed in amusement. It was the most glorious sound Lucas had ever heard. Double damn, this feisty, independent, spirited woman—a woman full of secrets and surprises—was getting to him. And he couldn't figure out how to stop it from happening.

"You are a hard case, Lucas, but I have made up my mind—"

"And may the Great Spirit help us all," he snorted in interruption.

"It is clear that you were sent to help me keep the magic of Christmas Eve alive for the children in Cahill Crossing," she continued, undaunted.

"No. Absolutely not," he said uncompromisingly.

She acted as if she hadn't heard him and just kept on talking. "There are dozens of new children in town. I have spent the past two months discreetly locating their homes. With your help we can distribute the gifts before dawn and no one will be the wiser."

"No. I'm staying out here where I belong," he said resolutely. "I've done my duty to society and that's that."

It was glaringly apparent to Rosa that she would have to drag Lucas—kicking, screaming and swearing—into society and she'd have to twist his arm a dozen different ways to enlist his help. And she would, too, she told herself determinedly. Even if he only felt pity for her after she confided her past to him, surely he would agree to help her. With that in mind, Rosa inhaled a deep breath and prepared herself to share the story she had never told another living soul.

"I had to leave home shortly after I turned eighteen because my widowed mother married a highly decorated naval commander. We moved from our mansion in Boston to Maryland. My new stepbrother decided the best way to guarantee control of the Greer-McKnight fortune was to force me into a potential scandal and shame me into marriage."

Rosa blinked, stunned, when she noticed Lucas's expression had turned so hard it could have been chiseled in granite. He was so intense, so utterly still, that she could only imagine what ruthless outlaws faced when he swooped in like the dark angel of doom to confront them.

For sure and certain, she always wanted to be on his side

if a fight broke out. He was not a man to challenge—if you valued your life.

"Go on," he demanded in a voice that reminded her of Dog's vicious growl.

Rosa swallowed hard and inhaled a fortifying breath. "Here is yet another secret I have shared with no one else," she began. "My stepbrother—"

"What's the bastard's name?" he interrupted sharply.

"It doesn't matter now."

"It does to me."

She smiled ruefully. Once a Texas Ranger always a Texas Ranger, she thought to herself. "Ah, where were you when I wanted to have the conniving scoundrel shot and stabbed a few times?"

"Chasing banditos and translating at powwows between Rangers, Comanches and Mexicans," he replied. "I don't have those other obligations now. *What's his name?*"

She shook her head and curlicue strands tumbled around her face in disarray. She reflexively flinched then told herself to relax when he reached over to comb the spring-loaded curls away from her cheek. She had her stepbrother to thank for her defensive reaction. However, she was discovering that, as vicious as Lucas could look when he was angry, he wouldn't hurt her.

He was an intriguing paradox of tenderness and overpowering strength. Furthermore, he was her guarding angel and she had nothing to fear from him.

When his fingertip gently caressed her cheek and jaw a surge of heat and pleasure that Rosa hadn't realized she was capable of feeling radiated through her. Her breath stalled in her chest as she stared helplessly into those obsidian eyes framed with long thick lashes.

He's the one, said a voice somewhere deep down inside her. *You don't have to be afraid anymore. Fate brought him to you for all the right reasons.*

She doubted Lucas would ever share the indescribable feelings and tingling sensations blossoming inside her, but she was certain he was the man she could have loved for all time—had she not been well past the usual marrying age and he had not been so cynical of society.

She wrapped her hand around his and pressed a kiss to his knuckles. She wasn't sure who was more surprised by the impulsive gesture. Him or her. She rarely displayed affection to a man, for fear he would take more than she intended to give.

She rushed on before Lucas asked her what that sentimental gesture meant. "Jubal, my stepbrother, asked me to join him upstairs during the party to introduce my mother to my stepfather's friends and military associates. Like a naive fool, I had no idea what he was about until he closed the bedroom door and pounced."

Lucas growled something she didn't ask him to repeat.

"I didn't care for the pretentious bastard from the moment I met him, but he earned my hatred and disgust in nothing flat. He tore the expensive gown I had designed for my mother's introduction into Maryland society."

Lucas snarled again, looking like a ferocious predator. Ah, how she wished he could have been there to deal with Jubal when she'd had to fight to prevent losing more than her temper.

"When he forced me down on the bed—" The awful ordeal came back in full force. Fortunately, holding on to Lucas with both hands and getting the humiliating secret off her chest was welcome therapy. "I managed to grab the bronze statue on the nightstand and I clobbered him with it," she hurried on. "I dazed him enough to escape onto the gallery. A moment later, one of his libertine cohorts burst inside. His timing was so precise that I knew Jubal had staged the incident to coerce me into cooperating with his grand plan."

Rosa half collapsed in her chair, relieved to have told the tormenting tale. She had considered telling her only cousin and dearest friend, Adrianna McKnight, but she hadn't found the nerve to do it.

This was the time, the place and this was the perfect confidant, she realized.

"Since Mother was happy again, I insisted that I wanted to follow my dreams of designing and selling clothing. I chose St. Louis to work as an assistant. Then I opened my first shop a year later. I managed to attract a great many clients who recommended me to their friends and my business boomed. But the bustling city, with its shallow high society and self-important aristocrats, reminded me of my past so I moved to Texas to make a new start in a new town."

"So you let everyone in Cahill Crossing assume you were a struggling boutique owner with rent and investor dividends to pay, like most of them are," Lucas remarked. "A shopkeeper of modest means by day and a secretive Saint Nicholas every Christmas Eve."

She nodded and smiled at Lucas. Another crack appeared in the stone vault that had sealed off his heart for over a decade.

"I plan to retain that image to fend off unwanted suitors like Jubal who would love to get their greedy fists on my fortune… Will you help me, Lucas?"

"No."

Her lovely face fell. "Why not?"

Lucas stiffened his resolve. "Because I am not what you need. Not for Christmas or any other time of the year."

He could tell his blunt comment had hurt and disappointed her, but double damn! He couldn't get involved in her world. He was where he belonged—skirting the edge of civilization—because he didn't really fit in anywhere.

She planted her hands on her hips and glared at him. "Lucas Burnett, you are a stubborn ass."

"I've been called worse, blondie." And he had, too. Hundreds of times.

"Fine then. Be mule-headed, but I'm still holding you to your vow of silence." She lurched around then said, "I'm going back to town now. I have a wagonload of secret cargo to stack in my storeroom after dark."

He arched a skeptical brow then stared pointedly at her leg. "On a bum leg? Doubt it."

She halted then glanced over her shoulder. Her chin elevated a notch and she looked down her aristocratic nose at him. Ah yes, here was the regal heiress who had fled high society to live in anonymity in Nowhere, Texas. He grinned—as he had done so many times since he'd made her acquaintance. He wondered if his face was going to crack wide-open, especially in these frigid temperatures.

"As I said earlier, Lucas, you will be well compensated for your time and trouble of rescuing me. Come by tomorrow and I will pay you."

With that, she donned her stylish-but-flimsy-jacket then limped toward the door. To his amazement, Dog rose from his favorite place beside the hearth to follow her.

Traitor, thought Lucas, glaring at his once devoted pet.

When she hobbled onto the stoop, Dog halted in the open doorway and looked back at him as if to say, "Are you coming or not?"

Lucas blew out a resigned sigh, surged to his feet and stalked over to grab his coat. Then he followed the hobbling blonde and the gimpy dog out the door.

Three days after Lucas had grudgingly accompanied Rosa to town to help her unload her cargo in the storeroom, she found herself grinning while she cut out the fabric for the gown she was designing for the mayor's wife. For all of Lucas's gruff resistance, he had softened up enough to help her—a little.

"Do you have all your plans organized for the party you are hosting on Town Square tomorrow night?" Melanie Ford, her assistant, asked, while she worked the foot-operated treadle of the sewing machine.

Rosa nodded to her invaluable seamstress. Melanie was a large-boned, heavy-set woman of thirty-five who was so skilled and efficient that she could make Rosa's creative designs come to life in record time. "I've asked the owners of Steven's Restaurant and Huber's Bakery to supply food and coffee for the festivities. The general store and dry goods managers are providing tables and chairs for our holiday gathering on the square."

Melanie slumped back in her chair to work the stiffness from her shoulders. Her hazel eyes twinkled. "This get-together will be even larger than last year, for sure. Talk of the town, in fact." Her smile faded. "Except I heard that some of the scarlet ladies and ruffians from the wrong side of the tracks plan to attend. If they chug down a few drinks to celebrate *before* they arrive, trouble might break out."

Rosa made a mental note to alert Tobias Hobbs, the city marshal. Of course, if Lucas Burnett accepted the hand-written invitation she had sent to him, she knew he could keep the situation under control without the marshal's assistance.

Lucas… She sighed inwardly then went back to work. She had known *of* Lucas for the two years she had been in business in town. Yet, after two days of being secluded *with* him in his cabin, he had restored her lost faith in the male of the species. He was so…everything! Ruggedly handsome, virile, capable and he possessed the integrity and sense of honor that men like Jubal Hawthorne lacked.

The bell above the door jingled, announcing an arrival. "Mail's here!"

Rosa strode from the workroom to the front of her shop. Although her shin was still a mite tender, she could walk without a limp. She veered around the racks of fashionable gowns that kept flying off the stands—at gratifying speed, she was happy to report.

"Here you go, Ms. Greer." Henry Stokes, who was thirty years old or thereabout, handed her two letters. "You have friends back East, I see."

Rosa smiled at the tall, thin busybody of a mail carrier who had bushy brown hair and pale blue eyes. "Indeed I do. Will you be attending Christmas on the Square tomorrow, Henry?" she asked, diverting his attention.

"Wouldn't miss it." Henry's smile displayed a few missing teeth. "Was hoping you'd save me a dance."

"You are very kind to ask, but I will be busy checking with the band, greeting guests and refilling refreshments. Besides, my dancing skills are meager at best. You would likely limp home with sore feet after I trounced all over them."

When Henry exited, Rosa pivoted to see that Melanie had propped her shoulder against the doorjamb and was smiling wryly. "I'm impressed with your ability to turn down men and make them think you are unsuitable. Ask me, what you need is a husband. Every woman needs one. You can't have mine, of course. He suits me perfectly."

Rosa had to agree. Cyril Ford, who managed the stage depot down the street, was Melanie's ideal mate. They got along splendidly. Not everyone enjoyed such compatibility, she knew. All too many loveless weddings and business arrangements were referred to loosely as *marriages*. Long ago, Rosa had vowed never to be wed*locked* to a man who used her for financial benefit, which is why she kept up her woman-of-modest-means persona.

Her thoughts trailed off when she opened the letter from her mother, who'd sent out another invitation to return to Maryland for Christmas. Her mother still didn't understand why Rosa had taken up residence in an upstart town along the path of the coming railroad.

A mocking grin pursed Rosa's lips when she read the part about "poor Jubal" who had been part of a scandal involving a wealthy aristocrat's daughter. The girl's father hadn't insisted on marriage. Instead, he had shipped Jubal out of town on a westbound train two weeks earlier, serenaded by the bellowing command never to return—or else.

"Merry Christmas to you, Jubal, you jackal," she murmured sarcastically.

Now, with her manipulative stepbrother out of the house, Rosa could visit her mother. But not at Christmas. She had toys and gifts to deliver—and it was going to be a long frantic night because Lucas refused to help her.

She opened the second letter, which was from Adrianna McKnight. Rosa shrieked in delight when she learned she had finally managed to entice her dear friend and cousin to move to Cahill Crossing. Rosa had invited Addie to Texas repeatedly to visit and inspect the ranch investment the Greers and McKnights owned as silent partners. Until now, Adrianna had responded, *It's tempting but the timing isn't right. Papa is ill.* But Rosa's maternal uncle, Adrianna's father, had passed the previous summer. Tempted with the possibility of adventure and excitement, Adrianna had decided to pack up and move to Texas.

"Everything all right out here?" Melanie asked as she poked her frizzy brown head around the corner.

"Everything is wonderful," Rosa enthused as she tucked the letters in her pocket. "My cousin is coming in a few months and an old enemy was run out of town on a rail. Things couldn't be better!"

"Will your cousin be buying up all your stylish creations?" Melanie asked.

"Definitely." Rosa strode hurriedly into the workroom. "She is exceptionally supportive of my designs."

"Then we had best get busy so we can finish all these orders before your cousin... What was her name again?"

"Adrianna," Rosa supplied as she plucked up the scissors.

"Right. Before *Adrianna* arrives in town."

Rosa set to work, her spirits riding high. Jubal had received his just deserts and Adrianna was coming to Cahill Crossing once the railroad tracks were completed in the spring. Now, if only Lucas...

She tamped down on the wistful thought. Just because she had developed an intense fascination for the local recluse didn't mean he gave a whit about her. But at the very least, she wished Lucas would come to regard her as his friend. Yet, if one considered the intensity of the kiss they had shared one dark and snowy night, one might think—

Rosa felt tingles of remembered desire coursing through her. She didn't consider herself an expert on kissing, but the embrace had seemed hot and explosive. Lucas had backed away from her before she was ready to let him go. Of course, men were men, she reminded herself. Lust was not heartfelt affection. What man would turn down an offered kiss? Not even Lucas, the cynical hermit, she suspected.

Rosa forced herself to concentrate on the task at hand. She had a holiday dress to complete in record time and a party to oversee. Despite her invitation—and she had sent Lucas two of them, just in case the exact date of the party slipped his mind—she doubted he would show up.

Chapter Four

Lucas scowled at his complete lack of willpower as he tethered Drizzle to the hitching post outside the general store—which sat next door to Rosa's Boutique. He had sworn to Dog repeatedly that he was not coming to the second annual townwide shindig Rosa hosted at Town Square for the holidays. But double damn, here he was, dressed in black, as usual. He was wearing the best clothes he owned. Which, by everyone else's standards, probably hadn't been fashionable in five years.

He glanced down at Dog. The ornery animal almost looked as if he were *smiling* in mocking amusement because his master had turned into a shameless hypocrite.

"Don't say a word," Lucas muttered at Dog then glanced every which way to make sure no passersby overheard him and called him crazy for carrying on a conversation with an animal.

Feeling awkward and uncomfortable, Lucas grumbled as he strode across the square. A large Christmas tree stood on each corner, decorated with paper ornaments and strings of popcorn. Lucas headed directly toward Rosa, who stood out like a beacon beneath the lanterns and torches that illuminated the dance area and refreshment tables.

Now that she had confided her background, he understood

how she could afford this elaborate spread for the holidays. Knowing her, he predicted she had asked the local shops to pitch in, in order to avoid any speculation about where she had acquired the money for this grand affair.

Lucas rolled his eyes, remembering the handwritten invitation she'd had a gangly teenage boy deliver to him. *The party won't be the same without you*, the note said. Then, a day later, as if he might have forgotten her invitation, another one arrived with the same teenager. Well, here he was, still uncertain why he'd shown up.

The locals kept glancing uneasily at him as if he were an outcast. Which he was, but he was the same outcast that had helped clear this area when it had been overrun with Mexican banditos and white outlaws, making settlement possible.

His thoughts trailed off when Rosa's voice overrode the murmur of conversation around him.

"Lucas! I'm so pleased you could come. You're just in time to meet some of my friends and acquaintances."

Lucas was uncomfortable with limelight. Nevertheless, all eyes zeroed in on him because Rosa approached him. Dressed in a sparkling white gown, she reminded him of his personal vision of what an angel—minus the wings—should look like. When he saw her glittering white cape swirling around her as she all but floated toward him, he thought, *ah, yes, wings included.*

To his stunned amazement, she pushed up on tiptoe to press a kiss to his cheek and said, "Happy holidays, Lucas."

Silence followed. He shifted uneasily from one booted foot to the other. Then Rosa clasped his hand and led him over to the cluster of people standing beside a refreshment table.

"Cyril and Melanie Ford, this is my dear friend, Lucas Burnett," she introduced. "He is the one who saved me from certain death when I was stranded in the blizzard last week."

Lucas inclined his head to greet the large-boned, frizzy brown-haired woman and her stout, broad-chested husband who was an inch shorter and a few years older than his wife.

"Melanie is my assistant and Cyril runs the stage depot," Rosa explained without releasing her hold on his hand.

Lucas was annoyed with himself for not stepping a respectable distance away from Rosa. Yet, like some moonstruck fool, he gave her hand a fond squeeze when she smiled angelically at him.

Double damn! The holiday must have turned him sappy. He wasn't the handholding kind of man and this was the first Christmas party he had ever attended.

"And this is Dog," Rosa went on to say as she hunkered down to give Dog a hug around the neck.

Dog nuzzled against her—a sap himself, apparently.

"If Lucas and Dog hadn't found me in the snowdrift I wouldn't be thawed out and alive to host this party."

To Lucas's amazement, the wariness he usually provoked in people fizzled out after Rosa finished hailing him as some sort of gallant hero. He had been accepted in town because she had given him a stamp of approval. Well, didn't that beat all.

"And this is Quin Cahill," Rosa said as she practically dragged Lucas toward the nearby lamppost where a man who matched Lucas in age, size and stature stood with a glass of punch in his hand. He had thick, dark hair and gray eyes that locked on Lucas with unblinking intensity.

"You two definitely should become acquainted." Rosa smiled brightly. "After all, your properties border each other." She leaned close to Lucas and he inhaled the tantalizing scent of her perfume. "Besides," she added confidentially, "you and Quin could both use a friend. His family is hither and yon and I don't know where yours is, either. You didn't bother to say."

"I don't have any family left," Lucas told her before turning his attention and extending his hand to Quin. "Pleasure, Cahill."

"Same here, Burnett," Quin replied then sipped his drink. To his surprise, Rosa wrapped his fingers around a glass of punch, pressed another unexpected kiss to his cheek then flitted off to attend her hosting duties.

Quin arched a dark brow and smiled wryly. "Interesting. Men have stumbled all over themselves trying to court Rosa, the Darling of Downtown. And she latched on to you."

Lucas shrugged nonchalantly. "Just gratitude." He sipped his punch—and realized someone had spiked it with liquor. "She thinks I'm her guardian angel since I saved her life."

Quin stared speculatively at Rosa's departing back then focused on Lucas. Thankfully, Quin let the subject die a graceful death. Lucas liked that about him.

"I've been meaning to contact you," Quin remarked. "I've seen some of the horses grazing in your pastures. I like the looks of them. I wondered if you would be interested in selling some to me."

"I've been selling beef and horses to the military at nearby Fort Ridge," Lucas replied, then took another sip of spiked punch. "I only give the army the offspring that don't show the color I'm breeding, of course."

"In other words, your selective breeding comes with a high price," Quin paraphrased, his gray eyes glittering with faint amusement. "Like the cattle I'm breeding? The average-looking steers and calves head up the trail to Dodge City, but the prize stock is pampered at my ranch."

Lucas grinned and said, "Maybe we can make a trade that will benefit both of us, Cahill."

A few minutes later, several men ambled by and Quin introduced Lucas. After a round of howdy-dos, Lucas heard a loud voice to his left. He and Dog went on high alert when Rosa surged forward to intervene in the shouting match between two men who appeared to have imbibed too much whiskey on the wrong side of town before attending the Christmas party.

Although Lucas had sworn two years earlier that he was officially out of the law-enforcement business, he handed his glass to one of his new acquaintances and strode off to quell the disturbance before Rosa accidentally caught a flying fist.

"Blasted female," he mumbled as he quickened his pace. "Independent and assertive aren't always noble traits."

"Amen to that, friend," Quin grumbled behind him.

Lucas glanced over his shoulder, surprised to note that Quin had come to back him up. And Dog made three.

"Hey!" A drunken tracklayer scowled when an inebriated ranch hand shoved him backward. "Git yer own girl. I'm gonna dance with this one."

"No, you are not," Rosa contradicted as she positioned herself in front of the attractive young woman who had drawn both men's interest. "Both of you are going to leave her alone."

"Then I'll take you, honey, and he can have the chit."

Rosa yelped in surprise when the unshaven scoundrel—who smelled as if he had bathed in whiskey—snaked his arm around her waist and yanked her back against him. She reflexively elbowed him in the belly. Which turned out to be a mistake. His grin became a spiteful scowl and he gave her a hard shake that rattled her teeth.

"Nobody rejects Fred Garner," he breathed down her neck. "I don't care if you are some la-di-da dress shop owner. You and me are gonna—"

Rosa blinked in surprise when the oafish tracklayer levitated off the ground and hung there with his boots dangling in midair. She glanced over her shoulder to see Lucas holding Fred by the nape of his tattered coat. When he growled threateningly so did Dog. Even the loudmouth ruffian had enough sense to shut up when Lucas bore down on him. His expression was as cold and hard as granite.

"Did you have something to say to the lady, Fred?" Lucas said in a low, vicious snarl.

"You that ruthless ex-Ranger mongrel?" the drunkard muttered.

"That would be me, Fred," Lucas assured him gruffly. "I've been itching to kill someone since I retired. You wanna be him?"

"Be nice," Rosa murmured. "Where's your holiday spirit?"

Lucas spared her a glance then glowered at the foul-smelling galoot. "Don't cross me or Rosa again, Freddie." He let Fred drop to his feet and watched him sway to regain his balance. "You get to live. Merry Christmas."

The stringy-haired hooligan made a show of straightening his grimy jacket then flashed Lucas a go-to-hell look. Lucas decided Fred needed more convincing so he grabbed his arm and spun him around to escort him off the premises.

"You want to deal with this besotted cowboy or can I have him?" Quin asked, holding the other troublemaker by the forearm.

"He's all yours. Might as well spread the cheer. Happy holidays, Cahill."

Rosa watched Quin quick-march the second ruffian across The Square. Lucas, Dog and Fred were a few steps ahead of them. She smiled, pleased that Lucas and Quin had bonded. Both men had been fodder for gossip. Lucas, because of his mixed heritage, his dangerous reputation and his refusal to venture into society on a regular basis. Quin because of the Cahill family tragedy, the rift between him, his brothers and sister and the mishaps at 4C Ranch that townsfolk referred to as the Cahill Curse.

When several female acquaintances appeared to check on her and Sylvia Bradley—the young brunette Fred had pestered—Rosa focused her attention on her guests. Her gaze drifted to Lucas at irregular intervals as he and Quin escorted the misbehaving ruffians off the premises. She wished for a private moment to thank him for intervening. However, she expected he would commence lecturing her about thrusting herself in harm's way, just as he had scolded her for traveling in the storm. But she could endure his tirade if it meant spending more time with him. She had missed him these past few days and she had been delighted that he had attended the party.

Be satisfied that you have made giant strides by getting him into town, she told herself. He was mingling in society and he had made a new friend. But still, she longed to be with him, to inhale his alluring masculine scent, to share more than a peck on his bronzed cheek, to run her hands over his sinewy flesh…

This is no time to be thinking those kinds of titillating thoughts! Rosa admonished herself silently then walked off to tend her duties as hostess.

It was late. He should go home.

Lucas sighed in frustration as he stared up at the light glowing in the upstairs window of Rosa's apartment above the boutique. Her party had been a grand success, except for the three interruptive fights that had broken out, he amended. Lucas and Quin had taken it upon themselves to deal with the troublemakers because Tobias Hobbs, the city marshal, hadn't been on hand when the arguments between tracklayers, soldiers from Fort Ridge and cowboys erupted.

His thoughts and his gaze drifted back to the upstairs window. Hell, who was he kidding? He hadn't attended tonight's holiday hoopla to socialize. He'd come to see Rosa…because not seeing her for several days had made him restless and dissatisfied.

Lucas grabbed Drizzle's reins then walked around the block to halt behind Rosa's shop. "Stay here with Drizzle," he told Dog.

When Dog whined in complaint, Lucas made a stabbing gesture with his forefinger. "*You* are in charge of Drizzle. *I* can take care of myself."

"Well, I used to be able to," he amended as he strode off. Now that he had become acquainted with Rosalie Greer everything had turned upside down. His wants and needs had changed. Lucas was headed for trouble and he knew it… and trouble was a shapely blonde with blue-violet eyes and lips as sweet and intoxicating as wine.

"Double damn, Burnett," he muttered at himself. "You really *are* turning into a Yuletide sap."

* * *

An unexpected rap sounded on Rosa's door. Alarmed, she grabbed the derringer from the dresser drawer. She intended to be prepared if Fred Garner showed up to take up where he'd left off.

Clutching her robe tightly around her, she aimed the weapon at whoever stood on the other side of the door. A Christmas *shooting* was the very last thing she wanted but she refused to be manhandled by one of the miscreants from Wrong Side who convinced himself that she owed him sexual favors.

Mustering her courage, she whipped open the door and aimed her derringer at the man's chest. Her mouth dropped open when she recognized Lucas lurking in the shadows. "Is something wrong?" she asked as she stepped aside to let him enter.

His dark gaze scanned her apartment, surveying her expensive furniture. She imagined he was comparing the items to his homemade furnishings and setting up a few more roadblocks as to why he should avoid associating with her.

But then, he is here, she reminded herself. Surely that meant something, didn't it? Was she getting to him the way he had gotten to her? Was it as unnerving and unfamiliar for him as it was for her?

Although Rosa didn't refer to herself as a man-hater, she had become a man-*mistruster* over the past eight years. Until Lucas had pulled her from a snowdrift and warmed her up—inside and out. Nowadays her thoughts drifted to him while she worked, while she lay alone in bed. She thought of him entirely too often!

Careful, Rosalie, you're going to get your heart broken for Christmas if you don't watch out.

"I wanted to make sure Fred didn't stop in to retaliate after you rejected him…. Nice place, by the way." His midnight-colored eyes resettled on her gaping robe that revealed the semitransparent lace on the bodice of her nightgown. "Nice lingerie, too. Did you design that?"

Heat suffused her face and desire coiled deep inside her when he stared at her with those penetrating obsidian eyes. Her silent warning about getting her heart broken flew right out the window. Rosa could almost guarantee she was going to do something reckless and impulsive. She had never wanted a man the way she wanted the raven-haired ex-Ranger who could set fire to her blood with one simmering stare.

And why couldn't she have him, if only for one night? She was a grown woman and she didn't have to answer to a protective father or brother. She made her own choices and she was prepared to live with the consequences.

Before Rosa could stop herself—and she probably wouldn't have even if she could have—she walked right up to Lucas, glided her arms over his broad shoulders and said, "I want you for Christmas."

"You sure about that?" he murmured as his arms came around her waist to draw her full length against him.

She focused on his sensuous lips then met his smoldering gaze. "Absolutely certain," she assured him breathlessly.

He lowered his head, his mouth a tormenting hairbreadth away from hers. "Then you can have me, Rosalie. As many times as you please... Ouch!"

The derringer she still held in her hand clanked against the side of his head when she wrapped her arms tightly around his neck.

"Give me that piddly thing," Lucas said, taking it from her fist to tuck in the waistband of his breeches. "You need something bigger and more powerful than that for protection."

His heart nearly cracked open like a walnut when she tilted her head back, letting her silver-gold hair cascade over her shoulders. She smiled impishly up at him and said, "I don't need a derringer when I have you—"

His mouth came down on hers with explosive need. Raw hunger pummeled him like a sledgehammer. Lucas groaned as he deepened the kiss and crushed her lush body to his. "I think I'd like that fancy robe and negligee better if you were out of them," he murmured against her earlobe.

She tensed momentarily as he walked her backward to the bedroom. Lucas halted to stare into her wide amethyst eyes.

"Jubal is here, in your head, isn't he?" he asked quietly.

She nodded then managed a faint smile. "He was, but he's gone now. In fact, mother's recent letter said a debutante's father ran him out of town and told him not to come back if he valued his life. Now I can visit mother without dealing with him. He's gone for good."

"Good riddance to him." Lucas skimmed his lips over her creamy cheek, loving the feel of her delicate skin.

"Lucas?"

"Mmm?" He kissed her eyelids and the tip of her nose, quickly losing interest in conversation.

"I don't expect him back. *Ever*." She stared earnestly at him. "You overshadow him, Lucas. You are everything he can never be."

Right there and then Lucas vowed that he would take all the time Rosa needed tonight. Whatever she wanted, however much she needed, he would give her. Even if impatient need gnawed at him, which it had begun to already.

On that dedicated vow, Lucas angled his head to savor the texture of her dewy lips. Gently, he drew her against him then hooked his thumb inside the silky robe and sent it gliding into a pool at her bare feet. When he skimmed his hand over the peak of her breast, he felt her tremble in his arms and prayed it wasn't fear but rather awakened desire that assailed her. She arched into him and moaned, so he assumed he had given her pleasure.

Difficult though it was, Lucas released her and stepped back. He held her gaze as he fumbled to unbutton his shirt. "If you've changed your mind, this is the time to say so."

To his relief, she shook her head. Silver-blond hair shimmered in the lantern light and lay temptingly against the full swells of her breasts. She reached out to rake her nails over his bare chest and he swore his legs were about to fold up like a tent. Hell, he couldn't even breathe normally while her hand swept down his breastbone to the dark furring of hair that disappeared beneath his belt buckle and double holsters.

"You're driving me crazy, you know that, don't you?" he wheezed as her index finger trailed along the band of his breeches to set aside the derringer.

"Good to know," she said with a wicked smile. "I wasn't sure anything less than a flying bullet could destroy the self-control of a legendary ex-Ranger."

"*You* can." Lucas was beginning to realize this lovely female was the one temptation in life he couldn't resist.

He hooked his arm around her waist and tumbled with her onto the frilly bed with its silky sheets. She snickered in play-ful amusement...until he slid the thin straps off her shoulders to flick at her breasts with his tongue. A wobbly sigh escaped her lips and Lucas smiled in masculine satisfaction when she snuggled closer. He wanted nothing more than to satisfy Rosa's needs and desires this night.

And double damn that Jubal whoever-he-was. That bastard had better not get in Lucas's way tonight or he'd have to hop an eastbound train to look the man up then shoot him down.

His vindictive thoughts scattered when Rosa glided her hand beneath the band of his trousers to discover he was unmistakably hard and fully aroused. Her long lashes swept up and she peered at him in surprise.

"You have the magic touch, Miss Secret Saint Nicholas," he teased playfully. "Can I remove my breeches or do you want to do it for me?"

Rosa grinned mischievously as she unfastened the placket of his trousers. "I think I'll design breeches for men that are faster and easier to remove."

"You do that," he said huskily. "Or maybe kilts and togas will become stylish for Western wear. I'm all in favor—"

When Rosa lowered her head to brush her warm lips over the hard length of his arousal she heard the air gush from his lungs in a whoosh. She couldn't believe she had become so bold and daring. She wanted to explore every inch of his masculine flesh, to make Lucas moan with pleasure until the want of her destroyed his willpower.

She could tell Lucas was trying to be deliberate and careful with her because he thought that cursed Jubal Hawthorne still might be skipping around in her head. But the bastard was long gone now and she had eight years of unfulfilled need roiling inside her. She had shed her inhibitions and she wanted Lucas to release his, too—

"Awk!" Rosa chirped in surprise when Lucas flipped her onto her back and loomed over her like the dark, ruggedly handsome angel he was.

"Lady, if you keep touching me like that it is going to get you into serious trouble," he rumbled huskily.

"Promises, promises," she taunted, amazed at the flirtatious side of her nature that had sprouted from nowhere.

"You are full of delightful surprises," he murmured, studying her as if she were an unexpected gift.

Her breath stalled in her chest when his hand tunneled beneath the hem of her nightgown, moved over the V between her legs, up her belly and ribs, and then encircled the tips of her breasts. Fire leaped in her bloodstream and she struggled to restart her heartbeat after he tugged the garment over her head and tossed it toward the dresser—missing it by a mile.

His dark, intense gaze swept over her in masculine appreciation. "My imagination didn't do you justice, Rosalie. I've wanted to do this since I stripped you down to your undergarments the night of the storm."

Then he brushed his clean-shaven cheek against her breast and his hand glided downward to trail from hip to kneecap then back up again. Inexpressible desire blazed inside her as he kissed and caressed her so slowly and tenderly that she wanted to demand that he make the burning ache go away— immediately.

Sweet mercy! She never dreamed hungry passion could

become instant obsession. She wanted him as close as he could get, wanted to hold him, touch him as intimately as he was touching her.

Repeatedly, he brought her to the crumbling edge of breathless need then gradually withdrew. Then he built the white-hot crescendo once again and she felt her body quivering as he teased her with his fingertips. Desperate, she clutched at his shoulder, demanding an end to this erotic torment. He had driven her as close to crazy as she had ever been and she wanted him so desperately that she shook with uncontrollable desire.

"Come here," she gasped and writhed and burned with the most indescribable sensations imaginable.

"Not yet, but soon, sweetheart."

When he clasped her by the hips and propped her against the headboard she started to ask what he was doing. But then he lowered his head between her legs and she felt his tongue and lips skimming her tender flesh. Rosa was unprepared for the burst of flames that scorched her, unprepared for the ravenous need clamoring through her. She swore she had been set on fire and had breathed her last breath as her body exploded with dozens more unbelievable sensations.

And then he pulled her beneath him and drove into her with long, slow, penetrating thrusts. Spasms of wild pleasure bombarded her as he moved above her, setting a hypnotic cadence that sent her spiraling from one dizzying pinnacle of rapture to the next.

Rosa hung on to Lucas for dear life as the world wobbled on its axis. When she heard him groan and felt him shudder above her, she wrapped her arms and legs around him and held on as if her very life depended on it. She knew without question that she had fallen in love with her dark angel. She wouldn't have given her heart and body to him if she weren't in love with him. For Rosa, it was all or nothing.

When Lucas eased down beside her, Rosa half collapsed. "If I die from too much amazing pleasure and I very well could," she panted raggedly, "promise you will deliver the toys and gifts."

He chuckled softly then pressed his full lips to hers. "Comanche promise, blondie... That good?"

She nodded and smiled, but exhaustion overtook her immediately. She slumped against his shoulder. His devastating lovemaking and the hustle and bustle of last-minute tasks for the town-wide celebration caught up with her. Her lashes fluttered against her flushed cheeks and her breath came out in a quiet sigh. She reached over to clasp Lucas's fingertips, giving them an affectionate squeeze that meant I love you, though she doubted he could interpret it, even though he was fluent in English, Spanish and the Comanche dialect.

A few minutes later, when Lucas knew Rosa had fallen asleep, he levered onto his elbow to study her exquisite face, surrounded by a halo of curly blond hair. A moment of regret threatened to overwhelm him, but he cast it aside. He knew he was Rosa's first experiment with passion. She was definitely his first time with an innocent. He had no right whatsoever to be grinning in triumph because he knew her more intimately than any man alive. But he liked knowing she belonged to him, if only for one night.

Speaking of which...Lucas inched away to retrieve his breeches—ones he had been eager to shed in his haste to bury himself in Rosa's welcoming warmth. In Rosa's silky arms, he had discovered the difference between rare, mind-boggling, bone-melting passion and meaningless sexual encounters.

Silently, he dressed, then tiptoed from her bedroom. He needed to leave before someone noticed his horse and dog waiting at the back door of the shop. If gossip started flying her reputation would be in shambles, whether she was the Darling of Downtown or not. Just look what had happened to Quin Cahill's family when folks began speculating on why his brothers and sister weren't coming home for Christmas.

You should have considered her reputation before you came upstairs. He scowled at himself.

Yet he knew a team of wild mustangs couldn't have dragged him away from her doorstep tonight. He had no self-restraint whatsoever when it came to Rosalie. He might have brought her to his cabin during the blizzard so she could thaw out but he was the one who had thawed out—mentally and emotionally. She made him want things he had never dared to expect from life.

Lucas decided to blame his lack of willpower on Christmas. His wish list had begun and ended with the want of that intriguing, violet-eyed blonde who had sworn him to secrecy. Then she had introduced him all over town, held his hand, kissed him on the cheek in front of her friends and acquaintances and made him feel as if he mattered to her. He had allowed her to drag him into society though he'd sworn up and down he would avoid it.

Now they shared another secret and he'd gone places he hadn't planned to go—and he meant that in the most intimate sense.

"What are you two looking at?" he muttered at Dog and Drizzle.

He swore his four-legged companions were silently admonishing him. More likely, it was his own conscience trying to nag him to death. Lucas knew he had made a wildly reckless mistake tonight. Yet it wasn't shame and guilt that hounded him now. It was the lingering memories of Rosa's delightfully playful nature and the astonishing passion that had burst to life between them.

"I'll feel guilty tomorrow, when I regain my good judgment," he said to the darkness as he rode home. "But definitely not tonight."

The glorious sensations of passion he had discovered while he was spiraling in Rosa's magical embrace filled his mind with wonder and warmed his body during the cold trek home.

Chapter Five

Rosa had seen nothing of Lucas since the night of the party when he had shown up unexpectedly at her apartment door—and introduced her to the incredible world of amazing sensations.

The very thought caused her face to flush with heat.

"You feeling okay, Rosa?" Melanie asked as she ironed the ruffle she had sewn onto the gown she was making.

Rosa waved her arm toward the wood stove in the workroom. "Standing too close to the fire."

She'd been too close to the fire all right—and the name of the flame was Lucas Burnett.

"Cyril and I are going to the church social this evening," Melanie said conversationally then she displayed a wide grin. "If you're attending, bring that handsome Lucas Burnett with you."

Rosa shrugged as casually as she knew how. "I invited him, but I'm not sure he can make it."

"You should know you two are the talk of the town," Melanie teased, her hazel eyes twinkling mischievously. "'Course, there were a half dozen eligible bachelors in Town Square, wondering why you favored the local recluse with your companionship and not them. Hmm…I'm wondering the same thing. What is going on with you two? And do not tell me it's gratitude on your part."

"I have told each of those men that I am not good marriage material," Rosa commented as she carefully cut the pattern for the satin gown she was making for one of her friends.

Melanie sniffed caustically. "Right. Too old. Too involved in starting your business. Too set in your ways and too opinionated."

"I am all those things," Rosa admitted honestly then hunkered over the cutting table to focus on her task.

Melanie studied her all too closely. "Then why appear in public with the ex-Ranger?"

Rosa set aside her scissors and worked the kinks from her back. "Because Lucas needed to mingle with society instead of spending all his time with Dog and the horses." *Liar,* she thought to herself. *You wanted to be with him and the party was the perfect excuse to invite him.* "Besides, it's the Christmas season. I wanted him to get into the spirit of the holidays."

"Uh-huh," Melanie said and smirked. "So that's why you two were holding hands and you placed a couple of pecks on his cheek? You were feeling the Christmas spirit, too. Right?"

Rosa stared her frizzy-haired assistant squarely in the eye. "I was trying to let everyone in town know that Lucas is a valuable, accepted member of our community. Also, I am greatly appreciative that he saved my life. Otherwise, I wouldn't be standing here on Christmas Eve afternoon, listening to you torment me instead of finishing that dress for one of our most impatient and particular patrons."

The pointed glance didn't faze Melanie. She waggled her eyebrows suggestively. "Yes, well, we all got the impression that you were more than grateful to Lucas. I'm grateful to Henry Stokes when he delivers the mail to our doorstep but I don't give him a kiss in exchange for a letter."

Gracious, had she been that obvious? Yes, Rosa supposed she had. Well, she would have to use it to her advantage then. She plucked up the scissors and went to work, but not before saying, "I had a second agenda. Having everyone think Lucas and I are an item is the perfect deterrent for holding unwanted suitors at bay. In fact," she added, tossing out an impish smile, "maybe I will *pay* him to be my escort during the holidays. Not only is there a party tonight but also one on New Year's, as well."

Melanie expelled an unladylike snort. "You don't fool me, Rosalie Greer. I know you too well. You like Lucas Burnett and I think he likes you back. In fact, when he snatched up that drunken hooligan for pestering you to dance with him, Lucas looked downright vicious and mad enough to strangle him."

"He's a former Ranger," she countered logically. "It's a learned reaction to put a stop to trouble, no matter who is involved."

"Fine, don't admit to me that there is something going on between you two." Melanie went back to her ironing. "At least be honest with yourself."

Rosa *was* honest with herself. She knew she had fallen hard and fast for the hermit and outcast who didn't think he fitted into society and didn't seem to care if he did. But she refused to put pressure on Lucas. She would count herself lucky if he attended the church social on Christmas Eve, but she didn't expect him to continue the policy after the holidays. Plus, she couldn't make him love her back if all he felt for her was occasional sexual desire.

However, she vowed to see that he was accepted and honored as a hero who had helped bring law and order to the area. That would be her gift to him. Acceptance and respect.

Her thoughts trailed off when the bell over the door jingled. "Yoo-hoo, Rosa! Is my gown ready for tonight?"

Rosa scooped up the elegant gown she had put the finishing touches on this morning and strode off to answer the customer's call. She tried to put Lucas out of mind but she wasn't the least bit successful.

And confound it, if he didn't show up to help her deliver

gifts in the middle of the night she wasn't sure she could finish her rounds without being sighted!

Lucas paced the confines of his cabin on Christmas Eve afternoon. Then he halted to stare at the note Rosa had sent with the same gangly teenager who had delivered the double invitations to her Town Square party, the same self-conscious teenager she suggested he hire to help with chores on his horse ranch. And so he had.

"Pushy female," he mumbled and grumbled then paced some more. "Church party on Christmas Eve." If he dared to show up at church, the white and Indian deities alike would likely send down a lightning bolt to drop him on the front steps.

He wasn't even sure what he believed, having been raised in the Comanche stronghold and introduced to white man's religion years later. Of course, his mixed breeding probably wasn't the only reason the Powers That Be might fry him to a crisp. More likely, it was his reckless tryst with Rosa.

Lucas's conscience had finally caught up with him and he regretted succumbing to his hungry need for a woman who was an integral part of civilized society. A woman who could buy and sell him if she had a mind to. They were so different! What had he been thinking?

He *hadn't* been thinking, that was the problem. Hungry need had been prowling through him since the night he met Rosa during the storm. That insatiable craving hadn't gone away, either. Not even after they ended up on her fancy bed, doing things to each other that, even days later, had the power to make his body throb and his sap rise.

He should have gone to the wrong side of the tracks the night of her party to ease his masculine needs. Not to her apartment. But he knew well and good that no other woman could satisfy the desire she alone had instilled in him.

Lucas blew out his breath and glowered at the elegant, hand-written invitation to the church social and her request to help her deliver packages in the dark of night. "Not going and that is that," he decided.

Dog was lying in front of the fire, as usual. He lifted his head from his oversize paws and said, "Woof." Whatever that meant.

A moment later Lucas knew exactly what Dog meant because footsteps resounded on the stoop. Gun drawn, Lucas opened the front door before his uninvited guest could raise his hand to knock.

"Cahill?" Lucas stared at the powerfully built rancher. "What are you doing here?"

"I came to offer to buy your ranch," Quin declared.

"No. I want to buy the piece of property on your ranch known as Comanche Bluff," Lucas countered. "It's where my people camped when we followed the buffalo herds that you and your kind nearly exterminated."

Lucas knew he was being rude and irascible but so what? He was nursing a conflict between good sense and unruly desire and it was seriously affecting his disposition.

"May I come in?" Quin asked, undaunted by Lucas's greeting scowl.

"No. Don't you have a home of your own?"

Quin snickered then barged in without invitation to look around. "You have permission to visit Comanche Bluff anytime you please," he offered generously. "But if you won't sell your ranch then how about a few of your horses?"

Lucas grabbed his coat to ward off the chill. "That I can do, Cahill. Not my best mares and foals, of course."

"Didn't expect that… Are you going to the church gathering tonight?" he asked as they stepped off the stoop.

"Don't know," Lucas murmured as he headed toward the barn and corrals.

"Me, either. Haven't decided yet. But it's better than staying home in a big, empty house, I suppose."

Or in a compact cabin filled with the lingering scents and memories of a violet-eyed female that I can't rout from my mind. Lucas sighed inwardly. Why hadn't Rosa become snowbound somewhere else? Then he wouldn't be fighting this exasperating battle that was keeping him up nights and coloring all his thoughts.

"Burnett?" Quin prompted, jolting Lucas back to the present.

"What?"

Although Quin flashed him a knowing grin, he didn't comment, just directed Lucas's attention to one of the yearlings in the corral. Lucas did his damnedest to keep his mind on the negotiations and off Rosalie. He even succeeded—for about thirty minutes.

Rosa checked her reflection in the cheval glass then pinned up an unruly corkscrew curl that dangled by her temple. She had made it a point to dress in the most delicate gown she owned so no one in Cahill Crossing would even think that a dainty female might be responsible for the surprise gifts that showed up on doorsteps long after midnight on Christmas Eve.

Unless a townsperson spotted her because a certain someone—named Lucas mule-headed Burnett—didn't help her distribute the toys so she had to do it herself in record time!

Rosa glanced up at the mantel clock. The church social and short evening service would begin in twenty minutes. It would take her that long to walk across town to the church situated near the school. Although the snow had melted days earlier, she required a heavy coat to fend off the cold breeze. After being snowbound in the blizzard Rosa had vowed to bundle up and never experience that kind of bone-deep chill ever again.

After she donned her coat, she pulled open the door then jumped back in surprise. Lucas stood before her, his hand upraised to knock. He had accepted her invitation? Another Christmas miracle.

"You're here," she said unnecessarily, and smiled like a witless idiot.

To her delight, he walked in and lifted her clean off the floor. Then he kissed her. Her arms involuntarily encircled his neck and she locked her legs around his lean hips. All too soon, Lucas set her to her wobbly legs and backed up a respectable distance. Rosa was having none of that. She grabbed him by the collar of his coat, jerked him to her and kissed him until she was forced to come up for air.

Then she gathered her composure and plucked up the gloves sitting on the end table. She glanced up to see Lucas staring at her with those penetrating midnight-colored eyes that had the power to bedevil and arouse.

"Is something wrong, Lucas?" she asked, trying to sound as nonchalant as a woman could get.

"Yes, but I learned while fighting intruders with the Comanche and battling outlaws with the Rangers that some problems you just can't fix."

She had no idea what that meant and she didn't have the chance to ask because Lucas glided his arm around her waist to escort her out the door.

"Quin Cahill came by this afternoon," he commented as they descended the steps.

"Good, I was hoping you two would become friends. Now that Quin, Bowie, Leanna and Chance have had a parting of ways after their parents' tragic accident, he spends entirely too much time rattling around in that big ole house on 4C Ranch."

"He bought six of my horses," Lucas reported as they stepped outside to greet the cold December wind. "I made a killing. He's a lousy horse trader. No self-respecting Comanche would pay that much for a mount when he can train another one easily enough."

Rosa chuckled at the playful twitch of Lucas's lips. "He wanted to buy Drizzle, didn't he?"

"Yep, but I told him Drizzle, Dog and I are family."

"Never underestimate Quin," Rosa warned. "He's liable

to return in a few months and offer to sell back one of your horses that he has trained to herd cattle, with or without a rider on its back. The man knows cattle and horses so don't let him fool you."

"My horses can open their stall gates and let themselves out," Lucas boasted teasingly. "Cahill has nothing on me."

Rosa silently seconded that but she didn't comment because Lucas grasped her hand as they hiked across Town Square. The want of him derailed her thoughts.

"Cahill isn't Comanche, Lord of the Plains. I am," he said, and grinned. "I like him, even if we have an ongoing debate about who knows more about livestock."

Rosa sighed contentedly as she strolled across town, hand-in-hand, with the swarthy ex-Ranger. She was already having a grand time and she had encouraged two lonely men to enter into a friendship that might benefit both of them. The evening so far, she decided, was about as perfect as it could get.

Melanie smiled delightedly, and her husband, Cyril, grinned when Lucas and Rosa entered the playground area between the church and school. Lucas experienced a moment of awkwardness when all eyes focused on him, just like the night of Rosa's party. This was their second public appearance. He received several annoyed glances from male partygoers that indicated his rivals weren't happy that he was Rosa's escort.

A sense of pride overcame Lucas as Melanie and Cyril walked toward them. Even if Rosa had invited him out of gratitude—and most likely a sense of obligation after their night of passion—they were an item. But gratitude and guilty obligation were the very last two things in the world that he wanted from Rosalie Greer. He wanted the impossible, he realized.

"How much did she pay you to accompany her so you could discourage her would-be suitors?" Melanie asked teasingly.

The question stung his pride like a hive of hornets. Is that what this was all about? He was running interference for her would-be beaus? Of course, he realized. That's what the public displays of affection were about.

"If you spread that nonsense around town, Melanie Eileen Ford, you are fired," Rosa insisted. "Don't tease Lucas. I'm just elated that he is joining in the festivities."

"Just having a bit of fun," Melanie said quickly. "Ask me, the two of you make a striking couple, don't they, Cyril?"

"Sure," Cyril agreed then shuffled his wife on her way.

Rosa pivoted to face Lucas. Then she pressed a kiss to his cheek but now he knew it was all for show. Suspected he was just a prop used in her charade to discourage unwanted suitors.

"That will cost you an extra two bits," he said, his voice gruff with the outrage he couldn't squelch.

She scowled at him and he gnashed his teeth, thoroughly aggravated with her. He allowed her to tow him into the shadows, away from the lanterns and the milling crowd. He had a few things to say to her and he didn't want an audience, either.

"Lucas Burnett, you are the furthest thing from my paid escort as you can get. You should know that without my having to tell you. I blurted out that comment in jest this afternoon because Melanie was trying to pry into our private affairs. I didn't know what to say when she insisted that I was exceptionally fond of you and that you were fond of me."

He bore down on her. "*Are* you?"

"Am I what?" she asked flippantly.

"You know, *fond*." Lucas had never felt so awkward or uncertain in his life. Nothing in his hardscrabble existence had prepared him for putting his heart on the line. His neck? Yes. He could face outlaws with guns blazing but he was in unfamiliar territory here.

Rosa drew herself up, squared her shoulders and tilted her chin to stare him directly in the eye. He liked that about her. She didn't sidestep issues with him, just gave it to him straight. He might not like her answer to his question but he appreciated her candor.

"Yes, I'm fond of you, Lucas," she told him. "And no, I don't mind that you escort me around town to assure other men that I am not interested in them and that I am not what they really need. Most men prefer younger, more impressionable women who haven't yet formed their own opinions and haven't spread their independent wings."

"Here we go," Lucas muttered under his breath. Rosa was handing him an excuse for making this their last evening together. She was going to let him think it was *his* idea to walk away from her.

"I enjoy running my shop and following my own dreams," she went on to say. "Just because you and I—" Her voice fizzled out momentarily. But Rosa, being Rosa, gathered her composure and forged ahead.

He admired that about her, too, but he still wanted to strangle her!

"I am trying to tell you that you are under no obligation whatsoever for what transpired between us. If consequences should arise, they will be my problem and I don't expect you to solve them. You can come and go as you please." She inhaled a deep breath and hurried on. "I am telling you here and now that if you walk me to my apartment door after the party, the same thing that happened last time will happen this time."

Lucas swallowed an amused grin, but she seemed so determined and serious that he tried not to laugh. "Well, in that case—"

"So, if you don't want to give a repeat performance," she cut in quickly, "then simply say good night at the door."

"I want to come upstairs," he assured her. "And you are under no obligation to let me think I'm more than your escort and your partner in passion if that is all you want from me."

Rosa gaped at him, wide-eyed. "All I want from you?"

"I know I'm not your social equal, even if you have made it your mission to introduce me all around town and shout to high heaven that I'm your guardian angel, a hero and a gallant knight all rolled into one."

"I don't have a social equal!" she shouted at him.

"You're right. You're in a class all by yourself and I am well aware of that. More so than anyone else in town," he added meaningfully.

She jerked her hands from his grasp and puffed up like a cobra. "That is not what I meant. Anyway, it doesn't matter. I'm in love with you, you blind fool and—"

Rosa slapped both hands over her mouth, wishing she could retract that blurted confession. Confound it! She had exposed herself as the hopeless romantic she never thought she would be after Jubal Hawthorne tore her dreams to shreds and made her wary of men's motives.

Mortified tears sprang to her eyes. She had embarrassed herself in front of the one man whose opinion of her mattered. To make the humiliating situation worse, he didn't utter a word. Just stood there, staring down at her with those dark, penetrating eyes.

Unable to meet his gaze, she glanced sideways to note that her upraised voice, if not her specific words, had called attention to her and Lucas.

Rosa spun on her heel so quickly she nearly threw herself off balance. With as much dignity as she could gather around her, she marched across the playground.

Lucas, her dark angel and knight in shining armor, didn't come after her, damn him. Which indicated that he didn't return her heartfelt affection.

He was probably relieved that she dashed off so he wouldn't have to figure out how to let her down gently.

Nothing like a domestic squabble in the churchyard on Christmas Eve to inflame gossip, she thought as she quickened her pace. The Cahills had nothing on her!

Tormented to no end, Rosa lifted her trailing skirts and broke into an undignified run to Town Square. Confound it! She had stumbled from one potential scandal with Jubal eight years earlier to another one with Lucas tonight. Now Lucas would never return to Cahill Crossing, for fear she would throw herself at him. Love was the last thing Lucas probably wanted from her. An occasional tryst during one of his infrequent visits to town was probably all the satisfaction he needed.

She'd have to pack up and leave, she thought in despair. All because she had made a supreme fool of herself by allowing her feelings for Lucas to bubble up like a geyser and spew out while a crowd milled about.

"Doesn't matter what he—or anyone else—thinks of me," she blubbered as she veered around to the back of her shop. She had a mission to undertake tonight when everyone was tucked into bed on Christmas Eve. She would make her deliveries alone, as she had last year, she promised herself determinedly.

And tomorrow, being Christmas, she would have a day of reprieve before she faced speculative stares and the noticeable absence of that brawny, dark-eyed ex-Ranger in her life—

Her thoughts exploded and she gasped in surprise when someone pounced from the shadows the moment she opened the back door of the shop. Rosa tried to bite the gloved hand clamped over mouth but her attacker rammed a pistol into the side of her neck, discouraging her from fighting back. She did, however, set her feet—but to no avail—when he pushed her ahead of him to scale the staircase leading to her apartment.

"Now unlock the door and be quick about it," he snapped gruffly.

Rosa opened the door, asking herself what Lucas would do when confronted with this dangerous situation. He would attack, she decided. Hands clenched together, she whirled around to wallop the masked man in the head. While he was dazed momentarily, she launched herself at him to grab his pistol but he clubbed her with it before she could yank it from his grasp.

Pain exploded in her skull and she wilted onto the floor in an unconscious heap.

Lucas stood there—as if he'd sprouted roots—for several minutes. What was he supposed to do after Rosa told him that she loved him then stamped off, as if she were *ashamed* of her feelings and didn't want him to know?

Did she really think she was in love with him? Why? What could he possibly give her that she couldn't purchase for herself? She was an heiress, for goodness sake. And he was... *not*.

He glanced around uncomfortably, noting that he was still the center of attention. "Double damn," he mumbled. Well, he was here. He supposed a glass of punch and a pastry wouldn't hurt him.

On his way to the refreshment table, Quin Cahill held out a glass to him and smiled wryly. "Looks like your Christmas goose is cooked, Burnett."

Lucas accepted the drink, stared in the direction Rosa had gone then expelled a frustrated sigh.

"Here's to friends and family abandoning a man during the holidays and leaving him to deal with the fallout," Quin toasted.

Lucas recalled what Rosa had said about the supposed Cahill Curse—whatever the hell it was—and Quin's family leaving town two years earlier. Sort of like the wealthy heiress—posing as a shopkeeper who made a modest living—shouting at you then darting away from the party and leaving you to deal with the aftermath.

"Women," Lucas mumbled then sipped his drink.

Quin clinked his glass against Lucas's then downed the punch. His teasing amusement faded and he stared directly at Lucas. "I don't know what just happened, but she *picked* you. She *rejected* everyone else. Figure it out, Burnett."

"Even you, Cahill?" Lucas asked.

"Not me. I've been too busy running the 4C by myself to have time for women. Not that I haven't noticed Rosa. She is an intelligent and exceptionally attractive young woman," Quin replied. "So...are you going to the service?"

Lucas glanced skyward, wondering when the Yuletide thunderbolt would strike him down. Then he realized it didn't matter. All that *did* matter was that Rosalie Greer had said she was in love with him, whether she wanted to be or not.

"I'm no expert on women, but you might want to give her time to cool down first," Quin advised. "Besides, this is a short come-and-go service. You light a candle, say a prayer then the parson wishes you good tidings of comfort and joy on your way out the door."

Maybe attending a prayer service was what a man who wasn't sure who or what he was needed to help him find his way. Also, he could use some divine assistance in formulating the right words to say to Rosa—*after* she cooled off, of course.

When Quin lurched around to follow the crowd inside, Lucas fell into step behind him. The citizens of Cahill Crossing might not forgive him for upsetting the Darling of Downtown, but maybe the Great Spirit would.

Lucas reckoned he would soon find out. Just to be on the safe side he sent a cautious glance skyward, in case of an oncoming thunderbolt.

When Rosa regained consciousness, she found herself tied to a chair. The velvet ropes from the drapery encircled her wrists. She blinked to clear her fuzzy vision then stared goggle-eyed at the blue-eyed, sandy-blond-haired ghost from eight Christmases past.

At least she *wished* Jubal Hawthorne were a figment of her imagination. Unfortunately, he looked very real while he stood over her, wearing expensive clothing that looked as if it had been slept in for two weeks. Apparently, he hadn't shaved since his eviction, either.

"Still up to your old trick of clobbering people over the head, I see," Jubal said as he gingerly touched the knot on his temple. "However, tonight isn't as painful as having a bronze statue slammed into my skull, Rosalie."

Anger and frustration consumed Rosa. She itched to get her hands on the despicable man who had so unfortunately influenced her association with men. That is, she amended, until Lucas had come along to dispel her mistrust.

"I'm in no mood for a stroll down memory lane," she snapped crossly. "What do you want?" As if she couldn't guess.

"Money, of course. Lots of it," Jubal replied. He looked down his snobbish nose at her apartment. "My my, this is a far cry from the opulent mansion you and your mother sold in Boston."

"It suits me perfectly," she retorted.

Jubal struck the arrogant pose she remembered so well. "I don't like roughing it out here in this godforsaken country, as you seem to. Therefore—" he tossed her a devilish grin, a look she well remembered "—if you don't want your reputation in tatters, after I boast that you and I had a wild affair on Christmas Eve, then give me money to tide me over until I settle in California and Papa can send me funds."

Despite the dull throb in her head, she tilted her chin in defiance. "Spread all the gossip you want," she said indifferently. "There is plenty of scandal swirling about me already tonight. I'm planning to leave town anyway so it matters very little what you add to flying rumors."

Jubal's refined features puckered in a scowl. "Damn it, Rosalie, I need money and I need it now!"

"Then find a job, you worthless buffoon," she sniped. "Your father has always bailed you out and made excuses for your reckless behavior. It wouldn't hurt you to make an honest day's wage for an honest day's work for once in your life—"

Her voice dried up when she heard footfalls on the staircase.

Jubal whirled, his pistol at the ready. "Get rid of your guest," he demanded in a quiet hiss.

A light tap resounded against the door and Lucas said, "Rosa, I'd like to talk to you."

The desperation in Jubal's expression alerted Rosa that Lucas was in danger of being shot—before he knew what hit him. The thought of losing Lucas to this disgusting excuse of a human being was unbearable. No matter what happened to her, Lucas was going to be safe, she vowed resolutely.

"Go away. I have nothing more to say to you," she shouted harshly. "I mean it. Get out of here!"

Lucas glanced down at Dog, who had insisted on following him up the steps to Rosa's apartment instead of remaining outside with Drizzle. When Dog growled and bared his teeth, Lucas knew his own instincts of danger were dead-on. He had heard the sound of fear mingling with anger in Rosa's upraised voice. Something was definitely wrong and it had nothing to do with their awkward encounter thirty minutes earlier.

He discreetly turned the doorknob, noting it was unlocked. Good. Breaking through a locked door could cause a crucial delay and every second counted if Rosa faced peril.

"I have something important to say to you," he said.

"I don't want to hear it," she called back. *"Go away!"*

Lucas went in low and fast. Dog was right beside him.

"Dog!" He snarled the command as he dived at the intruder, taking his storklike legs out from under him.

With a startled yelp, the man went down in an unceremonious heap. Dog leaped onto Jubal's chest then clamped his jaws around the wrist of his gun hand. The man yelped and dropped the pistol before Dog could bite off his hand at the wrist.

Lucas bounded to his feet to retrieve the pistol. Then he caught sight of Rosa, whose coiffure had come undone, leaving silky silver-blond hair tumbling off the side of her head like a misplaced fountain. She was still in one piece—thank goodness—but she was glaring pitchforks at her assailant. Lucas didn't have to ask who this dandified bastard was. He *knew.*

"Turn me loose and let me at him," she cried vindictively.

He complied. A smile pursed his lips when she shot to her feet and stamped off to loom over Jubal—who wasn't going anywhere since Dog was poised to go for his throat if he made any sudden moves. Lucas knew he wouldn't have to shout the command to Dog. The dog would act on his own accord, for he had become as protective of Rosa as he was of Lucas.

"How dare you come here asking for money, Jubal Hawthorne," Rosa shouted. "I don't care if it is Christmas Eve. I am not showing you the slightest generosity because you are a heartless libertine and you don't deserve it!"

Lucas bit back another grin when he realized Rosa was emulating the intimidating stance he used when confronting outlaws. He listened to her rake Jubal over live coals for a few minutes then he swooped in to hoist the haggard-looking dandy to his feet.

"I'll stuff Jubal in jail," he declared as he quick-marched him across the room. He halted by the door then glanced back at Rosa. "You okay?"

She blew out an agitated breath then nodded. More strands of hair tumbled from her lopsided coiffure. "Okay enough. Get the bastard out of my sight before I decide to shoot him full of buckshot."

After Lucas and Dog had hauled Jubal down the steps Rosa kerplopped on the sofa. She inhaled a half dozen cathartic breaths and regathered her frazzled composure. She had a slight headache but otherwise she was all right. No thanks to Jubal, damn his worthless hide.

She checked the clock on the mantel then rose to heat coffee. She consumed two full cups, hoping to warm herself from inside out before she ventured into the cold to deliver her gifts. After she bundled up in several layers of clothing, she opened the door—and lo and behold, her dark angel stood before her.

No doubt, Lucas had returned from incarcerating Jubal, giving himself extra time to formulate his speech so he could let her down *gently*—it being Christmas Eve and all.

"Jubal is resting *un*comfortably in his cell, I hope?" she asked.

"Yes, but he had an accident on his way to jail."

"Oh?" She arched her brow and stared curiously at Lucas. "What happened? Did he try to escape you?"

"No, he rammed his face into my fist three times," Lucas informed her. "He has a black eye, a bloody nose and a split lip."

Rosa met his dark gaze, wanting to throw herself into his arms but managing to restrain herself. She doubted she would be welcomed after she had blurted out the confession Lucas didn't want to hear.

"Thank you for doing what I wanted to do to Jubal but lacked the strength and skill for," she murmured.

"It was my pleasure." He shifted from one booted foot to the other then stared at the air over her right shoulder. "And Rosa…?"

She knew what was coming: the "I'm trying to let you down gently" speech. She couldn't deal with that. Not yet. It was too soon after her ordeal with Jubal and her public humiliation that had likely become the talk of the town at the fellowship social. Not to mention that Lucas didn't love her back. It was killing her, bit by excruciating bit.

"How was the service?" she asked, trying to stall so she could collect her rattled composure to face inevitable rejection.

"It was good…I stashed my wagon for transporting toys out back…I love you, Rosalie," he blurted out in the same breath.

Her mind whirled when he leapfrogged from one topic to the next, and then left her speechless with his unexpected confession.

Rosa regained her mental balance then narrowed her eyes at him. "You don't have to say that. You just feel sorry for me because Jubal showed up after I made a fool of myself at the church social."

"Sorry is the very last thing I feel for you," he insisted as he invited himself inside then closed the door behind him. "I told everyone that I was coming over here to apologize for what I said to upset you that sent you running home."

He was assuming the blame to salvage her pride? She wanted to hug the stuffing out of him for that.

"Then I told them I was going to ask you to marry me."

"You told them what?" she croaked, frog-eyed.

"You heard me, blondie. And don't feed me any more of that nonsense about being too old and too headstrong," he said as he unfastened her coat and tossed it aside. "And don't bother telling me that just because we...*you know*...that I'm under no obligation." He unbuttoned her second jacket and sent it flying in the same direction as the first. "You made me realize how empty my life has become. I brought you to my cabin and now I don't like being there because you aren't in it with me."

Her jaw sagged and her blue-violet eyes nearly popped from their sockets. "Do you mean that, Lucas? I want the truth... and nothing but from you."

He unfastened the men's trousers and long underwear she had pulled over two layers of pantaloons. He smiled in masculine satisfaction when she stood before him in a lacy chemise that barely covered her upper thighs. "Damn, Rosalie, you are so beautiful you take my breath away."

When he drew her lush body against his aching flesh, he felt as if he had found his place in the world. Wherever this spirited beauty was, that's where he belonged.

"Marry me, Rosalie," he whispered before he kissed her with all the love and affection that gurgled up from his heart and soul. "If you want to live here then we will. If you can be satisfied on my ranch then we'll stay there. Whatever you want—"

She pressed her forefinger to his lips and smiled radiantly at him. "I wouldn't marry anyone but you, and you can stop talking now, Lucas." She looped her arms around his neck and rubbed provocatively against him until he groaned in tormented pleasure.

"Whatever you say, love..." His voice trailed off when she unbuttoned his coat and shirt and splayed her hands over his chest, leaving his heartbeat hammering wildly beneath her roving fingertips.

She made undressing him a session in erotic torture—and Lucas loved every moment of it. Ex-warrior and ex-Ranger though he was, he fell back on her bed without putting up the slightest resistance. She teased him and tantalized him until he begged her to end the sweet torment of having her so close yet so maddeningly far away.

Lucas swore the top of his head was about to blow off when her moist lips and fingertips glided over his throbbing flesh. And then she sank down exactly upon him and every unfulfilled hope and impossible dream—that had seemed so far beyond his reach—crystallized around him. He knew he had found his soul mate…and she had silver-blond hair, the most incredible violet eyes and the most beguiling smile imaginable.

"I love you, Lucas," she whispered as she came apart in his arms and he shuddered helplessly against her.

Deliriously happy, he grinned into her angelic face then wrapped a ringlet of her silky hair around his finger to tow her down to his gentle kiss. "I'm hoping you'll invite me back to your apartment after we deliver the toys and gifts and spread the holiday cheer."

She nuzzled her forehead against his. "Or perhaps we could go to your cabin. I have a secret fantasy of tumbling around on that buffalo-skin blanket in front of the hearth."

"Whatever you wish," he granted without the slightest hesitation.

"You are what I wish," she murmured as she squirmed suggestively above him. "That and perhaps a few children of our own one day."

"Can't think of anything I'd like better myself, as long as I'm spending all the days of my life with you," he rumbled softly. "I need you as I need nothing and no one else, Rosa."

Passion flared up to warm the cold winter night and Lucas

and Rosa gave themselves up, body, heart and soul, to the love
that bound them together forevermore...

It was considerably later, while the children of Cahill Crossing were snuggled beneath the blankets on their beds, that
Rosa and Lucas made their secret deliveries to the right and
wrong sides of the tracks. They even left a little something
special for Quin Cahill, who was all alone on Christmas.

And not a soul in town figured out the identity of their
mysterious Saint Nicholas.

* * * * *

*Join Carol Finch and Harlequin Books
in November for Quin Cahill's story
of romance, mystery and adventure
in Cahill Crossing.*

A MAGICAL GIFT
AT CHRISTMAS

Cheryl St.John

Dear Reader,

I'm always delighted to participate in Harlequin Historical's Christmas anthologies. I hear from so many of you who look forward to them every year. Amidst the hustle and bustle of the season, we all need to make time for ourselves, and what better way than to escape into the pages of a holiday adventure?

I had always wanted to write a story that revolved around a train, so when I started planning this tale, I was quick to leap to the idea of a train robbery. A U.S. Marshal and a pampered society girl seemed a fun pairing. Jonah is all about duty, a loner who trusts in the power of his convictions. Meredith is a headstrong individualist, who dreams of a grand and perfect love. The only thing she fears is discovering that her life—and her plans—are somehow deficient. It was a lot of fun to throw the two of them together and watch love bloom.

I hope you enjoy this holiday break and lose yourself in the pages of these stories.

Wishing you a Christmas filled with the best gift of all—love!

Cheryl St.John

A Magical Gift at Christmas is lovingly dedicated to my family, who bring me much joy, and of whom I am exceedingly proud:

Jay, Mike, Jennifer, Zach, Jaden, Brad, LeighAnn, Erin, Ryan, Adam, Eric, Jared, Jessica, Alexis, Jared II, Kristin, Elijah and Elliana. I love you.

Chapter One

Colorado, 1865

The farther north the rocking train traveled, the harder snow fell, turning the landscape into a blinding white vista and obscuring the view from the windows.

U.S. Marshal Jonah Cavanaugh lounged casually in his seat, the brim of his hat pulled low, his eyelids lowered. To others he appeared an average cowboy taking a lazy nap, but in truth he'd analyzed every passenger in three cars and deliberately remained in this one.

Assigned to protect a shipment of payroll gold headed for Denver, he was one of four lawmen aboard. A decoy train had departed an hour before this one, designed to draw away attention. Obviously, that hadn't worked.

Across the aisle and up four rows, a partially balding man with his coat collar turned up craned his neck to study the landscape and then looked at his pocket watch. He was known by several aliases, but his given name was Roscoe Bloom. His likeness had been plastered across papers since about '59, when he and his long-since-hanged brother had pulled off a stage robbery, killing the driver and three passengers.

Bloom turned and glanced at the unsuspecting travelers in

the seats across from him, giving Jonah a view of his profile.
Roscoe wasn't aging well.

Jonah considered his options. Calling Bloom out in a
crowded passenger car wouldn't be the smartest choice. But
he couldn't wait until the train reached the next water tower.
Currently the rails led the train between rocky hillsides, but
only a mile ahead they'd reach an open area, where Roscoe's
partners would join up for an inevitable attack.

Once Bloom turned his attention back to the window, Jonah
got up and made his way to the back of the car and silently let
himself out. The clack of the rails was muffled by the cushion
of snow on either side. He climbed the rear ladder, reaching
the top, where bitter-cold wind bit his skin and made his eyes
water. He crawled forward, leaping from the passenger car to
the coal car, where he climbed down and entered, making his
way forward until he reached the engine.

At the surprised look on the stocky engineer's face, Jonah
opened his coat to reveal his star. "Marshal Cavanaugh.
Assigned to the shipment," he called above the roar of the
steam engine.

"Trouble on board?"

"Trouble ahead for sure," he replied. "Don't stop, even if
there's something on the tracks—slow down and try to push
your way forward. Maybe there won't be a block, but at the
least there'll be riders with guns. I'm going back to uncouple
the mail car." It was the only thing he could think of that would
give him time to hide the gold.

"Luggage car and the Abbott's Pullman are behind it."

"Can't be helped. Abbott'll have to go without his hot toddy
tonight." Jonah didn't want to be responsible for a civilian, but
there wasn't time to figure out anything else. "Three other
marshals will stay on the train with you. Good luck."

"And to you, Marshal."

Jonah exited the engine and again made his way atop the
rocking train, carefully balancing himself, wary of the slick

moisture. He did his best to keep his boots silent atop the passenger car in which Bloom traveled.

He reached the mail car, where he told Marshal Zeke Faver what was happening.

"Where's Thorpe?" Faver asked, referring to another of the lawmen.

"Still in car two. Troy's in the other."

"I'll get word to them. We'll be ready."

"Send help back as soon as you can." Jonah waited for the man to enter the car ahead before he hung off the back and turned the lever that uncoupled the last three cars.

He steadied himself on the narrow platform and watched as the rest of the train pulled forward and the car upon which he stood slowed on the tracks.

This stretch of land was fairly level, so within a matter of minutes, the mail car rolled to a stop.

To the north, falling snow obliterated the departing train from view and eventually the rumbling sound disappeared. Silence enveloped the countryside.

Jonah touched the .45 at his hip, resting his fingertips on the steel for seconds. Turning, he entered the mail car, checking that the strongbox holding the gold remained safely stashed behind several bags of mail. He would bury it in case Bloom's gang came back once they discovered the missing car.

Railcars often had a shovel for removing debris from the tracks, so he searched, but didn't find one. Heading out back, he checked the baggage car and found a shovel stored in a bin.

"Hello? Hello! Is anyone there?"

The woman's voice caught him by surprise. Had Abbott brought his wife along? The Pullman belonged to Cornelius Abbott, the rich tycoon who owned the C&O railroad and traveled in luxury in his own custom-built car. Jonah had seen it numerous times as he traveled the rails protecting gold shipments. Now he'd have to deal with the man and his wife. The gold was his priority, but with this development, he'd just become responsible for more lives.

He laid down the shovel, impatient to get back to his task. He'd have to go let Abbott know what was happening. Hopefully the fellow would stay out of the way in his car and let Jonah take care of things.

Stepping onto the iron grate, he stood four feet away from the Pullman. On its platform, made of scrolled ironwork, stood a remarkably pretty young woman. She wore a pale fox coat—paler than her honey-colored hair—and stood grasping the fluffy collar closed at her throat.

What the hell?

"What's happening?" she called. "I saw the rest of the train disappear up ahead."

"What are you doing on that Pullman?"

"It belongs to my father. Why have they left us behind?"

"Afraid I'm responsible for that," he told her. "Marshal Cavanaugh," he said by way of introduction, holding his coat open to show her his star.

"Meredith Abbott," she replied. "Now that the niceties are out of the way, would you mind telling me why we're stranded here?"

"If you'll call your father out, Miss Abbott, I'll be glad to explain."

"I can't do that."

"Is he all right?"

"I'm sure he's perfectly fine—in Denver, waiting for my arrival this evening."

"Who are you traveling with?"

"I'm capable of traveling on my own," she told him with a saucy lift to her chin. "I have a gun, and I'm an expert shot."

Just in case he was getting any ideas, he supposed. A young woman traveling alone? What kind of father let his daughter roam around the country without protection?

"No doubt you can hit a clay disk with amazing accuracy, but protecting yourself from outlaws and renegades is another thing." And now he was stuck with her.

She widened her eyes in what surely couldn't be exhilaration. "Are there outlaws and renegades?"

"At least one on that train headed north and most likely a passel more up ahead, waiting for the gold."

"What gold is that?"

"Payroll." He jerked a thumb over his shoulder. "In the mail car."

"Of course." She glanced at the sky. Her hair was now covered with a layer of flakes and she blinked away those that fell on her lashes. She straightened her posture and looked back at him. "Now what?"

He had to hand it to her for not falling into hysterics or fainting dead away. "I'm going to bury the strongbox in case the robbers head this way."

She nodded as though considering his words. "That sounds wise. May I help?"

"Stay warm inside," he told her. "You have a coal heater in there?"

She nodded.

"Much of a supply?"

"A bucket full."

That wouldn't last long. "I can find coal along the tracks. And if need be I'll gather wood. We'll keep warm enough," he assured her. "Load your gun and stay inside."

He turned and headed inside the mail car. A female on her own. Another predicament to deal with.

Meredith watched the marshal go, disappointed he'd turned aside her offer to help bury the gold. Her heart had started pounding as soon as she'd seen that train winding to the right along the tracks ahead and felt the car in which she rode slowing to a halt.

She entered the Pullman and hung her coat on a brass hook to dry. The interior of the car was comfortably warm, but she looked at the single bucket of coal. Tearing her gaze away, she went to a window, pulling a velvet drape to the side and tying it back with a tasseled cord.

Snowflakes layered the marshal's black hat as he strode through several inches of snow on the ground, a metal chest on his shoulder. He wore a holster at his hip.

The sight of him leaving her here alone sent a dart of unease skittering down her spine. She had warm clothing and boots, but she had no idea which direction to travel should he not come back and help never arrive.

Thoughts racing, she made a mental inventory of food and supplies. He would return. Not wanting to know where he took the strongbox, she turned away from the glass.

There had to be something helpful she could do. She glanced at the coal bucket again. He'd mentioned coal along the tracks, and she hadn't comprehended. The thought came to her that the chunks probably fell from the coal cars.

In her father's closet, she found a woolen scarf and donned it, followed by her fur-lined boots and fox coat. She dumped the coal from the bucket onto a corner of the Persian carpet and carried the bucket out of doors.

She couldn't get lost with the tracks to follow, and her coat was plenty warm. The problem was finding the coal beneath the mounting layer of snow.

The snow would only get worse, she reasoned, so she went back in and carried out a slender broom. With it, she swept snow in wide circles, moving six to eight feet out from the tracks. In several spots, her search revealed lumps of the porous black substance. The bucket was half filled by the time she straightened and spotted Marshal Cavanaugh returning with shovel in hand.

He joined her, using the back of the shovel, and working on the opposite side of the tracks until they'd again filled the bucket.

"I'll take this in and dump it. Let's continue as long as we can," he called to her. "It'll only get harder the more snow falls."

Though her feet were cold and her nose running, she nodded her agreement. An hour or so later, they were working a lengthy stretch from the Pullman. Meredith's back ached from sweeping and bending over. He carried the last bucket and they trudged back.

"Don't know how long we'll be here," he said. "The snow isn't letting up. We should probably check the luggage car for more guns and food."

"Won't that be stealing?"

"Would you care if they were your belongings and someone else was in this predicament?"

"Probably not."

He set the full bucket on the platform and gestured for her to lead the way inside the luggage car. It smelled like leather and damp wool, and wasn't a whole lot warmer than outside, but it was dry. She shook off her coat near the door and put it back on.

Trunks and steamers were stacked along the sides and banded with leather straps anchored to the walls. The marshal unfastened them and lifted down half a dozen trunks.

Meredith experienced discomfort opening the first one and touching someone's personal belongings, but he glibly dug through another, finding a sheathed knife, a woolen hat and a pair of gloves. She followed his lead, and on her third trunk, she discovered neatly folded quilts layered in tissue paper. "Someone won't be happy about this."

She removed the whole stack and stuffed the tissue back into the trunk.

A sound stopped her as she bent to add the quilts to their growing pile of provisions. She looked to the marshal. He'd obviously heard the noise too, and was standing dead still, his head tilted to one side. Slowly, he set down the silver matchbox he held and reached for his holster. In a fluid motion, he slid the pearl-handled gun into his palm and cocked the trigger with a thumb.

Meredith held her breath in anticipation. Had one or

more of the train robbers been hidden among the baggage all this time?

With his free palm, the marshal gestured for her to get down.

Her skirts swished as she obediently squatted in place, her mouth dry. She strained hard to hear any movement.

He had removed his hat to try on one of the wool caps, and now his black hair stood in sweaty peaks as he crept toward the spot where the sound had come from. Something rustled again now. He crouched lower until he reached a crevice between a stack of valises and another of carpet bags.

Even though she'd been watching and expecting the next exchange, his quick move elicited a started cry from her throat, and she clapped a hand over her mouth.

The man sprang into action, sending bags toppling and creating an open place to reveal whatever or whomever was hidden behind the luggage.

He stood motionless for several seconds while, behind him, she waited with heart pounding for gunfire to explode. Instead of shooting anyone, he slid the revolver back into its holster.

What of the danger? She craned her neck to see around him.

At last he turned his head and spoke to her. "You'd better come here."

Meredith scrambled to her feet and darted to where he waited. He took a step back to make room for her, and she moved in close.

Huddled behind the toppled stacks of carpetbags cringed two wide-eyed, terrified children.

Chapter Two

Jonah stared, still wrapping his brain around what his eyes were telling him. This just kept getting better. Two more lives in his care.

"Those aren't train robbers," she said with a note of disappointment lacing her tone.

He frowned at her and then looked back at the youngsters. He didn't know much about children, but the boy and girl were probably somewhere between five and ten years old, with tousled dark hair and large brown eyes. The youngest, the little girl, stuck her thumb in her mouth while studying him with wary concern.

"You two alone?" he asked.

The boy nodded.

"Where are your folks?"

The boy got to his feet. "Our ma's dead. Our Pa went to Denver, and we're goin' after 'im."

"How did you get in here?" he asked.

"Watched while the men was loadin' the cases, and when no one was lookin' we snuck in." He looked toward the back door. "Why ain't we movin'? Are we to Denver?"

Without answering, the marshal turned to Meredith. "What are we going to do with them?"

"How should I know? I don't know anything about children."

"My sister's hungry," the boy said. "She ain't had nothin' to eat for a couple o' days."

The Abbott woman's attitude softened with her next words. "We'll get you both something to eat." She reached for the girl's hand. "What's your name?"

It was the boy who replied. "She's Jillian."

"What's your name?" Jonah asked him.

"Hayden Langley. Are you a truant officer?"

Jonah blinked at that. "No. I'm a United States Marshal."

The boy shrank back against the side of the car. "Are you takin' us to jail?"

"Children don't go to jail," Jonah replied.

The boy didn't appear convinced. "We'll wait right here 'til we get to Denver."

"You'd get mighty cold and hungry waiting here, because the steam engine's gone off without this car," Jonah informed him. "So come out of there and let Miss Abbott fix you a meal."

They exited the luggage car, with Jonah carrying supplies and Meredith holding the girl's hand. Jonah observed that his tracks to and from the spot where he'd buried the gold were already hidden beneath layers of fallen snow.

As Meredith ushered the children inside her Pullman, he stopped her with a hand on her thick fur sleeve. "The smart thing for me to do now would be to head for the nearest town and alert the law. Send them back for the gold."

She met his eyes. Up close hers were vivid blue and seemed to see inside him, but they showed no sign of fear. "Are you going?"

"Without a horse it would take me a day or more. I can't leave you here alone with two helpless children. Not in this weather."

And not with the possibility that Bloom's men might come searching, but he didn't say that aloud. There was no telling what had happened when the train reached the spot for the intended robbery. "I guess we wait it out, then," she said. "When the train doesn't arrive this evening, they'll alert the closest authorities."

"Reaching us in this storm will be the problem."

"As well as a problem for the thieves," she stated logically.

He nodded in agreement. The storm just might be their salvation.

They entered the car, where she removed her boots and coat and changed into a pair of soft-looking gray leather slippers. The inside was as elegant as anything Jonah had ever seen. The beams along the ceiling and the paneling on lower half of the walls were glossy mahogany. The gilt-framed mirrors and paintings of hunting scenes belonged in a mansion.

The room in which they stood wasn't wide, but made up for size in length, with a corridor to the left, leading to more space behind the wall. A fluffy white cat lay upon a long plush divan upholstered in deep wine-colored velvet with fringe trim. The animal blinked at them in disdain and swished its tail in the air before getting up and ducking underneath the piece of furniture.

Leather chairs, secured tables and lamps made the space appear as a gentleman's study. Gleaming brass adorned hinges and cabinets, and shelves with brass rims held books and writing supplies. She wasn't exactly roughing it while she traveled.

"Come along," she said, leading them toward the corridor. Jonah followed the children along the paneled hallway and they emerged into a kitchen area, which held cabinets and bins made of steel, a rectangular table with benches, and an ice chest.

The room was equipped with a narrow stove. "You didn't mention a stove," he said.

"You only asked about the coal heater. There are three of those actually." She peered at the stove now. "I've never used it. When Father travels, Mr. Montgomery accompanies him and prepares his meals. I most often bring along prepared items. If there's a dining car, I eat there."

"What's back there?" he asked, gesturing to the continuing hallway.

"Sleeping quarters and the necessary." She turned and explained the facility to the children. Both were amazed and ran right back to examine it.

"Weapons or ammunition?" Jonah asked.

She took him to an overhead cabinet in her father's sleeping room and opened it for him. He looked over the hunting rifle, a set of pistols and tins of bullets. "What about your gun?"

She turned away from him, raised the hem of her skirt and turned back with a derringer.

"That's only effective at close range."

"I can shoot the pistols, too."

"If there's trouble, go for those."

She nodded her understanding. "Of course."

"We'll partition off those rooms to hold the heat out there in the first room. We might be here a while."

"So we'll all sleep out there?"

"Got a better idea for conserving the fuel?"

"No."

"Okay, then. Mind if I go look for blankets and what have you to cover the corridor?"

"Help yourself." She turned her attention to feeding the children and sliced bread and cheese.

They ate hungrily and politely thanked her. She melted snow on the heater and filled a basin in which she bathed them and washed their hair. Hayden pitched an indignant fit, but she scrubbed him anyway. He was so dirty, he had crust behind his ears.

"This will have to do for now," she said. "But we're going to do it again tomorrow until you sparkle."

Not amused, he frowned. "Men don't sparkle."

"When they're eating at my table and sleeping on my furniture they do," she disagreed.

Jillian sat near the coal heater, drying her hair. "I sparkle, don't I, Miss Abbott?"

Indeed, Meredith thought, the child's appearance was much improved from the streaked face and matted hair of an hour ago. "You shine," she replied.

The wind howled down the stove pipe just then, and the car rocked slightly.

"Will the wind tip us over?" Hayden asked.

"This coach is seventy feet long and weighs over twenty-five tons," she assured him. "A little wind isn't going to blow it over."

The marshal had returned from his task of nailing up quilts to overhear the last. "I thought the train seemed a trifle slow on the hills."

"Usually they limit the cars ahead or add another engine when they pull us."

"The other engine was rerouted as our decoy train." He stepped to the window and surveyed the landscape. In the late afternoon light she got a good look at his features. Narrow nose, chiseled jaw and chin, a high forehead creased with white lines and a full expressive mouth. She carried a cup of coffee to him and he straightened to accept it.

His eyes were a golden-brown, shining like gemstones, the centers shrunk from gazing out into the bright snow. "Thanks."

"Are you hungry?" she asked.

"What do we have?"

"Bread, cheese, crackers, cookies and a box of chocolates. There's flour, sugar, rice and coffee, as well."

"I'll set snares before it gets dark," he said. "Tomorrow we'll have game. For now I'll eat whatever's handy."

After he'd eaten the same fare the children had enjoyed and had another cup of coffee, Jonah trudged up a hillside and set snares, bending tree branches to guide the way back. The snow was well over a foot deep now and still falling heavily. Eventually darkness settled, and they nestled inside the luxurious Pullman. As long as they had to be stranded in a blizzard, these were the best conditions he could imagine.

The children looked different than when they'd found them that afternoon. Their hair and faces were clean, though the Abbott woman had used a foolish amount of their fuel supply to melt snow and bathe them. She'd done her share of gathering coal, however, so he kept his silence—for now. Tomorrow he'd have a talk with her about rationing.

He pulled the velvet curtains closed over the short windows and placed all the pillows used for adornment on the furniture in the deep sills to absorb cold, sound and hopefully even bullets. He doubted anyone was out in this storm, but his instincts, always on alert, told him to prepare for the worst.

She had pulled a narrow mattress from the rear of the car and made Hayden and Jillian comfortable upon it with quilts and a brocade counterpane. Upon a fainting couch, she settled a pillow and blankets for herself and gestured for Jonah to take the wide divan. He had placed his boots near the heater to dry, so the blankets felt good on his cold feet.

"Who's expecting you in Denver?" he asked.

"My parents are there," she answered. "My father is seeking governorship soon, so he's attending all the holiday social events. Christmas is just three days away."

He'd forgotten.

"There's a ball at the governor's mansion tomorrow evening. That's my destination."

"Don't think you're going to make it."

"One of my father's associates is a young man with political aspirations himself. He was to be my escort, and…"

He waited for her to go on.

"He gave every indication that he'd made plans to propose."

"Has he been courting you?"

"We've attended several social functions together, and he's come to dinner at our home on occasion."

"Has he kissed you?"

Before replying, she glanced at the children, who had

immediately fallen into exhausted slumber. "I don't see that it's any of your business."

"Just making conversation."

Silence stretched between them for several minutes before she said, "I don't know your given name, Marshal Gallagher."

"Jonah."

"You may call me Meredith," she said. "These are unusual circumstances, so I don't see a need for formality."

"Did you find out anything more about where those kids came from?"

"Hayden mentioned Polk City, but I didn't prod. I figured tomorrow would be soon enough to ask. It's obvious they've gone without proper care and food."

In the dim light from the slits in the door of the coal heater, the fluffy white cat was visible as it came from hiding to leap up and join Meredith on the couch. From several feet away Jonah heard the animal's contented purr as she stroked its fur.

"Did you decide it was safe to come out now that the children are sleeping?" she asked softly. "I'm not sure what to make of them, either."

Jonah had spent his life sleeping on railcars, in a bedroll under the sky, in hotels, or occasionally as a guest in the home of a lawman, but this was the first time he'd shared quarters with a pretty socialite, a couple of rag-tag orphans and a cat.

Often, he had a criminal in his care, with the duty of delivering him to a jail or court, but for the most part he looked out for himself.

Suddenly he'd found himself responsible for the lives of the others whose soft, even breathing created a loud critical chorus in his head. If he was alone, he'd have taken off and made his way to the closest town. He couldn't risk exposing Meredith Abbott and those kids to the elements. He reassured himself that even though they were sitting ducks, this was the safest place for them. Even if they were attacked, this structure was made of steel, and they had plenty of guns and ammunition.

For now, this was the best he could do.

Chapter Three

Meredith awoke to the smell of something baking. The marshal's spot on the divan was empty, and the children nowhere to be seen, but she heard them. Pulling on her silk robe, she padded to the kitchen, where the smell of coffee reached her, and her mouth watered.

"Morning," Jonah said from the tiny stove, where he was plucking biscuits from a pan with his bare fingers, tossing them back and forth, then finally dropping them on a china plate.

"You made biscuits?"

"Found preserves too. Have a seat."

Jillian already had red smears on either side of her mouth. She licked her fingers and studied the plate heaped with more biscuits.

Jonah plucked one from the pile, sliced it open and spread preserves on it for her.

"This is the bestest breakfast I ever had," she said to the marshal, surprising Meredith, because she hadn't said anything at all the day before.

"I've eaten my share of biscuits on the trail," he answered and poured dark, steaming coffee into two china cups.

Meredith got sugar from a cupboard before sitting and adding a spoonful to her cup. Jonah drank his black.

She tasted the strong brew. She preferred tea, but this had smelled too good to pass up, and it was already prepared.

"I'll check the traps later this morning," he said, sitting to eat. "Most likely we'll have a nice fat rabbit at noon."

"Possums is good, too," Hayden said.

Meredith stared at the biscuit she'd taken. Desperate times called for desperate measures, and she could eat possum if that's what had happened into the marshal's snare. She tried not to dwell on the breakfast that would have greeted her in the hotel dining room had she made it to her destination last night. Fluffy yellow eggs, ham, hollandaise sauce and fresh fruit....

She bit into the biscuit and found it surprisingly tasty.

"Can I go with you out to check the snares?" Hayden asked.

Jonah glanced at Meredith. "Seems I recall seeing some boy's clothing in one of those trunks we rifled." He looked back at Hayden. "Long as you have dry clothing for our return, you can go with me."

"What about clothing for you?" Meredith asked.

"My saddlebags are in the mail car."

"Can I go, too?" Jillian asked.

"Stay here and help Miss Abbott," Jonah told her.

Her crestfallen expression showed her displeasure at being left behind.

"We'll do some sewing," Meredith suggested.

Breakfast ended, and Jonah left with Hayden at his side. Meredith removed the pillows he'd placed at all the windows to let in daylight. She and Jillian watched their two forms, stark against the white background, as Jonah tramped through the snow with Hayden following in the footsteps he'd cleared. Snow still fell, and the wind gusted. Above their heads as far as she could see the sky was a gray haze.

After busying herself washing the dishes in a small amount of melted snow, Meredith folded and stacked their bedding in her sleeping area. She brushed Jillian's hair and fashioned it by pulling the front away from her face with ribbons and leaving the rest flowing down her back. "You have such pretty hair," she told the child.

"My mama had pretty hair," Jillian told her. "When she was sick, I sat on her bed and brush-ded it for her."

"I'm sure she liked that."

She nodded. "Then she went to heaven and we din't see her any again."

"I'm sorry."

"Do you have a mama?"

"Yes. Her name is Deliah."

"Do you gots a brother?"

"Two of them. One is older than me, like Hayden is to you, and the other is younger."

"Where are they?"

"Morgan lives in Philadelphia with his wife. He's an important attorney—a businessman. Peter is attending university."

"What's university?"

"School. Have you gone to school?"

She shook her head. "Hayden used to go, but not after Mama went to heaven."

"What did the two of you do after your Mama—went to heaven?"

"The sheriff took us to a openage. We din't like it there, so we run-ded away."

"Where did you go?"

"We hid in our old cabin, 'til some people came to clean and wanted to live there. We couldn't find nowhere safe, so Hayden said we was gonna go get our pa."

Meredith couldn't imagine children as young as these left to fend for themselves. Hadn't their mother made provision for them? Where *was* their father?

Meredith had been pampered by her parents and their servants for as long as she could remember. She'd never gone hungry or been cold at night; in her family, even their winter outings were made comfortable with covered carriages and hot bricks at their feet.

She looked around this lavish Pullman she took for granted, comparing it to the drafty barren cabin she imagined Jillian had called home. Her thoughts traveled to the enormous decorated trees in two of the rooms at her family home in Philadelphia, packages with satin bows and candles burning of an evening.

"What did you do for Christmas when your mama was with you?" she asked.

"We went to church and sitted in the back row. Up front was a pretty tree with glass balls, and when no one else was there, we sat close to smell it and see the shiny stars. Mama bought us a meat pie for supper."

"That's sounds very special," Meredith told her with a smile.

"Is it Christmas?" Jillian asked.

"Almost. Tomorrow is Christmas Eve and the next day is Christmas."

"How many is that?"

Meredith reached for the little girl's sturdy hand and helped her hold up three fingers. "This is today." She folded down that finger. "And this is tomorrow." She tucked that one under and then touched Jillian's index finger with her own. "And this one is Christmas."

"That's not very many."

Voices reached them from outdoors, and they hurried to the window to see Jonah and Hayden returning. Hayden had a pale gray animal flopping on his shoulder as he trudged through the snow, a wide grin on his face. Jonah carried an armful of wood.

"A wabbit!" Jillian cried. "We're havin' a wabbit for dinner."

Thank goodness the possums had steered clear of the snares. Meredith had never tasted rabbit, but the idea didn't sour her stomach as much as the thought of possum. If she didn't like rabbit meat, she'd eat crackers.

She opened the door.

"Hand me down that knife I found yesterday," Jonah said. "It's inside the liquor cabinet. And pass out the fire poker. It'll make a handy spit."

She found both items. She and Jillian watched through the glass as Jonah showed the boy how to skin and clean the animal. Jonah rolled it in the snow to clean it, then speared it lengthwise with the poker. Before too long they had a fire going, the rabbit roasting above it.

"I kin smell it," Jillian said reverently.

The door opened, and both of them rushed toward it.

"Want to put these in a pot of water?" Jonah held out a lumpy kerchief, roots dangling from an opening on one end.

She took it from him. "What are they?"

"Wild leeks and burdock root. I washed them off with snow, so just boil 'em."

"They're safe to eat?"

He grinned. "And pretty tasty, too."

"Okay. Come on, Jillian."

Sometime later, they sat around the table in the kitchen, with the tantalizing scents of meat and vegetables making Meredith's stomach growl. "I must say the meal smells quite good."

Jonah's cheeks and nose were red from the cold, as were Hayden's. After she'd served the children, she heaped a portion onto a gold-rimmed china plate and set it before him. He picked up a monogrammed fork. "Have to say I've never before eaten rabbit on such fancy dishes. Most times I eat it right off the spit with my fingers."

"The good Lord gave us fingers 'afore He gave us forks," Hayden added. "That's what my ma used to say."

"Well, that's true, I suppose," Meredith replied with a smile.

Jonah waited until she'd spooned out her own serving and tasted a bite before he dug into his meal.

The meat had been roasted to perfection, and tasted surprisingly good. Meredith ate the vegetables with appreciation for the marshal's ingenuity. Hayden and Jillian cleaned their plates in no time. Meredith scooped out the last remaining bits of food onto their plates, and they ate appreciatively.

"Can we have this again tomorrow?" Hayden asked.

"Reckon it'll depend on the critter that wanders into our snare," Jonah replied.

"What if it's a fox?" he asked.

Meredith cringed, but looked to Jonah for his reply. He grinned at the boy. "Might have to make somebody a hat."

"Oh, boy! I hope we catch a fox!"

Meredith thought of the coat that kept her so warm, for the first time actually considering how many animals it had taken to make it.

"I wanna hat, too!" Jillian said.

"I'm sure we'll have enough skins to make you a hat. How about mittens?" Jonah asked.

Jillian smiled from ear to ear, and Meredith recognized how easy it was to please these children. They were nothing like her spoiled niece and nephew, who had more than they needed and pouted when they didn't get their way or had to eat their vegetables.

Meredith stacked their plates.

"I saw a set of bones in a trunk in the mail car. Do you know how to play?"

The children looked at Jonah with quizzical expressions.

"Bones?" Meredith asked skeptically.

"Yes, it's a game with rectangular pieces made from bone or ivory—I think the ones I saw were ivory—and they have sets of dots on them. You play your bones on the matching numbers and try to block others from playing theirs."

"You're talking about *dominoes,*" Meredith said.

He shrugged. "Okay. Does anyone know how to play dominoes?"

"My mother never allowed me to play, but I've watched my brothers." Meredith tried to keep umbrage from her voice.

"Why couldn't you play?"

"She claimed it was a men's game and not for ladies. I most often played the piano while the men enjoyed their games."

"Nobody's here to care if you break the rules," he told her. "I'll go find the bones."

Before long, he returned with a set of dominoes in a velvet drawstring bag, as well as a cribbage board and an elegant leather case holding checkers. He dumped the ivory tiles onto a low table. Meredith sat on the divan and the kids knelt on the floor. Jonah got a cushion and seated himself. "First we each draw seven bones from the bone yard."

"Jillian don't know her numbers," Hayden said.

"That's all right," Jonah said. "Jillian, you can learn as we go. For now I'll count out seven for you." And he proceeded to do so. "You go first. Just pick any one of those and lay it in the middle of the table."

"This one looks pretty." Jillian selected a domino and slid it to the center.

"Each side of the one you played has six dots," Jonah told her. He counted the dots aloud. "Now it's Miss Abbott's turn, and if she doesn't have a six, she passes her turn."

As much as Meredith enjoyed playing the game that had always been forbidden to her, she especially enjoyed listening to the marshal count the dots on every last domino so that Jillian had a concept of the numbers and the game.

"How many pearls are on Miss Abbott's earbob?" he asked.

Jillian studied the pearls dangling from Meredith's left ear. "One, two."

"Perfect," her teacher declared. "How many are there if you count both of her earbobs?"

"One, two and one, two."

He nodded. "Yes, each one has two." He slid two extra dominoes from the bone yard to her place on the table. "Two here." He slid over another two. "And two here. Now we count them all together." Jillian counted aloud with him. "Can you find four on one of the bones?"

She studied the dominoes at length. Finally, her serious

expression softened, and she reached to point at a tile. "This one!"

Meredith met Jonah's gaze and they shared a silent exchange.

"You're a smart girl."

After a couple of games, Jillian yawned. She climbed onto the divan and within minutes fell asleep. Meredith got a book and sat near her. Jonah set up the checker game. "Know how to play this?"

"Yes, sir."

Turned out Hayden not only knew how, but was quite good at it. At one point when he had one of Jonah's kings trapped, he laughed and slapped his knee. The two of them reminded Meredith of the gray-haired men she'd seen playing board games near a stove at the post office in Denver.

It was the first time she'd thought about Denver all day. Surprising how she'd nearly forgotten, when she was about to miss the Christmas ball and the proposal she'd seen coming this evening.

"You look lost in thought," the marshal said.

"I was thinking about the ball this evening."

"You would have attended with your young man?"

"More than likely, yes."

"And you think he was ready to offer for your hand?"

He couldn't tell in this light, but he guessed she blushed. "I think so."

She was a strikingly lovely young woman. Her eyes had a greenish cast in this light. Though she appeared every bit the elegant socialite, there was a softness around her eyes and mouth that lent her an approachable appeal. While she was headstrong and opinionated, she'd been nothing but kind and generous toward him and the young stowaways.

"Would you have accepted?" he couldn't help inquiring.

"He's exactly the sort of man my father would have me marry. He's very like my father and brothers. He has political aspirations, and I've been prepared for marriage to someone of his standing."

"How did you prepare?"

"I attended school. I studied deportment, etiquette and manners. I learned how to manage a home and a staff."

"Servants," he clarified.

"Yes."

He stacked the board games.

"What aren't you saying?" she asked.

"You said he's the sort of man your father wanted you to marry."

"He is."

"What about you? Is he the sort you want to marry?"

"Yes. Of course."

"Well, then I'm sorry you won't make it to your party. I'll keep you safe and get you to Denver to meet up with your beau."

"He's not a beau," she disagreed with a soft shake of her head that made the pearls on her ears swing

"Sounds like he is."

"He's a serious marriage prospect. Someone with whom to plan a future. If I choose to marry him, I shall run a grand house, entertain important guests and even travel."

"Sounds…grand."

"You're being flip."

He raised both hands and if surrendering.

"What about you?" she asked. "Have you a wife? A girl back home?"

Chapter Four

Jonah had been expecting the question. He'd inquired about her romantic interests, after all. "My life isn't suited to that sort of thing. I rarely stay in one spot for longer than a day or two."

"Sounds lonely."

"Solitary. I like it that way."

Once Jillian woke, Jonah taught Meredith how to make biscuit dough. She did a fair job, and they ate cheese with them. When it grew dark, he again covered all the windows with pillows. That evening, Meredith read to them from a book of poetry and then from a copy of *Emma*.

"What is this story about?" Hayden asked after a chapter.

"Emma is a matchmaker," Meredith explained.

"What's a matchmaker?"

She laid down the book. "I don't suppose this story is exciting enough for children, is it?"

"Do you got any pirate stories?"

"I'm afraid not."

"I like the book just fine, Miss Abbott," Jillian told her. "I don't understand all them words, but your voice is pretty, an' it's toasty warm in here. The blankets are soft and smell good. We had yummy food, din't we?" She gave the others a sweet smile. "This is a good day."

Meredith had no reply. Empathy for the child's situation welled up in her chest. If being stranded in a snowstorm could be counted as a good day, Meredith wasn't sure she wanted to know what the worst days had been like. Though she suspected well enough....

She couldn't meet Jonah's eyes because of the overwhelming flood of emotion that would be revealed.

"I liked listening, too," came his deep-timbered comment.

She hadn't been prepared for his approval, and she experienced a heady rush of self-consciousness she hadn't felt around him before. In that moment their situation changed. They were a man and a woman trapped together in a snowstorm, secluded from their normal lives and from everything familiar...and now acutely aware of each other.

She picked up the book and read aloud another chapter.

Everyone grew tired early. Jonah bundled up and went out of doors to search the perimeter of the railcars and study the landscape beneath the night sky. When he returned, Meredith and the children were snuggled into their places, and blankets had been prepared on the divan for him.

He locked the door and made sure the coal heater had enough fuel to last several hours before he lay down. He'd fallen asleep when a sound woke him. He didn't recognize the noise, but he got up and went to pull away one of the pillows and peer outside.

An enormous brown bear was investigating the area where they'd built their spit and cooked the rabbit.

"What's out there?" Meredith's soft voice came from near his shoulder.

He took a step back so she could see. As soon as she moved in front of him, her delicate scent reached him, eliciting a quick response. Rather than smelling like perfume, she carried a mild combination of clean clothing and fragrant soap.

Her swift intake of breath revealed her surprise at the scene out of doors. "What's it doing?"

"Investigating. Bears can smell for a mile or better. Might have smelled our rabbit."

The animal turned toward the railcar and stood on its hind legs.

She took a step back, bring her soft curves right against him. "Is it going to attack the Pullman?"

"Nah. It's just curious. If it knew we were watching, it would likely run away."

She shivered, and he felt the tremors along the front of his body. It took all of his willpower not to wrap his arms around her.

"Are you sure it won't try to get in?"

He rested a comforting hand on her shoulder. "I'm sure. He's just looking for easy food. We don't have anything, except the innards from that rabbit, that he can smell or find, so he'll be on his way."

"I thought bears hibernated all winter."

"They can sleep for weeks at a time, but they don't go the entire winter without eating. Weather was nice enough for foraging only days ago. This fellow probably got surprised by all the snow. Like we did."

Meredith had draped her insubstantial robe around her shoulders, and now she tugged it around her more tightly.

"You should get back under your covers," he suggested.

She turned, and he let his hand drop from her shoulder, but she was trapped between the window and his body. He didn't have the willpower to move away and let her go.

She could probably see his face in the glow of moonlight on the snow that streamed through the window, but he couldn't see hers. She surprised him by reaching up and tracing his jaw with her cool fingers. He wore a couple days' worth of stubble, which she must have found interesting, because she brushed her fingertips upward and back down.

He caught her hand. "What are you doing?"

"I wondered all day what that felt like."

He couldn't have been more surprised.

"My father's attendant shaves him in the morning and again before supper. Only once that I can recall did I ever see my brothers with hair on their faces. They'd just returned from a hunting trip."

Her hand was soft, yet strong, with long fingers. He turned it over in his and discovered her ring with his thumb. He'd noticed it before, of course. It was a square ruby set into a wide gold band that she wore on her index finger. On each side of the gemstone in worn gold was a lion's head in profile.

"Your ring looks like something a medieval king would wear, rather than a young woman's jewelry," he commented.

"It belonged to my grandfather," she said. "My brothers inherited parcels of land and houses, along with stocks. My inheritance is in the form of a dowry, available only upon my marriage. I asked my mother for the ring, because I remember my grandfather wearing it on his little finger. He was a kind man."

"You haven't said much abut your mother." He finally eased back and led her to the fainting couch, where she sat and raised her feet to tuck them under the covers. Jonah perched on the leather-upholstered footstool.

"She's quite beautiful."

"Could have guessed that."

"She's kind. She's involved with numerous charities. She makes planning a banquet or a gala look easy, though it's actually complicated and time-consuming. The servants respect and adore her, and most have been with us for many years. She's generous to their families."

"You're close, the two of you?"

"I love her very much. I don't often see eye to eye with my father, and she's often caught between the two of us." She shrugged. "She defers to him, of course."

"What do you and your father disagree over?"

"I wanted to go to university and have the same opportunities as my brothers. He wouldn't allow it. I was sent to a boarding school, but escaped at every opportunity. He finally gave up on keeping me there and allowed me to come home."

"What did you do after that?"

"He consented to let me work at his campaign office, as long as I stay out of the limelight and remain in the background. I actually have a staff and a budget now, but it was hard won. And I had to promise to marry by the end of next year."

Jonah said nothing, merely listened.

"I think he's hoping my husband won't allow me to continue with the campaigns or that perhaps I'll transfer my energies to my husband's campaigns."

"What do your brothers do?" he asked after she'd been silent for several minutes.

"Morgan is a C&O attorney. He's married and has two children. Peter is still at university, but upon his graduation he'll be given a position as a surveyor. They were trained up in the railroad business alongside my father. He has high expectations for their futures."

"And your future?"

"My only responsibility is to snare a husband with excellent prospects."

"I doubt that will be a problem."

"Especially not with the dowry inheritance, right?"

"I was thinking more that any man would appreciate a wife so clever and capable…as well as beautiful. Rich or not."

She didn't say anything for a moment. In the moonlight he made out her hands as she spread them on top of the covers. It was out of character for him to speak so openly to a woman he'd only met a few days ago. But the unusual conditions created an air of intimacy and familiarity.

"This fellow waiting for you in Denver…?" His question trailed off.

"Ivan," she supplied. "Ivan Kingsley."

"This Kingsley fellow, is he likely to want you to join his business or his campaigns? What does he do?"

"He's in banking," she replied. "And our conversations have never reached that point."

"Will you still say yes if he wants you at home raising babies?"

She shrugged. "I don't know. Probably not. He's young, ambitious and successful. He's not the worst prospect out there. And I may never find a husband willing to allow me to do as I wish."

He was sure a great many women had settled for husbands or had been forced into marriages that weren't of their choosing. At least she had a say so. Jonah intended to check out this Kingsley fellow as soon as he had the opportunity, however.

He stood and walked silently to the heater, where he added a scoop of coal before moving to the window. "Our night visitor is gone," he whispered. He placed the pillow back in the opening and lay on the comfortable divan and covered himself. "Good night, Meredith."

"Good night, Jonah."

He liked his name on her lips. Entirely too much. Because he wasn't a rich, successful businessman who esteemed a position in government. He was a U.S. marshal who'd roamed the country without putting down roots or making connections. The only people he knew in high places were those whose gold and trains he guarded.

Nearly all his earnings had gone into savings, however, because he had nothing upon which to spend it. One of these days he was going to buy a spread and settle down to raise a few horses.

So far one-of-these-days hadn't arrived. He had only the foggiest picture of how the future would come to pass. A wife would be good. A couple of children maybe. He'd never given kids much consideration. Kids had always presented as a liability, victims to their parents' thoughtless actions. He'd never considered all the children raised as Meredith had been, in loving families.

Looking at Hayden and Jillian, however, he suspected the

percentage left fending for themselves was greater. Somebody needed to look out for kids like them, instead of bringing more into the world.

When had he become a philosopher? He scoffed at himself. If it ever became his job to fix life's problems, the world would end tomorrow.

He checked the .45 under his pillow and closed his eyes.

Christmas Eve arrived and with it the sun. Sparkling snow as far as the eye could see hurt Meredith's eyes when she stepped out of the Pullman. Beside her, Jillian and Hayden were bundled, Hayden with a shovel and Jillian with a broom. Meredith carried a shovel of her own, along with a bucket, and they made their way along the tracks, until she looked back and guessed this was as far as she and Jonah had searched for coal the last time.

She instructed them on moving snow from the ground, so lumps of coal could be discovered. The snow was deep and heavy now, and Jillian didn't have the strength to shovel for long. Hayden was surprisingly strong and adept at the task, however, so he shoveled, and once the chunks were revealed, Jillian gathered them. Meredith worked the opposite side of the tracks.

Early that morning Jonah had taken food and a rifle and followed the rails in the opposite direction to explore what lay beyond and look for animal or human tracks, if any.

He didn't return until well after noon. "There's nothing as far as the eye can see," he told her when they were alone. "But it's stopped snowing."

She'd been thinking of that, too. The weather was good for them, because it meant someone could come to their aid now, but it also meant the robbers might be the first to reach them.

Chapter Five

"The train has either arrived in Denver or was waylaid by Bloom's gang," Jonah said. "We have no way of knowing if the other marshals shot them or if the outlaws surrounded the train and figured out the mail car was missing. They'd have been forced to wait out the storm. Anything else would have been suicide."

"But by now help should be on the way, shouldn't it?"

He nodded. The engineer or the other marshals would have alerted the law. "They'll put a plow on a locomotive and make their way to us."

"It could be today yet," she suggested. "We might be in Denver for Christmas."

"Or tomorrow," he suggested, considering all the logistics.

"Well, we're here now," she reasoned. "I want to make Christmas Eve as special as possible for Hayden and Jillian."

"What do you have in mind?"

"Well..." She thought a moment. "It would be lovely to have a tree to decorate."

"I can provide the tree, but what about decorations?"

"Let me worry about that."

"All right. I brought back a pheasant for supper," he told her. "I'll dig for more roots."

"That sounds perfect."

While Jonah went in search of a tree, Meredith worked out her plan to celebrate the holiday. In her sleeping compartment, she opened the carved wood doors on the armoire and took out a stack of hatboxes, which she opened on the bed. Finding several hats adorned with feathers, she plucked them free and filled one entire hatbox. From other hats she removed wax cherries, paper birds and silk flowers, until a second box was filled.

After tossing the barren hats back into the armoire, she located her emergency sewing kit and threaded needles. Carrying the overflowing boxes out to the main area, she arranged them on the divan. "These will be our tree decorations."

Jillian and Hayden examined the feathers and assortment of objects with muted reverence. Finally, Jillian turned wide brown eyes on Meredith. "These is the most beautifullest decorations in the whole wide world, Miss Abbott. We will have the bestest tree ever there was."

Never had Meredith yearned so achingly for the simplest of things, such as a bowl of popping corn or a basket of cranberries. But obviously, these children didn't recognize the hardship, which was somehow even more sad.

When Jonah returned, they were ready with their makeshift ornaments. He had fashioned a stand from pieces of a crate. They stood the tree atop the low table and added the flourishes with painstaking care. Once again Jonah left and this time returned with pinecones he'd gathered in a piece of burlap.

Jillian squealed as though he'd brought them something valuable, and he was soon involved in an attempt to thread a needle so she could hang the cones.

With a laugh, Meredith took the needle and thread from him and had it ready in seconds. Jillian looked around for the footstool, and Jonah helped her arrange it near the table, then steadied her as she stood upon it and hung her prized ornaments. The pinecones all ended up on the same side of the tree, but neither Jonah or Meredith mentioned it or rearranged them.

Hayden had discovered a method of securing two feathers together and adding another garnish, like a wax cherry or a paper bird, and then hanging the finished piece from a limb.

"You have something there," Jonah told him. "Those look as good as any store-bought ornaments."

"I agree," Meredith concurred. She'd be making a beeline for the milliners when she finally reached Denver, but for now, it didn't matter a whit. These objects were bringing more pleasure as tree decorations than they ever had as hat adornment.

Once the tree was at last finished, they cleared their mess and stood back to admire their creation.

"It's the most beautifullest tree in the whole wide world," Jillian proclaimed, her sweet voice laced with awe.

Meredith met Jonah's gaze and recognized the emotion he couldn't completely hide.

If her trip had been uneventful and she had arrived at her destination as planned, Meredith would have been at the governor's mansion this evening, dressed in her emerald velvet gown and elbow-length white gloves, dancing to an orchestra and making polite conversation with a hundred people she barely knew. Instead, she was stranded somewhere in the foothills, surviving on biscuits and wild game, and caring for a couple of abandoned children....

It was the best Christmas Eve she could remember.

Hayden and Jillian embodied precisely what the spirit of Christmas was all about. It wasn't about lavish parties or expensive gifts. It was about a person sharing what they have with others, even if they possessed no more than a smile... Christmas was about people looking into their hearts and finding love and compassion for others.

"We have pheasant for tonight's supper," Jonah told them. "But I've been saving something for tomorrow."

The children were attentive. "What is it?" Hayden asked.

"I'll be right back." Jonah grabbed his coat and headed out the door. Several minutes later he returned with something rolled in a piece of canvas. As he unrolled it, the aroma reached Meredith. Her mouth watered.

"Oh, it smells so good," Jillian declared.

Jonah presented them with a savory-smelling, hickory-smoked ham. He grinned.

"Someone had *packed* this?" Meredith asked, incredulous.

He nodded. "Yup. The entire trunk smelled like a smoke-house. Probably intended as a gift for someone."

"Too bad for the intended receiver," Meredith said. "But fortunate for us." She took the ham from him and headed for the kitchen area. "Maybe I'll slice just a little to dice into our biscuits this evening. We're going to owe a whole lot of people for the items we've used when we get to Denver."

"I'll be more than happy to pay double whatever this ham cost," he said.

She laughed. "Who's cooking that pheasant?"

"I'll get right on it. Come help me, Hayden."

Roasted pheasant, biscuits and burdock root wasn't a traditional Christmas Eve supper, but the meal tasted delicious. They enjoyed the bits of ham and cheese Meredith had sprinkled into the biscuit dough.

Jonah broke off another bite. "You might write a cookbook once you're home," he told her.

"The instructions for most recipes would be simple," she agreed. "'Find yourself a savvy outdoorsman to snare a rabbit and roast it to a savory tenderness.'"

They laughed together.

Jonah couldn't help but admire the way Meredith jumped right in and accomplished any task she set her mind to. She hadn't once complained about the conditions or lack of amenities, as most women of her status would have, but instead approached every trial as though she was ready and capable to create a solution. And she had.

She was bossy and quite obviously used to having her own

way, but she was also competent and generous. She'd never shown fear, and had made certain the Langley kids were unaware of the imminent danger.

At first glance, she'd appeared a snooty female whose only purpose in life was attending parties and looking good on the arm of a political candidate, but the more he was around her, the more he recognized she was not who she seemed. Meredith was the furthest from shallow that a person could be and trapped by her circumstances. She'd been born into that family and raised to be like them.

The children were picking up plates without being asked.

"Is there anything more you would you like to do?" he asked softly. "Besides marrying well and helping with your husband's career advances?"

"The cookbook isn't a bad idea," she said. "Although I've never cooked until you showed me how to make biscuits, so I probably lack credibility." Her eyes revealed the same humor her words conveyed. "I've tried my hand at painting and was a disappointment to my instructor. I'm too impatient to get the colors and shadows right. People's faces were decidedly frightening, with lopsided mouths and drooping eyes."

"You sew, apparently."

"Only very basic and primitive stitches to get me by until I can reach a seamstress."

"You said you can shoot."

"Quite well, actually. Short of a Wild West show, there's not much call for a woman with dead-eye aim, however. My father would frown upon it if I took a job as an executioner or took up big-game hunting."

Jonah laughed out loud at her comedic sense of self-deprecation. "And how many trophy heads could you even fit on your walls?"

"Not that many."

Hayden looked at them as though they were crazy, which only had them laughing again.

Her expression sobered. "I want a well-to-do husband and a position on his staff."

She would do well in a job like that, Jonah figured. He wasn't any kind of an expert on matters of the heart—or on females for that matter—and practicality would serve a woman well, but didn't women dream of a grand passion?

"What are you thinking?" she asked, as though guessing he had questions.

"I'm thinking you'd be good at anything you set your mind to." She gave him one of those smiles that knocked him off-kilter.

By the time they'd finished their meal and cleaned up, it was dark out. Jonah covered the windows as he always did, and they lit a single lamp.

"I held on to something else I found," he said.

Hayden and Jillian sat forward on the divan, where they'd perched beside Meredith. "What did you find, Marshal?" Hayden asked.

Jonah pulled a Bible from under his coat near the door. "This."

"Another book?" Jillian asked. "What does this one be about?"

"About a lot of things," he answered with a grin. "But for tonight I'm gonna find the part about the first Christmas."

"The manger story?" Hayden asked.

"That's the one." Jonah sat and thumbed through the well-worn pages, and Meredith couldn't help wondering who the Bible belonged to. Maybe a preacher man traveling aboard the train, from the looks of it.

"Here we go," Jonah said. He spread the book open and ran his finger down the flimsy page. "'And it came to pass in those days that there went out a decree from Caesar Augustus that all the world should be taxed.'"

"What's a decree?" Hayden asked.

Jonah looked to Meredith.

"It's a new rule," she explained.

"Do it hurt to get taxed?" Jillian asked.

"Only hurts your pocketbook." Jonah took this one. "A tax is something that the people in charge, like kings or rulers, make people pay in order to own land or buy things or just to live in the country. In this case the ruler was Caesar, and he wanted every person counted so he could make them pay him." He would have liked to tell them about the tea taxation in Boston in more recent history, but for tonight they should probably try to get through this story.

Both children waited for more.

In the end they had so many questions that the story of the baby Jesus's birth took longer than expected, but that was okay, because they were smart, and they had the evening to pass.

"Is there more about the baby Jesus in that book?" Hayden asked.

"There's a lot more," Meredith answered. "But the rest of the story is about him as a grown-up."

"I wanna hear it," Jillian said with an eager lift of her brows.

"We can read more another time," Jonah promised.

"Let's sing a couple of Christmas songs before you go to bed." She got up and went to the corner, where a fringed cloth covered what Jonah had assumed was a table or cabinet. Instead, a small pianoforte was revealed.

Jillian clapped her hands and squealed in delight.

Jonah hoped she wasn't expecting him to know any songs.

After locating a stack of sheets that looked like music, Meredith slid a dainty bench before the instrument and seated herself. Flipping pages, she settled on a piece and placed her fingers on the keys.

Jonah was used to off-key honky-tonk music, so the lilting tones she produced took him by surprise. He'd never heard the song, but he enjoyed it, especially once she accompanied her playing with her surprisingly rich and husky-toned voice. There was nothing sweet or angelic about Meredith's voice—

n fact, it brought to mind sensual images that definitely didn't
coincide with the carol about bells and Yule logs.

"You didn't know it?" she asked.

He shook his head.

"I probably wouldn't have if I hadn't taken eight years of
instruction."

He raised his dark brows. "Eight years?"

"Excessive, I agree. I nagged so persistently to learn to ride
and shoot that eventually my mother gave in and let me take
lessons as long as I kept up the music class."

"Can you shoot as well as you play?"

"Better."

"Play more!" Jillian's plea turned Meredith back to her
sheet music.

The next few hymns were more familiar, and the children
sang along with the choruses.

Eventually, Jillian's eyes were drooping, and Meredith sent
her to the necessary, as she called it, and then made her comfortable on the mattress.

She fell asleep snuggled right up against her brother, his
hand stroking her hair. Jonah gave Hayden a smile. For now
they were safe and warm, and had probably just enjoyed one
of the best Christmas Eve's in their short history.

Jonah couldn't remember a holiday as good as this once
since his childhood. Christmases passed without much fan-
fare. A good turkey or roast beef dinner at a restaurant was a
treat, and if he wasn't on the trail, a quiet night in a hotel room
completed his celebration. He'd eaten dinner with another
marshal's family once, but he'd felt out of place and excused
himself early.

Meredith recovered the pianoforte, and Jonah sat admiring
the little tree in the dim light from the oil lamp he'd turned
low. "We'd better get out those guns from the other room and
have them at the ready."

Now that the storm had let up, their real troubles had begun.

Chapter Six

She gave a single nod. "All right. We'll be back shortly," she said to Hayden.

Together they took guns and ammunition from the cabinet Meredith unlocked. Jonah grabbed a Winchester carbine with elaborate gold embellishments. "Your father knows his guns."

"He's a collector."

"The models that came before this weren't as powerful. The two single actions in the case there are better weapons than those were, but this lever-action beauty..." He ran his finger over the nickel plating.

"It can be fired several times without reloading," she supplied.

"Show me you know how to load it."

She took the rifle from him, selected the correct carton of bullets and, using the gate on the side, loaded the magazine. One by one, she checked the ammunition in each weapon until he was satisfied she could handle the task.

When Jonah told her they needed to fill the copper tub in the necessary with snow, she cast him a skeptical frown.

"Need to keep water on hand," he explained.

She saw his logic and helped him haul snow through the car. "Are you convinced the outlaws will attack soon?"

"Snow let up today," he replied. "All they have to do is follow the rails to reach us."

She quirked her mouth to the side as she considered. "Maybe we shouldn't just sit here."

"I thought it out. We could try to make a run for the nearest town, though I'm not completely certain of its location without doing a little scouting first. The youngins would hold us up, making traveling slow. The chance of getting caught out in the open, in the cold, worries me more than staying put and waiting for help. This car is sound enough for us to hold off an attack. Staying put is our best chance of keeping them safe."

"All right," she agreed without hesitation. She was trusting him with their lives. All he could do was hope he'd made the right decision.

"It could get dangerous if they show up," he warned her. "I want you to focus on covering one side of the car, and I'll be on the other. Shoot to kill, Meredith."

Her wide eyes were solemn as she nodded her understanding.

"We have a good chance if we keep our heads level and plan. We'll push the tallest furniture in front of the windows and lean other things over them. We should teach Hayden how to reload the guns."

Her expression showed surprise, but resolve quickly replaced it. "He's a smart boy. He can do it. I'll go get him."

For the next half hour Hayden got instruction on how to load the chambers and magazines. Jonah quizzed him on which ammunition filled which gun, and the boy picked it up without error.

Jonah explained to Hayden what was most likely going to happen. It was wiser to inform him and have him participate in their defense than to risk one less set of hands at the critical hour.

"Let's carry these out and place them under the divan and in the chest," Meredith suggested. "Close at hand, but not so that Jillian will be afraid."

"You're going to do just fine, boy," Jonah said to Hayden. "Before long, we'll be out of here and on our way to Denver."

Jillian remained sound asleep, looking as peaceful as Jonah wished he felt. He was accustomed to perilous situations, but normally it was only his neck and a strongbox of gold at risk. The stakes were a lot higher in this predicament.

Once the guns were stowed away, they pushed a cabinet in front of a window and nailed a carpet over another.

"What about the windows in the other places?" Hayden asked with solemn concern etching his brow.

"Real wise of you to think of that," Jonah replied. "The others are all too small for a person to get through. They could shoot out the glass, but they can't enter."

Meredith tucked Hayden into his bedding and exited the room. She returned a while later to hand Jonah a steaming cup. Reaching for it, he recognized the trembling of her fingers on the handle. Taking her wrist and the cup at the same time, he set the cup aside and enveloped her hand with both of his. "You're scared."

She glanced over at the now sleeping Hayden. "No," she disagreed. "I'm not."

"Everybody gets scared, Meredith. Fear keeps us on our toes."

"I'm not afraid."

"Why are your hands shaking?"

"I'm cold."

He liked that she was proud and didn't want to show weakness. She survived in a household of men without being one of those simpering females who got her way by feigning tears or throwing tantrums.

"Drink your coffee," he said.

"It's tea."

He led her to the wide divan, where his covers had already been arranged, and guided her to sit, then handed her a cup. "Drink your tea."

She took it from him and sipped. He got his own cup and

sat beside her. The hot sweet liquid was indeed tea, and it tasted good.

"Possible the lawmen will get here first," he said. "Men could come from town or bring a locomotive from Denver. We're just getting ready for the worst-case scenario."

"I trust your preparations, Marshal."

Either she trusted him the way she said or she was just too darned stubborn to admit she had misgivings.

"You're the most fearless female I've ever met."

"Thank you."

"Did the tea warm you up?"

"A little."

He draped his arm across her shoulder and felt her trembling. Taking both cups, he set them on the floor. "Lie down and rest. I'll keep you warm."

She gave him a questioning look.

"Look at Hayden and Jillian, warm as a litter of pups."

She eased onto the divan and he stretched out behind her, wrapping his arm around her and conforming his legs to the bent shape of hers. He made sure his belt buckle didn't poke her.

Her clean scent, like soap and fresh cotton, teased his senses, a hundred times more evocative than a cloying perfume. Against his chin, her hair was cool and silky, catching against his whiskers when he moved to pull the blankets up over them.

"Better?" he asked.

"I would have been just fine."

"I needed some comforting tonight," he told her.

"What sort of comfort did you expect I'd provide?"

"I may have had a few disrespectful thoughts about you, but while you're in my care, I'm committed to keep you safe—safe from me as well as from anyone else."

"Supposing the comfort *I* asked for came in the form of a kiss?" she asked. "What then?"

A dart of anticipation arrowed through his chest. "I'd be

obliged to comfort you any way that eased your troubled mind."

"A request like that would be forward. Definitely unseemly."

"Desperate times call for desperate sacrifices."

"Indeed." She rolled to her back, bringing her closer, her hip pressing against him. Her warm softness was a fierce temptation. He wanted to reach for her and pull her flush against him. But he steeled himself.

Jonah rarely acted on impulse. Impulse got a person into trouble—or got him dead. He prided himself on thinking things through and making wise choices, even in a tight situation. But he didn't want to think over her request for a kiss. He simply wanted to kiss Meredith Abbott.

She raised one hand to lie her palm against his jaw. Her cool touch set his already tingling nerve endings ablaze. Without letting another second slip away, he leaned toward her.

Meredith expected him to claim her mouth in forceful urgency, but he didn't. He covered her lips with his in a tender exploration that surprised and delighted her. She hadn't expected the warmth of his lips...or the pleasurable softness.

She had never anticipated a touch so gentle and innocent could take her breath away and create inside her a deep yearning for more. She had to be crazy to want this man she barely knew to kiss her. She had to be shameless to enjoy it so thoroughly.

What she'd imagined might be awkward, bumping noses or stilted breathing was instead the most natural experience in the world. The mechanics of a kiss didn't enter her mind once, while the pleasure and sensuality of the moment took complete control.

Indeed, she was shameless. It was the most instinctive thing in the world to raise her hand and caress the contours of his jaw, thread her fingers into his satin-soft thick hair and grasp his scalp as though holding him securely would satisfy her growing desire to get closer.

Jonah touched her, too, his hand now stroking her shoulder

and upper arm through her clothing, moving until his fingertips met skin above her collar and sent shivers along her neck and then her cheek. With a single fingertip, he drew a circle around her ear, eliciting a breathless sound of pleasure from her throat.

She drew back slightly and he released her. She pressed her forehead to his and remained that way with his breath fluttering across her chin, her lips tingling and her heart racing inside her breast.

"I lied," she managed breathlessly.

His voice was hoarse when he asked, "About what?"

"About kissing Ivan Kingsley." Doubly shameless to confess her lack of sophistication! "I never have."

Jonah moved back to look into her eyes.

"I got impatient waiting for him," she explained. "The time never seemed right to question his interest. I figured if he really wanted to, he would have. Don't you suppose?"

"Something's wrong with the man."

She smiled.

The cat chose that moment to leap onto the divan, obviously surprised at not finding Meredith alone. Balancing on her hip, the fluffy feline took a wary step back.

"It's all right, Hercules." She stroked her pet's long white fur to assure him he was welcome. "You may lie with us. Come on."

Jonah figured nestling with a cat was a small price to pay for the pleasure of cozying up with this spellbinding woman. He wasn't sure what it was about her that drew him, because according to appearances she was untouchable. Beautiful. Rich and pampered. Headstrong and competent. But here they were, sharing a bed for the night...engaging in a first kiss....

A heart-stopping first kiss.

He'd been teasing about desperate times, but their frightening situation obviously had a lot, if not everything, to do with her request for a kiss. He hoped the kiss had given her the comfort she needed to rest. He didn't have any crazy idea that she saw something in him that revealed even an ounce of compatibility, because there was nothing. He was a loner.

He wasn't going to take advantage of the situation or her uncharacteristic vulnerability. He had a duty to perform, and she'd unwittingly become part of it. He had to keep her safe and deliver her to her family…and the man waiting for her.

The fool who had never even kissed her.

Jonah wanted to feel bad about that—about kissing her when he wasn't the one with intentions of marriage…but he couldn't. The memory of their kiss would last him a good long while. And he didn't regret it one bit. He hoped she didn't, either.

Once they got out of here, they'd both go about their lives. He'd give her no reason for remorse.

Her soft even breathing told him she slept.

He closed his eyes and tried to do the same.

Sounds outside the Pullman woke him.

Jonah jumped over Meredith to grab a rifle and dart to the window. In the breaking dawn, he made out two men bent over a trunk toppled in the snow.

Behind him, Meredith asked, "What is it?"

"It's Bloom's men. Pile all the blankets and pillows on top of Jillian and order her to lie still."

She did as he ordered, assuring Jillian that the marshal was going to take care of them. The sound of Meredith cocking the Winchester assured him she was prepared for instructions.

"Help me set the divan on end in front of that window."

Hayden helped the adults maneuver the piece of furniture into place.

Jonah checked outside once more. "Now the couch over that one."

They had all the windows blocked now, save one on each side, from which they'd fire, and they left the pillows stuffed into the deep sills. "Hayden, grab me the hammer I left near the door."

The boy obeyed and they took their positions. Jonah peered out. The two outlaws had discovered a bottle of liquor and were passing it back and forth.

Jonah had a decision to make. Obviously Bloom's gang had gone straight to the mail car without finding what they wanted and were now searching the baggage. This Pullman gleamed in the sunlight; it couldn't have missed their scrutiny. He'd bet a dime to a dollar there was someone standing outside the door in wait.

When the men didn't find the gold, they'd do everything in their power to get inside this car. He could only guess how many there were, but he could eliminate two right now.

Another man in a parka stepped into view.

Three.

"Hand me the Winchester," he whispered and reached back.

The solid barrel pressed into his palm. He set his rifle down and instinctively glanced at this one, assuring himself it was ready to fire.

He picked up the hammer with his left hand, wedged the barrel beside the pillow, held his breath and took aim.

Chapter Seven

He broke the window, dropped the hammer, then quickly regained his grip on the rifle. Three rapid successive shots.

Three men toppled over in the snow.

With any luck half of their adversaries were out of the picture. But Jonah couldn't be sure. And now those remaining would be fighting mad.

A loud curse rang out. "Shit, Harry, somebody just shot 'em dead!"

"Slide the hammer to Meredith," he ordered Hayden.

Gunfire erupted, as he'd expected. The sound of bullets pinging off the side of the Pullman had the terrified little girl screaming beneath the covers.

"Stay put," Meredith said sternly. Glass broke behind him.

He glanced over his shoulder to find Meredith at the window, the hammer already on the floor, a Spencer repeating rifle in her white-knuckled grip.

Near him sat Hayden, ready with a revolver and a hinged walnut case filled with bullets. It had been the boy who'd handed him the Winchester. "Good job, son. We're going to be fine."

Hayden nodded, his brown eyes round as saucers.

Silence reigned for several minutes.

Meredith's heart pounded so hard, she could hear blood pulsing through her body at an alarming rate. She took several deep breaths of the cold air to calm herself. She wouldn't be of any help if she couldn't hold her hands steady or see straight.

One at a time, she wiped her clammy hands on her wrinkled skirt, thankful she'd fallen asleep in her clothing. All the while she kept her alert gaze on the view outside the window.

Jillian cried into the blankets. "I peed in the bed," she sobbed.

"It's okay, Jilly," Hayden said to her.

"We'll get you clean clothes when we can," Meredith said softly. "Try not to cry, all right, sweetie?"

"Arright. I twy."

Movement caught her eye, and Meredith jumped. Below the line of her vision, right below where she stood, she spotted the top of a battered brown hat, moving quickly.

"Someone's right under the window!" she gasped at Jonah.

"He can't get through the wall, Meredith," he told her. "Don't look around the pillow to show your face, but keep your gun pointed out. Don't be afraid to fire if you get a chance. Remember, he'd shoot you if he got a clear shot."

"That's comforting."

"Wasn't supposed to be. It's a fact. Shoot or be shot."

"Okay." She swallowed hard. Was the outlaw lurking right on the other side of the exterior wall of the Pullman? The disturbing thought elicited a shudder that darted down her spine. "Thank you, Daddy, for buying a steel-fortified railcar," she whispered.

A craggy, whisker-stubbled face beneath shaggy hair and a brown hat sprang up in front of her.

She cut off her scream midway to panic, aimed and squeezed the trigger. The hat sailed backward. The man grabbed what was left of his bloody ear and fell below her line of vision.

"I didn't get a good shot, but I hit him!"

Jonah didn't have time to respond, because at that moment

more shots were fired. Glass splintered as the windows behind the pieces of furniture broke.

Hayden crawled across the floor and pushed a revolver toward her. "Use this 'un when that runs out."

From the west, fifty or sixty feet from Meredith's side of the car, two riders forced their struggling horses to wade through snow. One of them was the man with the bloody ear. The deep drifts hindered the animals' speed, making the riders easy targets.

The outlaws fired at the Pullman. Meredith's first instinct was to duck down and hide. She had to resist the urge to flee, however. There was no place to go anyway, and if she didn't do her part to hold them at bay, these outlaws could overtake them.

She leveled the rifle, peered along the barrel and squeezed the trigger three more times.

Hadn't they been expecting resistance on this side of the car? Why had they ridden into plain view? One of them slid from the saddle, crouched behind his horse and led it back the way they'd come.

His partner yelled at him and threw a canteen, apparently hitting the first man, because the fellow yelped. Meredith got a shot at the second outlaw as he ran to catch up. He crumpled to his knees. From that position, he raised his arm and fired at her.

She ducked as the rest of the window glass splintered inward and rained across her hair and shoulders.

"You all right?" Jonah yelled.

"Yes." She shook off the shards, then crept back up to peer outside. Neither man was in sight. "I got one in the leg."

"Here." Hayden shoved a revolver at her.

She exchanged it for the rifle, and he hurried to reload.

The interior of the Pullman smelled like gunpowder, but the acrid odor soon dissipated in the frigid air flowing through the broken windows. "Put on your coat and hat, Hayden."

He did so and dragged her fur coat to her. "Wear this, Miss Abbott."

After a quick search of the landscape, she slipped on her coat, glad for its heavy warmth.

"Throw out the gold and we'll ride out!" came a male voice from Jonah's side of the car.

"I don't have it!" he shouted back.

"Tell me where it is."

"Can't recall."

A bullet dinged off the exterior of the car, punctuating the outlaw's frustration.

Jonah glanced at her. "How many were on that side?"

"Two, from what I could tell."

"Two over here," he said. "And two out of the four are wounded."

"Maybe they'll give up."

"Not likely. With three of 'em dead, each one gets a bigger cut of the gold now. They'll wait us out. Hope to run us out of ammunition and food."

"Is that likely?"

"We've got a dozen or more of your father's guns and ammunition for each. More weapons than a few men can carry on horseback. This car is like a steel fort."

"I never appreciated it when my father extolled the praises of this rolling hotel," she lamented.

More bullets hit the exterior of the car and several slugs pounded into the bottom of the plush divan covering one window and hit the back of the antique cabinet at another.

"My father was wise to keep all his first editions at home."

Jonah slanted her a glance to see if she was being derisive, and assured himself she was.

A bullet struck the chimney of an oil lamp affixed to the wall, shattering the glass. They held their positions.

After that things got quiet. Jonah didn't let up on his vigilance. They waited until half an hour had passed.

"Take Jillian to the necessary," he said softly. "Crawl and

keep her as quiet as you can. When you come back, Hayden will take a turn. Grab something we can eat and drink." He looked at Hayden. "You're doing real fine, son. Remember to keep your head down."

"Yessir."

Meredith laid the revolver beside the rifle on the floor and crawled to where Jillian lay. "Come on, sweetie. We're going to clean you up a little."

The child's brown hair was a tumble of knots, her face red from crying. She cast her brother and Jonah each a look before joining Meredith on her hands and knees and heading back through the corridor.

"I thought o' sumpthin' bad, Marshal."

Jonah looked at Hayden. "What is it?"

"What if they throw burnin' torches through a window?"

"That's a real possibility," he replied honestly. "That's why I put blankets under the melting snow in the big tub. We have to keep a watch out and, if something catches fire, put it out with a wet blanket. Can you help me check for fire? We have to keep an eye on the other rooms, too. The windows are small, but a torch could fit."

"I'll help."

"What made you think of that?"

"My pa told me that he was locked up once and his friends throwed a torch into the sheriff's office to get the lawman to run out. When the sheriff ran out, they went in and got my pa."

Jonah had wondered often about these kids' parents. This story made it sound as though their father had been busted from jail. He'd bet anything the sheriff in this story got shot. He knew how a jailbreak took place. "Why was your pa in jail?"

"They said he robbed a bank, but they got him mixed up with somebody what looked like him."

Jonah said nothing, only nodded to say he'd heard. The children's father was a fugitive.

Jonah could find people who didn't want to be found.

* * *

Meredith took Jonah's watch point so he could make his own trip to the necessary, he returned quickly.

They moved Jillian's mattress and bedding to the corridor, where there were no windows. Meredith supplied her with a box of jewelry to keep her entertained. The girl tried on an emerald necklace and pinned an opal-and-diamond brooch to her plain cotton shirt.

"Likely they'll lie low until dark." Jonah checked from his vantage point and then crossed to speak to Meredith. "They're probably cozy in one of the other two cars for now, taking turns sleeping. Once it's dark, I could slip out and move along the ravine to the south in hopes of discovering their whereabouts."

The thought of him going out there terrified her. He could be discovered and killed. "They might be watching for you to do something like that."

"Most likely."

"I don't want you to leave."

He held up a palm. "All right. I won't."

"Promise me." She kept the urgency from her tone, but her panic was there beneath the surface.

"I swear I won't leave unless we have no other option left and we both agree."

"Thank you." Emotion threatened to rise up. She fought it down. She was a levelheaded woman, up to the challenge of staying alert. She had to help the marshal, needed to protect Hayden and Jillian. She was competent, more than able to do this. She liked the way Jonah's admiring looks made her feel. She wouldn't let him down. "This may be my first gunfight, but we're going to get through this."

He caught her around the neck with a strong hand and pressed a reassuring kiss on her lips. Holding her so he could look into her eyes, one corner of his mouth quirked into a grin. "You're the only woman I'd want to be surrounded by outlaws with."

He released her, and she had to steady herself before taking her place at her window. Heat rose in her cheeks and searing gratification tingled in her limbs. He respected her in a way no one ever had before. He treated her as an equal and expected much from her. He made her feel extraordinary…something she'd never felt before. Jonah's belief in her gave her credibility and confidence.

He settled at the other window, and she tried to keep her gaze on the view outside, not the man who'd taken to making her heart pound whenever he came near. Last night had been exhilarating. After the kiss they'd shared, she hadn't imagined she'd be able to sleep, but she'd felt safe with his arm around her and his warmth along her body.

The whole scenario had been inappropriate, and her mother would have had a fit of apoplexy if she'd known. But she never would. Meredith intended to hold what they'd shared close to her heart, an experience that was only hers that no one could change or control. She'd been in charge of her own life these past couple of days and she'd liked it.

Jonah asked her opinion, listened to her concerns and desires. He'd promised not to go exploring because she felt strongly about it. He validated her feelings.

This last kiss had probably been prompted by the adrenaline running high in such a stressful situation, but she didn't care if it wasn't heartfelt on his part. He made her feel important.

She forced her attention back to the scene on the other side of the window. Before long her nose was cold from the biting air, so she grabbed a scarf from a nearby table, folded it into several layers and tied it over the lower half of her face.

"Are you warm enough, Jillian?"

"Yes, Miss Abbott."

She glanced at Hayden. He'd fallen asleep leaning back against an upholstered chair.

The rest of the day was uneventful, but Jonah reminded them not to let down their guard. Not long after the sun had lowered behind the horizon and the countryside as well as the interior of the Pullman became dark, the sound of something falling came from one of the rooms in the rear.

"Go!" Jonah swung a hand to indicate the back of the car.

Meredith jumped up, and Hayden took her position, pointing a long-barreled Smith & Wesson into the darkness.

With trepidation, she crept past Jillian, warning her to stay put. It didn't take long to find where the sound had come from. Orange light flickered from inside her father's sleeping compartment.

As could have been expected, gunfire exploded, and from the opposite end of the car came the sounds of Jonah and Hayden returning fire.

Grabbing a blanket from the copper tub, she gave it a couple of twists and ran with the surprisingly heavy armload. Fire licked at the corner of her father's bed, the burning silk giving off an acrid smell. It took all her strength to stay protectively low and still swing the heavy wet blanket. Quickly, she beat out the flames.

As soon as she'd accomplished that, she found the curtains in her compartment ablaze and repeatedly struck them with the blanket. Now the wool was singed and starting to dry, so she bolted back to the necessary and traded it for the other.

She crouched in the corridor, her heart pounding, waiting for the next development.

"You all right?" came Jonah's urgent query.

"Yes, I'm fine. I put out two fires and am waiting for another. The blankets were an excellent idea."

"I'll remember that next time I'm in this predicament."

"This is what you said they'd do."

"It's what I would do if I wanted in."

She thought over that remark.

After a couple more attempts with the burning torches and gunfire, things quieted down. Forty minutes passed uneventfully.

Meredith crawled to peer into the darkness where Jonah's

and Hayden's forms were barely visible in the dim moonlight. "Have they given up?"

"Could be they figured out that tactic wasn't working. Someone from atop the car hammered the stovepipe loose and pulled it out the roof. I had to bank the coals in the heater."

Meredith was already freezing, her coat and the front of her dress soaked. "I have to change before I catch my death of cold."

"Go. Bring back warm clothing for everyone."

She fumbled in the darkness and donned a skirt, a shirt-waist, and a fitted jacket, then located a wool coat and pulled it on.

"Take off that brooch," Jonah said when she joined him. "Glittering like it does, it'll make you a target."

She hadn't even noticed the gemstone brooch on the coat and quickly stashed it in a pocket.

"It's snowing," he told her.

Her hopes sank. She gave herself a minute to muster them. Their rescuers were already close at hand. It wouldn't be long now. "Are you hungry? The children need to eat."

"Couple slices of ham will suffice."

She turned, but he caught her hand. "Don't know that I ever met a female as brave as you."

She swallowed the lump in her throat and squeezed his hand. "We're going to get out of here."

"Soon," he agreed.

Meredith piled a plate with pieces of ham and crackers and placed it on a tray with cups of water. She stopped in the corridor to give Jillian a share and then pushed it across the glass-littered carpet so Hayden and Jonah could get theirs. She went back into the corridor to eat with Jillian.

The little girl was wearing necklaces over her coat. Bracelets dangled from both wrists, diamond earbobs hung from her ears, and her wavy dark hair was messily swept up with half a dozen pearl-encrusted combs.

"You're looking lovely today, Miss Langley. Let's get some more clothing on you. I'll pull wool socks on over your shoes."

Jillian obediently let Meredith bundle her, even managing a weak smile. When Meredith was satisfied, Jillian sat to eat and poked a slipping piece of ham into her mouth with a fingertip.

Hercules meowed and joined them on the thick covers. Meredith broke him off pieces of ham and fed them to him. "You're being a brave kitty and staying out of the way, aren't you?"

Jillian chewed and swallowed. "I looked for him, but couldn't see him anywhere."

"He has hiding places where he feels safe."

"When are those bad men going to leave?"

She wished she had an answer, one she was confident about. "I'm not sure. Soon, I think."

A sound from the front end of the car caught her attention. "I heard something," she called to Jonah.

"What did it sound like?"

She crawled to the corridor opening so he could hear her, without her yelling. "Metal, I think. Like the sound when the Pullman is affixed to the train."

"Likely they've uncoupled us."

"Why?"

"Not sure."

She thought about what he'd said before. "What would you do? If you wanted in?"

"Depends what resources I had at hand. How much did you say this car weighs?"

"More than twenty-five tons."

"They can't tip it."

"Or pull it," she added.

"They may have brought along something to get into a safe or a strongbox."

"A crowbar?"

"D-Y-N-A-M-I-T-E," he spelled.

Chapter Eight

Her heart leaped. She crawled the remaining couple of feet to the end of the corridor to look at him.

"As a last resort only, because they want it in case they need it to extract the gold."

"Where would they use it?"

"A door would be logical, but they know the first person who tried to come in would be…"

"S-H-O-T," she supplied.

"You spelled dead," Hayden said.

Jonah inclined his head. "Smart boy."

"Why ain't someone come from a town yet?" he asked.

"Could be Bloom and his men spotted them before they could get here."

"In the dark we could make a run for it afore they bust in," Hayden suggested.

"They might be watching," Meredith replied.

Jonah looked her way. "It's almighty cold out there. Nobody'd want that watch. We'd have difficulty surviving if we risked it."

She thought of the falling snow and said nothing.

"But we should be prepared," he added. "Do you have a satchel?"

"Yes."

"Wrap slices of ham and crackers enough for a couple of days. One cup. Gather matches and all the ammunition for the Spencer, the Winchester and two revolvers. Bundle it up tight and affix a belt to it for carrying over a shoulder. Roll a couple of blankets tight for carrying, as well. Have it all at the ready."

She did as instructed, praying they wouldn't have to risk leaving their haven, but resigned to doing whatever it took to keep them alive. She made sure the revolver in her coat pocket was loaded and ready.

"See if you can get some sleep now." She stroked the little girl's hair and tied a scarf around it. Most of her hats were too big, but she rolled a small one under her boot to soften the felt, and then fitted it on Jillian's head. "Keep this on."

After piling the satchel and blanket rolls against an interior wall, she took up her rifle and relieved Hayden at the window. "You might as well rest now. I found extra clothing for you. We need to stay bundled."

He did as she asked and went to lie down near his sister.

"Is there more than one trap door?" Jonah asked in a quiet tone.

"Only the one in the kitchen."

"I pulled the icebox over it."

"I saw," she said.

"You know what you asked me?" he said a minute later.

"Which time?"

"About what I'd do."

"Yes."

"More and more I think I would set off a blast. Maybe under the car. Or on top. Anywhere the car was vulnerable enough to make a hole."

His words were disturbing, but she trusted his judgment. "We'd be vulnerable. We might get separated in the confusion. They could get the children. Or kill us."

"Could happen."

"We shouldn't be here when they set off an explosion."

"That's what I'm thinking."

"Are you thinking we sneak out?"

"I'll start the heater in the rear. Rising smoke will make it look like we're here. The snow will cover our tracks. We can make our way into the foothills and take cover."

"All right, Jonah."

"It'll be cold," he said. "We can't make a fire."

"It's our best chance. Now?"

"Now."

"I'll get Jilly." Obviously Hayden had been listening to their conversation.

Jonah double-checked the guns, stuffed his pockets with bullets and hefted the satchel on one shoulder. He stretched the other bundle toward Meredith. "If you can carry the blankets, I'll get Jillian."

Quickly, she ran into the corridor and came out with the furry white cat. Until that moment he hadn't seen the second satchel open and waiting. "You're not taking that cat."

"I'm not leaving him here to get blown up. Or worse."

He tried to reason. "Meredith—"

"I've done every last thing you've asked of me. But I will not leave Hercules behind." She placed the cat in the leather satchel, closed it and fastened the buckles. Picking it up, she reached for the blanket rolls and stood at the ready.

Arguing with her wasn't going to do any good, so he picked up Jillian and led the way to the door. "Quiet now," he ordered. "Don't say a single word until we're far away. Do you understand how important it is to keep silent?"

"Yessir," replied Hayden.

"Yessir," echoed Jillian. "I won't cry, neither."

"That's right. You're a brave girl. Hayden, you walk behind me and Meredith you bring up the rear. Get down as low as you can. There's a ravine just a short way from the rails. That's where we're heading to get out of sight."

Snow fell, but didn't blow much as their little party exited in silence. Meredith pushed the door shut and they headed away from the Pullman.

Responsibility was always a part of his job, but Jonah had never felt the weight as heavily as he did now, taking this woman and these children into the cold winter night.

Even bundled so she could barely move, Jillian managed to cling to his neck, and she wasn't heavy. Their feet made soft crunching noises as they waded through the snow.

He turned to observe the railcars silhouetted against the backdrop of snow. All three sat in stillness, a slender curl of smoke rising from the front end of the Pullman where he'd left the heater burning. The enormous car gleamed in the moonlight. Another thread of unease wove its way into his mind, but he'd made his decision. There was no turning back. He had a task at hand, so he focused on their safety.

Once they reached the ravine, much of his anxiety faded. They'd made their escape undetected, and now they could work their way north and find a place to navigate into the foothills, where signs of their passing would be obliterated by trees, pine needles and snow.

Hercules complained loudly from the valise, and Jonah was thankful the feline had waited until they were out of earshot.

Jillian had fallen asleep, her weight growing more clumsy to carry. He propped her over his shoulder and carried on.

"Are you all right, Hayden?" Meredith asked softly from behind.

"Yes'm. My feet are cold, though."

"You're doing great," Jonah assured him.

As they trudged farther from the tracks and left the ravine behind, their journey took them up the incline and into the trees. Meredith and Hayden's labored breathing joined the sounds of their boots in the snow.

The pungent scent of the evergreens enveloped them. Jonah kept a watchful ear tuned for animals, since it was too dark to see one. That bear had gone back to his cave by now, and hopefully no others would cross their path. The last thing he needed was to be forced to shoot a wild creature and alert Bloom's gang to their whereabouts. As it was, the men would have no reason to notice they were missing until they attacked or set off dynamite and got no response.

The wind picked up, sending showers of needles and gusts of snow down from the tallest trees. He broke off a long branch for later and shook the snow from it. Still they made their way upward. As they left the wooded area, the moon on the snow made it easy to find a way up the rocky hillside. It took another fifteen or twenty minutes of searching and winding around boulders to locate an overhang, under which they could all fit and remain out of the wind and snow.

There might have been animal remains or feces, so Jonah used the branch to sweep the area while they waited. "Hand me the blankets."

Jillian roused only long enough to glance around and assure herself she was safe, then drifted back to sleep.

"Sleep now, Meredith," Jonah told her. "When you wake, I'll take a turn. We need to get rest so we can stay alert."

He didn't need to say it twice. She took the cat from the satchel, affixed a leash to its collar and tucked Hercules beneath the covers between herself and Jillian. Hayden lay beside Jillian and next to Jonah.

"You, too, Hayden. You can take a watch with Miss Abbott in the morning."

Hayden lay down and within minutes snored softly. The boy had gone through as much stress as Jonah and Meredith, hadn't complained once and had been as brave as any grown man Jonah had ever ridden with. He was an extraordinary young man. Jonah vowed to find the Langley fellow and not desert these kids until he was assured they'd be well taken care of.

He counted stars to keep himself awake. Listened to the sounds of the night. Occasionally, he got up, stretched, and paced in front of the overhang, assuring himself enough snow had fallen to cover their tracks. As dawn broke through the clouds, Meredith woke and sat up.

"Did you sleep?" he asked softly.

"Surprisingly, yes. It made a difference not feeling trapped."

"My eyes feel like sandpaper." He lay down and fell asleep within a few minutes.

Meredith used Jonah's branch to sweep a path and cleared a circle not too far away where she and the kids could relieve themselves. When they woke, she took Jillian and showed Hayden the path. She cut them bits of ham and rationed the crackers. Each of them used the cup for snow, letting it melt on their tongues. She couldn't help thinking of the steaming pots of coffee Jonah had boiled for them before the outlaws had arrived. She could almost smell it now, and her mouth watered. She shivered. The ham made her thirsty, so she let more snow melt on her tongue.

After he'd slept a few hours, Jonah awoke and ate.

"I'm going to climb farther up and see if I can find a spot that overlooks the Pullman. Likely they'll make a move today and learn we're gone."

Having thought to tuck a book into their stash of provisions, Meredith opened it and read to the children while he was gone. Hayden fell back asleep, and she realized he'd gone without rest nearly as much as the adults.

Upon returning, Jonah wrapped a blanket around his shoulders and seated himself. "I found a vantage point where I can observe them. I could make my way down and shoot at least one from a distance. After that they'd wise up and stay out of sight, but there would be one less threat. I'd be gone a long time, because I can't leave tracks to lead them back here. I'd find another vantage point and wait."

He didn't see fear in her eyes. She appeared to think over his suggestion. Finally, she nodded. "Take out more than one the first time."

"I'll do my best. Let's carry out the ham and cover it with

snow so animals don't smell it, and if they do, you're safely away from it. Take your best shot while it's eating."

At that her eyes widened, but he'd had to warn her.

"Don't shoot at a bear, though. A bear will eat and move away from your scent, unless you startle it or attack it."

"Go." She got up to carry out his instructions with the meat.

He stood and caught her sleeve. He couldn't straighten to his full height under the rock ceiling, and his position forced him to lean over her.

She looked up into his eyes.

"I *will* come back for you."

"I know."

"No one can find you here."

"We'll be fine, Jonah."

He wanted to kiss her. His gaze dropped to her lips, now chapped from the cold and wind, and he wanted to press his mouth against hers and feel her sweet warmth.

She knew what he was thinking, because her eyelids fluttered and even more color than what the cold created rose in her cheeks. "You may kiss me."

She never stopped surprising him. Hayden was probably watching, but Jonah didn't care. He loved that she was fearless and headstrong. He loved that she spoke her mind and asked for what she wanted.

He hadn't realized how cold his nose and cheeks were until he pressed his lips to hers and found hers warmer. Apparently, she didn't care that his face was cold, because she returned the kiss in wholehearted, unrestrained abandon. He was the one who ended it and glanced at Hayden.

The boy was petting the cat while deliberately not watching them. "I'll be back for you," he said to the boy.

Hayden looked up then, but said nothing.

Jonah turned and left them in their shelter.

Chapter Nine

Midmorning, from a ridge on the opposite side of the tracks, Jonah discovered the perfect vantage point from which to observe Bloom's gang below. They went about what he figured was their plan to dynamite the car. If he went now, while they were absorbed in their task, he might catch more of them together.

He crept down and made his way closer. Their unsaddled horses were tethered at the front of the mail car, under a crude lean-to created from a tarp and stripped lodge pole pines. Smart of them to protect their mounts. If he didn't have so much climbing to do, he'd take the horses. But he could move around more easily unburdened.

The outlaws couldn't get away without their mounts, though. While the four men were busy between the Pullman and the luggage car, Jonah crept up and pressed his gloved hand over each horse's nose to quiet it and familiarize the animals with his scent. Rapidly, he untethered all seven and led them north, then down the ravine, where he removed the tethers. Without saddles and in this weather, the beasts were likely to simply wander off. He was counting on it.

Jonah slapped two on their rumps, and they took off, the

others joining them. He watched to make sure they had a good start, then darted back to find cover and creep closer.

One man was under the Pullman. One sat on the platform of the luggage car, and the other two were crouched near the track. One of those two was Roscoe Bloom.

Jonah took aim at Bloom, held his breath and fired three times in rapid succession.

Bloom collapsed over into the snow. The man beside him crumpled and the one on the platform shouted, grabbed his neck and flattened himself against the rear wall of the car. Seconds later, he let himself inside.

Jonah didn't wait to see what would happen next or if the outlaw under the Pullman came out shooting. He turned and hightailed it back up the hillside on the opposite side of the tracks and away from where he'd left Meredith and, the children. He wouldn't lead them to her.

He figured there were some hoppin' mad robbers down there if they'd discovered their horses gone. He didn't think they knew the Pullman was empty yet, so they had no idea who had fired upon them.

From his vantage point above the tracks, he observed the scene below. No movement. No one headed after him.

Apparently, they'd gone back inside whichever car they were using. One of the men was surely licking his wounds. Jonah wondered how they liked it now that the shoe was on the other foot, and they were the ones holed up in a railcar. Feeling pretty satisfied with himself, he almost didn't hear the low rumble behind him.

The hackles on the back of his neck rose. With unhurried movements, he turned.

A cougar perched on a boulder above him, its ears pitched backward, its teeth bared. A quiver of anxiety rippled through Jonah's cold limbs. He eased his revolver from its holster and lowered the Winchester. The .45 would fire more rapidly and was still fully loaded.

There weren't a lot of options. Risk his location being discovered…or a wrestling match with the prospect of having his throat slashed open.

The enormous cat leaped toward him. Jonah fired four times and it landed on the rock at his feet with a solid thud.

Checking the railcars, he saw no movement. He reloaded both guns and headed out.

An hour later, he'd canvassed the entire area. If anyone followed his tracks, they'd be led in circles. Eventually he worked his way behind and above the overhang where he'd left Meredith and as darkness fell, he called out. "It's me."

Jillian ran to him, grabbed his leg and clung for dear life. "Oh, I missed-ded you!"

He patted her back through layers of coats and wraps and gave her a reassuring smile. "I missed you, too."

"Did you bwing a wabbit?"

"Not this time. We can't have a fire just yet. There are still two bad men down there."

Meredith picked up on his hidden message. Two more down. She and Hayden exchanged a satisfied look.

"One more is hurting tonight," he added.

"How about some ham?" Meredith asked.

"Better than nothing," he replied. "Though it will likely be a while before I want another ham dinner."

"You sleep first," she said, after he'd eaten a small portion.

He made himself comfortable and closed his eyes.

Meredith was dreaming of taking a hot bath when the distant sound of a train whistle disturbed the pleasantry. Annoyed at first, she buried her head below the blanket and deeper into the collar of her coat, but the piercing sound came again.

She sat straight up.

Jonah was already out from under the overhang. She shrugged out of the blanket and dashed after him. On his heels as he took long strides and climbed the hillside, she determinedly kept up. Her heart raced with anticipation.

They reached a flat rock that overlooked the landscape

below. Sure enough, coming from the north puffed a loco-motive with a coal car and one freight car behind it. A huge wedge-shaped plow on the front shoved the deep snow to each side. The whistle sounded once again, louder this time, echoing up to where they stood.

From the mail car, two figures, tiny from this height, darted away and headed east up the other side.

Before the engine slowed to a stop, the wide door rolled open and men poured from the freight car and gave the outlaws chase.

Meredith squealed and grabbed Jonah, trapping his arms at his sides. He smiled, broke free and turned her around. "Let's go!"

They gathered the children and their meager belongings. He led the way in the straightest path available down the hillside.

In the distance shots rang out, volleying across the canyon.

They neared the tracks. Now men were searching the cars, two standing at the rear of the Pullman.

"Daddy!" Meredith spotted her father and ran toward him. Jonah followed with the children.

"Meredith!" The tall deep-voiced man ran to meet her and enveloped her in an embrace.

"You're well? I've never been so frightened in all my life." He framed her face with both hands and pressed a kiss soundly on her forehead. His astute gaze took in her disheveled appearance. "Are you all right?"

"I'm fine. Thanks to Marshal Cavanaugh." She detached herself to step back and wave Jonah forward. "Jonah—er, Marshal, this is my father, Nicolas Abbott."

"Marshal," Abbott said, reaching for Jonah's hand and shaking it heartily. "They assured me you'd take care of my daughter, but I was concerned. I haven't slept a wink since the train arrived in Denver without her."

"Cavanaugh!" came a shout from one of the lawmen.

Jonah set down Jillian beside Meredith and shook hands with Jeremiah Thorpe, one of the other marshals who'd been on the train he'd abandoned. "What happened when you came into the open?"

"They came at the train like we figured. Faver took a bullet. He's doin' good. Then they saw the mail car was gone. Turned and high-tailed it outta there. We got Faver to Denver, but it was a slow trip in that blizzard. After that we waited for the storm to let up so we could head back for you. Looks like you're both safe, but where did these two come from?" The other marshal looked over Hayden and Jillian with a question on his face.

"We need to talk about that," Jonah replied. He turned to Meredith's father and jerked a thumb over his shoulder. "That fortress saved us."

Abbott seemed pleased at that. "She's a beauty, isn't she?" On closer inspection he frowned at the bullet holes scattered across the entire side and the broken windows. "A little damage is a small price to pay for my daughter's life."

Meredith shot a glance at Jonah. It was far more than a little damage, and her father would see that once he got inside.

"Oh. And this." Jonah handed Abbott the Winchester. "Handsome weapon, sir."

Abbott looked at it. "This was probably fired more these past days than the entire time I've had it. I shot a few clay pigeons a year or so ago." He extended the rifle. "You keep it."

"Thanks, but I couldn't take it."

"You saved my daughter's life."

"I was just doing my job."

"Take it now or I'll ship it to you later. It's yours."

Jonah accepted the gift. "Thank you."

"I'm not the one who deserves thanks. Thank *you*."

Jonah merely nodded. He called to Thorpe, who had turned away. "Have them check under the Pullman. I'm pretty sure they'll find dynamite ready to be lit."

"Why didn't they light it?"

"They came under fire and ran to hide."

Thorpe instructed his men. Within a few minutes they produced a bundle of explosives. "I can't wait to hear this whole story."

"We ate wabbits! An' had a Chwistmas twee." After her cheerful revelation, Jillian clung to Jonah's leg until he picked her up again.

The lawmen took the bodies to the freight car while the railroad employees coupled the disengaged cars to the engine.

"All aboard!" shouted the engineer.

Jonah joined the lawmen, and Meredith ushered the children back into the Pullman. Her father joined her, and she saw the devastation through his eyes.

"You must have been terrified." His voice was gruff with emotion.

"We can use the heater back in your compartment," she said and led the way, carrying the satchel that held Hercules. "And there's not as much glass." She stirred the coals, which were still hot, and added more. Once Hayden and Jillian were settled on the bed, she opened the valise and let out an angry Hercules. He arched his back, so that his white fur stood on end, gave her a scathing look and darted under the bed.

She and her father took chairs. His gaze went to the scorched corner of the mattress and silk counterpane.

"I wasn't as frightened as I might have imagined. Not nearly as much as you're thinking. There wasn't time to have a fit of vapors. There was only time to react wisely and do what needed to be done."

"Your mother is going to be so relieved to see you. Mr. Kingsley, as well. He visited our hotel every day to see if we had news and to comfort us. He's such a nice young man."

She said nothing, but closed her eyes as the train got underway and the car picked up speed. "At last we're on our way to Denver."

Chapter Ten

Soaking in a tub had never felt so good. After two nights of lying on a rock ledge, with only her coat and a blanket for padding and experiencing the bitter cold, her body ached all over. The steaming hot water soothed her muscles. Finally, she felt clean. Her dry skin absorbed the oil her mother had lavishly poured into the water, while the soothing scent drifted around her.

She had bathed the children first, and then tucked them into the wide bed with satin sheets. Meredith smiled at how lovely Jillian's glossy dark hair had looked, clean and brushed and dried before the fire.

Hayden had figured out she meant business about his ears and fingernails and set to work on them until his scrubbing met her approval.

The City Marshal who'd met them at the station had immediately wanted to take them into his custody, but she had convinced Fred Swope that after the trauma they'd been through, the Langley children needed to stay with her.

She advised him, perhaps a little too bossily, to search for their father while she got them clean and fed them and saw to it they were comfortable that night.

Her father had told her that Ivan would be by to see her

later that evening. She tried to muster up some enthusiasm about that, but she was exhausted and wanted nothing more than to take her bath, then join the children in plush comfort and sleep with no one waking her. She asked him to make her excuses and assure Ivan she'd see him tomorrow.

Her mother had wept and hugged her and supervised the filling of the tub three times. She'd laid out Meredith's clothing and fussed until Meredith kissed her cheek and told her she'd love to tell her everything after she'd slept for several hours. The woman had taken the hint and reluctantly excused herself.

"I'll check on you during the night," Deliah assured her.

"Thank you, Mother."

Before she fell asleep right here in the cooling water, Meredith stood and dried herself, then folded her robe around her and padded out to slip into her nightclothes.

She fell into exhausted slumber and dreamed she was sitting beside Jonah on the seat of a buggy. The day was warm, with the scent of lilacs on the air. They crossed a bridge and rode through an arbor of blooming trees, where apple blossoms rained from the sky like huge flakes of feathery light snow.

Jonah reigned the horses to a halt and held her by the waist to set her upon the ground. In the next moment, she was in his arms. She'd never wanted anything as badly as she wanted him to kiss her. She leaned into him and strained upward.

He released her to turn away. "I can't kiss you."

"Of course you may," she urged.

"No. Not now."

"Why not now?"

"You're a married woman, Meredith. We won't be seeing each other again."

Meredith woke with a sinking sensation in her stomach. She lay without moving, the urge to cry welling up and threatening to spill out. She'd never felt so disappointed and sad.

The dream receded and reality swam into focus. Jillian lay

beside her, smelling little-girl clean, and on the other side of his sister, Hayden's deep breathing reached her ears.

They were all safe.

They'd made it to Denver.

She wasn't married to anyone.

A puzzling sense of relief washed over her. It had only been a dream. But it had seemed so real, and the memory of her deep despondency was vivid.

She closed her eyes.

Her mother had breakfast sent to Meredith's room. "You don't even have to dress if you prefer comfort today."

But of course she did, donning a blue-and-gray silk dress with a ribbon-trimmed taffeta overskirt. One of the deputies had delivered a bag containing her jewelry, and she opened it to select earrings and a watch brooch.

After arranging her hair, she brushed and braided Jillian's hair, as well. "After breakfast we'll shop for clothing and shoes for you and your brother. New coats, too."

"Can I get a bwue dress like yours?" Jillian asked.

"We'll have to see what's available. We can have one made, but it won't be ready today."

"You look so pretty, Miss Meredith."

"Thank you, sweetie. You're awfully pretty yourself."

Meredith's mother ate with them, and it became apparent that she, too, was touched by these children's story and their charming innocence. Jillian dropped a splat of preserves on the white tablecloth and attempted to wipe it off with her napkin, making an even bigger mess.

"Here, honey, we'll just cover that with a clean napkin so you can finish eating." Deliah covered the preserves, wiped Jillian's hand and sat back down. When she found Meredith grinning, she gave her a sheepish smile.

"We'll speak later," Meredith said. She had a lot to tell her mother, but she wanted to let her know about the Langley children's situation. "Will you join us on our shopping trip?"

Deliah gave her a delighted smile. "I would love to. I don'
want to let you out of my sight, actually."

After being cramped up for so long, it was a pleasure t
walk along the paved streets of the city. Their hotel was onl
a few blocks from most of the shops, so Meredith decline
a buggy, and her mother indulged her. The children peere
in windows, pausing often to comment. Jillian skipped, he
braids bouncing against the back of her coat.

"Christmas was dreadful," Deliah told her, hugging her arr
through her coat sleeve. "I couldn't eat nor sleep for worry."

"It must have been awful for you." Meredith gave Deliah'
gloved hand a pat. "It wasn't so bad. We were warm and saf
in the Pullman. I don't have a hat left that hasn't been plucked
but the children and I even decorated a little tree."

They reached a shop she wanted to enter, and the rest of th
morning was spent trying clothing on the children and goin
from place to place until she was satisfied they had prope
clothing, shoes and coats.

They enjoyed their noon meal at a bustling café. Hayden
now wearing his new clothing, sat a little straighter and copie
the two women's behavior by placing his napkin on his lap an
thanking the server who brought their food. He ate a heaping
mound of potatoes with dark gravy and started on the slice
beef.

Jillian had taken her cues from Deliah and ordered braise
chicken with carrots.

"Meredith!"

At her name, she turned and spotted Ivan crossing the roor
toward them, holding his hat against the front of his coat. Sh
rested her fork on the edge of her plate. "Hello, Ivan."

He glanced around, spotted a chair and dragged it to thei
table. Deliah moved to that seat so he could sit near her daugh
ter.

"I waited at the hotel for an hour," he claimed. "I had hope
to see you first thing this morning. Are you well?"

His brown hair was neatly combed, as always, and he wor

a tailored suit with gray trousers and a black coat. His white shirt had a stiff collar, and gold cufflinks winked at his wrists.

"Yes, I'm fine. Ivan, this is Hayden Langley and his sister, Jillian. They shared the adventure with us. Children, this is Mr. Kingsley."

Jillian gave him a wary smile and Hayden reached to shake his hand.

Ivan glanced at the boy's hand, but spoke to Meredith without taking it. "When I heard you had arrived in Denver safely, I went straight to the hotel. Your father told me you were too weary to see anyone."

Hayden dropped his hand with a disconcerted look, but resumed eating.

"We were all exhausted last night," she answered. "I slept like a rock."

"You'll dine with me this evening, of course. I have to return to work now, but I had to see you and know for myself you were all right."

"The marshal took good care of us."

"I'll come by for you at seven." His demeanor suggested he would have liked to say something more, but he stood and excused himself. He adjusted his hat upon his head before exiting the café.

"He came by the hotel every day," Deliah said. "He was as concerned as the rest of us. Your ordeal made the headlines of the *Rocky Mountain News.* Everyone was talking about it and waiting to hear of your return."

For the first time, Meredith took notice of the people at the tables around them. Several patrons gave her a smile or a brief wave. "How do they know who I am?"

"Your portrait was printed with each article."

Resigned to being the topic of local news, Meredith sipped her tea. "I hope you gave them the one where I'm wearing the lavender dress with the scalloped tiers and the matching shawl."

"Of course. It's your best."

"Mother, would you mind seeing the children back to the hotel so I can attend to some business? There are a couple of visits I need to make alone."

"Regarding the little ones?"

"Yes."

"Of course, dear. We'll stay for a slice of pie and then go to our rooms and nap."

Meredith stood and gave her mother a peck on the cheek.

She'd never visited a lawman's office, so she hailed a carriage and asked the driver to deliver her to the City Marshal. Fred Swope recognized her, not only from the newspapers, but from their encounter the day before. "Miss Abbott."

"Marshal Swope. I've come to discuss the children's situation."

"Cavanaugh has been in and out, too. He's waitin' on telegrams. We figured out who Langley is. Seems he's wanted in several states."

"He's a *criminal?*"

"I'm afraid it's a certainty, miss. In cases like this, the children hafta be placed in the custody of a safe facility."

"An orphanage."

"Yes, miss. It's the best place for them."

"They've already run away from a place like that. I don't see how another one would be an improvement."

"They can't stay with you. You have no legal hold on them. If you bring them in today, my wife will take care of them until other arrangements are made."

Her heart sank and her breakfast threatened to come back up. But above the escalating fear rose indignant anger. It wouldn't further her cause to be rude to the man, who was only doing his job, so she cautioned herself and took a deep breath. "What will happen if I don't turn them over to you?"

"Then I'm afraid I'll have to come get them."

She thought over the consequences of not complying. The children would only be more confused and hurt. "This is the only way?"

"Until we can get a judge's ruling on where to take them."

"How is it they can stay with your wife and not with me?"

"She's a married woman. A law officer's wife. We have youngins of our own and we've taken in orphans before."

"Very well. I'll bring them this afternoon. Do you know where Marshal Cavanaugh is staying?"

"The Oxford. Thank you for cooperating."

Turning quickly before he saw her distress, she exited the building. The driver helped her into the carriage.

"The Oxford Hotel, please." As soon as the driver had closed the door, she promptly burst into tears. After blindly searching for a handkerchief in her reticule, she finally located one and buried her face. She was stronger than this. She wasn't a simpering female. Anger fueled this blubbering, and she had yet to curb that emotion.

The thought of seeing Jonah sobered her. She didn't want him seeing her red-faced or out of control. She dried her tears and dabbed on face powder from her gold compact. A dab of lip color followed. There now.

She would be taken seriously as long as she kept her emotions in control. She'd never let anyone glimpse an insecurity.

Once they'd pulled up before the unfamiliar hotel, the driver took her gloved hand and aided her step to the ground.

Inside, an enormous Christmas tree stood in the middle of the lobby. At the desk, she asked for Jonah's room number and climbed two sets of stairs to reach it. Her heart thudded as she stood before room thirty-seven, her hand raised. She rapped on the panel and waited. After two more louder knocks, she accepted that he wasn't there.

Disappointed, she took the stairs back down to the lobby.

"Meredith!"

At his voice, she stopped in her tracks and found him ten feet away. "Jonah."

Chapter Eleven

They met halfway and faced each other. Seeing him here, in an unfamiliar setting, was odd. He looked good. He'd shaved and had a haircut. He wore the same coat however, and held his familiar hat. "Look at you," he said. "Is there a party?"

"No, I came to find you."

"Are the kids all right?"

She tampered down the jolt of fear that threatened to overtake her at his question. "They're fine for now. But that's what I need to talk to you about."

"I have news, too," he said. He glanced around the spacious area. "Let's sit over there."

He led her to a grouping of overstuffed chairs not far from the decorated tree and pulled one close to another so they could sit facing each other. There was no one else nearby, and she appreciated the privacy.

"Why are you here?" he asked.

She took a breath. "Marshal Swope needs to take Hayden and Jillian into his custody until a judge decides what to do with them." She looked into his dark eyes and read his compassion. "He claims they'll be sent to an orphanage. I won't let that happen. That's why they were in that luggage car, remember? Running away from a place like that."

"It's worse," he stated simply.

"What's that?"

"Their father is dead. I spent the morning sending telegrams to lawmen around the country. Heard back from a sheriff in Kansas. Seems Langley was shot during a holdup."

"Oh." Meredith couldn't muster up any sympathy for the man. All her concerns were for Hayden and Jillian, who were truly orphans now.

"This will make it easier for a judge," he explained. "Now there are no living parents or legal guardians, so he can make an informed decision."

"Still, it lands them in an institution."

He lifted a shoulder. "There aren't many options."

"I can adopt them."

"I suppose you can. You'll be married soon. The authorities will require that a married couple take them."

The dream rose in her thoughts, along with the very real distress she'd felt over the belief that she was married—and not to this man. "Yes."

His eyes revealed nothing he might be thinking.

"I guess I will be married soon. And then I can ask for custody. A judge would be in favor then, right?"

"I don't see why not. You could make a good home. You care deeply for them already." He paused. "Have you seen Kingsley yet?"

"Only briefly. We're having supper tonight, though. My parents said he called on them every day while I was missing."

"I like your father. Wasn't at all what I expected."

"What did you expect?"

"A stuffy railroad baron who threw his weight around. He's genuinely kind. And he adores you."

"I could use a lot less adoration and a little more respect."

"You deserve it."

His words touched her. "Thank you." She considered the news he'd delivered. "How are we going to tell the children about their father?"

She hadn't stumbled over the word *we.* It had come out quite naturally. If he thought anything of it, he didn't let on.

"They don't need to know how he died," Jonah replied. "But they need to know he's out of their lives now. Can't have them running off to find him again."

"Will you come with me? To tell them? We only have this afternoon, and then I have to deliver them to the City Marshal."

"I'll come with you." He stood and reached for her hand.

Grasping it, she got to her feet. "I have a carriage outside."

They arrived at the hotel, and she paid the driver. Together they entered the grand foyer and took the open curved staircase to the next floor. At the end of the hall, she turned the key in the lock on a set of double doors and entered first.

She saw the suite through his eyes, with its elegant furnishings and tasseled draperies. Her mother was seated in a chair, reading. She looked up and gave Jonah a curious once-over.

"Mother, this is Marshal Cavanaugh. Jonah, this is—"

Deliah sprang to her feet and enveloped Jonah in a hug. His expression of surprise amused Meredith, and she grinned.

"You dear man," she said on a rush of emotional fervor. "I can't thank you enough for protecting Meredith. You saved the life of my precious daughter. I'll be forever indebted."

He extricated himself from her zealous embrace and removed his hat. "Pleasure to meet you, ma'am. Can't take that much praise for how things turned out. Your daughter here is darned clever on her own. She could've survived without my help."

"Nonsense," Meredith denied. "He's completely responsible for keeping all of us safe. You should probably throw a party for him, Mother."

Deliah's face lit like the brightest candle. "Indeed!"

Jonah's brows lowered over dark eyes and he scowled at Meredith.

She couldn't help but laugh.

"Where are Hayden and Jillian?" he asked, ignoring her foolery.

She led him to the bedroom, where they lay on a high bed with a canopy.

Both had heard their voices and immediately sat up. "Jonah!" Jillian cried and bounded up to wrap her arms around his neck.

He allowed her hug, and then shook hands with Hayden and ruffled his hair. "You got taller. And those new duds look fine on you."

"See my dress?" Jillian asked, not to be outdone.

"I noticed it was mighty pretty."

Meredith touched the little girl's shoulder. "Let's fix your braid, and then we're all going to sit and talk, all right?"

Deliah had ordered tea, and they all gathered on the divan and nearby chairs and sipped the hot brew. She had even cooled the children's with milk.

Jonah had handled a lot of unpleasant tasks in his life, but telling these youngsters about their father was one of the most difficult things he had ever done. Facing that cougar had been less traumatic. But he had thought out what he'd say, and he explained it to them so they understood the permanence of Langley's death, but not so they'd think less of the man for his nefarious ways.

Both cried, with Hayden holding back as best he could, and Jillian sobbing against Meredith's breast. Even Mrs. Abbott got out a handkerchief and wiped her eyes more than once. Meredith stoically comforted them without showing her own distress, and he admired her all the more for her strength.

He'd been determined to find their father. Only days ago he'd vowed to himself that he wouldn't desert these children, and now that they knew the truth, his vow was more important than ever.

Once their young charges had grown calm, Meredith opened the next subject that had to be addressed. "I have to tell you about the law now," she began. Halfway through the explanation, her voice broke. She composed herself and carried on. "Mrs. Swope is going to take very good care of you. There are other children for you to play with."

Both children accepted their fate without a show of hysterics or emotional pleading. Their serene acceptance was almost worse, because it exemplified the hopelessness they'd experienced in their young lives.

"I won't make you promises I can't keep," Meredith said with so much emotion in her husky tone that Jonah got up and went to the window, where he stood without seeing. "What I promise you is that I'm going to do everything in my power to make sure you have a real home. A home with a family who wants you and loves you and takes care of you. I give you my word—my *promise* that I won't stop trying until that happens."

"Awwight, Miss Meredith." Jillian hugged her. "Don't be sad."

Meredith quickly checked the little sob that escaped her lips. Jonah turned to see her gather herself. "We're going to do something together now. We'll play a game or read a book. And then I'm going to take you to the City Marshal's office."

"Does he got a jail there?" Hayden asked.

"Sure does," Jonah replied. "I'll show it to you."

"Do we gots to sleep at the jail?" Jillian asked.

"No, you'll have nice comfortable beds at the marshal's very own house," Meredith assured her.

"Okay." Jillian hopped down from Meredith's lap. "Let's pway."

Jonah perched on the divan. "I'll stay if it's all right."

Meredith gave him a grateful smile.

Deliah looked from Meredith to Jonah and back, observing their interaction. She pulled the wall cord to summon a staff person and ordered more tea as well as cookies.

No matter the fare, neither of the children ever left behind so much as a crumb. More than once Deliah had raised an eyebrow over how much they consumed, but her expression was one of compassion, rather than censure.

Much as he wished he could, Jonah couldn't stop the clock. The afternoon grew long, and Meredith resignedly packed all the children's new clothing, shoes and books she'd purchased for them. Jonah carried the two pieces of luggage to the door.

Mrs. Abbott gave each child a watery smile and a motherly hug. Hayden was his usual inquisitive self, inquiring about the fate of the remaining outlaws and the gold.

"The gold arrived safely at its destination."

"'Cause that's your job, right?"

"Right."

The bellman snagged a carriage for them, and they crossed the busy section of town. Jillian squealed with delight at the sights from the window.

Jonah watched Meredith and her reactions. Likely she was thinking this would be their last time together, the four of them. He could see the strain in her elegant features. She had so many qualities he admired, he sometimes forgot how breathtakingly stunning she truly was. She didn't behave like any of the attractive women he'd ever known, and as far as he could tell, she wasn't even aware of her beauty.

The carriage pulled up before the brick building that housed the City Marshal and the jail. Meredith closed her eyes briefly, and then opened them to help Jillian to her feet. Jonah got out first and reached back to help them, one at a time.

Inside, Marshal Swope was seated behind his desk. A deputy poured a cup of coffee from the dented pot on a small cast-iron stove. Jonah set down the luggage near the door.

"I'm glad you came, Miss Abbott," Swope said to her.

"I had no other choice."

He nodded at Jonah.

"This is Hayden," Jonah told him. "And this is Jillian."

"Howdy do?" the man said. "Grady here is gonna watch over things while I take you to my house."

Hayden raised a hand to shake Jonah's. His slim hand felt so fragile in Jonah's grip. Jillian reached for Meredith, and Meredith knelt to hug the little girl, her skirts pooling around her. Straightening, she smoothed Hayden's hair, pressed her hands together under her chin and watched them go.

Tears streamed down her cheeks. It was the first time Jonah had ever seen her cry, and he didn't like the fist that tightened in his chest at the sight. He didn't care that the deputy was behind them, he took the steps that separated them and pulled her into his arms. Their bulky coats prevented him from feeling the extent of her trembling and the exquisite softness of her curves. He wished for a moment they were still cut off from the world, still alone and able to drop pretenses.

In reality, he was the last man her father would ever approve of for his daughter. And Jonah didn't know anything other than what his years of protecting gold and chasing outlaws had taught him.

"I'll see you back to your hotel, and then I'll talk to Swope about getting this in front of a judge."

"No, you stay." She pulled from his gentle embrace. "The sooner you speak with him, the sooner things will move forward. I'll see myself back to the hotel."

He didn't argue with her. She was perfectly capable of making her own decisions and getting around the city. "I'll let you know when I know something."

"Even the smallest detail," she told him. "I want to know everything."

Once he agreed, she moved to the door and let herself out.

Jonah had never felt empty inside, like he did at that moment. He was a loner, and he liked his life that way. He always had a plan and a ready solution, but he couldn't fix this.

He needed to wrap things up here and get back to his job.

Chapter Twelve

Meredith experienced an unfamiliar melancholy. Deliah sensed her need to talk and sat quietly while her daughter explained every detail of what had happened during their entrapment aboard the Pullman. Meredith left out a few intimate details, but she suspected her mother heard what she didn't say, as well as what she did.

She didn't want to lie down and be unable to sleep, so she kept busy. She sent clothing out to the laundry and ran a few errands. When it grew late, she dressed for supper and fashioned her hair.

Ivan arrived promptly at seven, helped her with her coat and escorted her down to a waiting carriage.

The hotel dining room would have suited her, but Ivan liked the busy restaurants where he was spotted by colleagues who greeted them and columnists who printed their names in the society news. Voters were everywhere.

"I'm disappointed you missed Christmas Eve," he said.

"It wasn't my first choice to be stranded in a blizzard, either."

"I'm just glad you're safe and have returned to us."

A waiter arrived and uncorked a bottle of champagne.

"I want to celebrate." He handed her a glass and raised his.

"To your deliverance from the weather and those outlaws—and to us."

She touched her glass to his and sipped the bubbly beverage. She loved champagne.

She told him what had happened with the children that day.

"They're better off with people who can take care of them." He caught the eye of someone at a nearby table and gave a stiff-armed wave and a broad smile.

Shrimp salads arrived, and she ate half of hers. He had ordered for both of them, without knowing she'd had beef at noon, but she looked at the slices on her plate, thankful it wasn't ham. She cut and enjoyed steamed asparagus with creamy hollandaise sauce.

"I'll have coffee and the lady will take tea," he said to her waiter.

"Actually, I'd like coffee, too."

He gave her a surprised look. "The lady will have coffee, as well."

When they'd finished eating, he reached inside his jacket and withdrew a small black velvet box.

Here it was, she thought frantically. The proposal she'd missed on Christmas Eve was still forthcoming. It was what she'd been looking forward to. Her heart skipped an erratic beat. Why was she dreading what came next?

"Meredith, we've shown that we are compatible in so many ways." He named off their shared liking for theater and books and their similar upbringings. "The next step is marriage. I've spoken with your father and he wants only your happiness. I assured him I could give you that."

Her father had forced her promise that she would marry before the end of this new year. Of course he liked Ivan. They were alike in nearly all ways.

"You know my aspirations for one day attaining the position of governor. I can't promise it would be anytime soon, but already I can offer you a stately home and excellent social standing. You will lack for nothing."

Not to mention her inheritance upon her marriage. That was a tidy sum. Meredith waited, thinking over his words. Was that it then? Had that been his proposal?

She didn't fool herself that there was anything romantic about his proposition. It fell short of her expectations, but she wasn't saying no. If they married they would be able to adopt the Langley kids. "What month were you planning a wedding?"

"June would be convenient and conventional."

"What about sooner?"

He raised his eyebrows. "We can certainly discuss an earlier date."

She rested her napkin beside her plate and finished her champagne. "I need some time to think about it. At least a few days."

He blinked his surprise. Had he expected her to fall at his feet in grateful acceptance? "Yes. Take all the time you need."

She slid her chair back. "I'm tired, Ivan. I'm ready to go back to my hotel."

"I'll pay the check and go get your coat."

"I'll get my coat." She left him standing beside the table and headed for the hat check room.

She missed her fur, but it had been sent for cleaning. The young man found her sapphire blue wool coat and helped her into it. She tipped him and stood just inside the door, waiting for Ivan. Her head swam with questions about what she should do next. Marrying him would provide the solution she needed to keep Hayden and Jillian from a fate in an orphanage.

She'd promised she would do anything required to place them in a loving home. Even if it meant marrying Ivan.

Her father would be pleased.

Ivan joined her and led her outside, where a flurry of snow-flakes greeted them. The falling snow reminded her of the trek she and Jonah had taken into the wilderness when they'd escaped the Pullman.

She pushed that from her mind to focus on the here and now.

They reached her hotel, and Ivan assisted her from the carriage.

"Thank you for the lovely dinner."

"I should see you inside."

She didn't want to invite him and offer him a drink as she'd done before. She wanted time alone. "No need to bother. You've seen me to the hotel entrance. I'll contact you in a day or two."

His expression showed his mystification with her brisk manner. "Good night, Meredith."

"Good night." She hurried inside and dashed up the stairs.

She let herself into her room quietly, so her mother wouldn't hear her from the suite next door. In the dark, she found her way around to undress. She efficiently changed into her nightgown and robe. The layout was familiar. Because her father spent nearly all his time here now, she stayed here nearly as much as at her family home. Her mother still preferred Pennsylvania, so the division had changed things. At last Meredith lit a single lamp in the bedroom and stretched out upon the bed.

A week ago she'd been focused on her arrival and the proposal that awaited her. That proposal had only been delayed, and it hadn't taken place amid the gaiety of the holiday celebration.

Only one thing had changed between leaving Philadelphia and arriving in Denver. Two children had stolen her heart.

Everything else was the same. Her father still expected her to marry soon. Ivan was still her best prospect.

Why did she have so many misgivings now that he'd actually proposed? Why did she have such a burning need to escape his presence? Maybe she suspected he would make up her mind for her. Maybe she feared she was too weak or didn't have a good enough reason to say no. She hated facing those possibilities.

She fluffed the pillows and forced herself to relax. She still hadn't caught up on sleep, and now this dilemma had been added to the list of worries that kept her awake.

In the back of her mind, a glaring flaw waited to be recognized. She didn't want to take it out and examine it. She'd always harbored a secret fear of feeling ordinary. One of her flaws had always been dreaming too big and wishing for the perfect love, the perfect life and then being disappointed that reality wasn't as grand or as satisfying.

She didn't want to cloud her decision with foolishness or unrealistic dreams. She didn't want to be disappointed.

But there it was, a fact. The reality. Ivan hadn't mentioned love.

There was too much at stake to be swayed by emotion.

The lamp burned down. Meredith lay in the dark, listening to the muted sounds of the street below. She slept and dreamed of Hayden and Jillian living in an orphanage, writing her letters and begging her to come for them.

When she woke, she knew what she had to do.

In the days that followed, Meredith talked over marriage to Ivan with her mother.

"Are you certain you want to take on the responsibility of children who already come with a set of life problems? It can be difficult to establish a married life without children—or with your own babies. How does Ivan feel about this?"

Straightaway she sent a note to Ivan, asking him to meet her in the hotel dining room that evening.

Once they were seated, he gave their order to the waiter.

"I prefer the salmon."

She'd interrupted, and he gave her an odd glance.

"I would like salmon for supper," she clarified. "Not the brisket."

Ivan gave the waiter an apologetic shrug. "The lady will have the salmon."

The hotel employee hurried away.

"Have you come to a conclusion?" Ivan asked, once they were alone.

"I have to talk to you first, because actually the final decision will be up to you."

"What do you mean?"

"Well." She straightened her silverware, planning how to approach these things. "First, and this is really just a small thing, but something I feel strongly about, I prefer to order for myself. I'm perfectly capable of selecting food and seeing myself about the city without an escort."

"Surely that will change once you're married and you have a husband to do those things for you."

"No. It won't. Will that be a problem?"

"I suppose not. Not if it makes you happy."

"Good. Now, this other subject is life-changing and I understand it will take some thought."

"You have me curious."

"It's about the Langley children."

"What about them?"

She could tell he'd already forgotten them until she brought them up. "I promised them I'd do everything in my power to give them a good home and a family who wants and loves them."

"The law will work on that, won't they?"

"The law will send them to an orphanage, where they may or may not find them homes. And there's no guarantee they'd be good homes."

"We could offer financial support, could we not?"

"I want to adopt them. Make a family for them and raise them."

He blinked and his mouth opened and shut before he could get something out. "I'm sure there's another family who would take them."

"I *want* them."

"I don't think you know what you'd be letting us in for here."

"I believe I do. I've made them a promise. I intend to keep it."

"You can keep it by visiting them."

"I want to adopt them, Ivan. Have you heard what I'm saying?"

"They are the offspring of a criminal, Meredith."

"That makes no difference to me."

"They're bad seed. They could grow up to murder us in our sleep."

"They are not bad seed." Her hackles rose at his callous remark. "They are smart and funny and so far have survived a difficult childhood. And I want them."

"You sound like a spoiled child."

She pressed her hands flat on the tablecloth and drilled him with a challenging stare. "I'm not a child. I am not making this decision lightly. If you can't agree to allowing us to adopt them once we're married, then I can't marry you."

A muscle in his jaw ticked. He wasn't pleased, but she had to know where they stood. She had her mind made up.

After a moment, he relaxed his posture. "Very well. If you're certain this is what will make you happy, I will agree."

Meredith didn't feel the relief she hoped for. Their meals arrived, and she ate because her body needed the fuel. She didn't taste a thing.

"Can you make a decision now?" Ivan asked.

"I believe so. We will talk tomorrow. Thank you for meeting me." She laid down her napkin and stood.

He started to get to his feet but she raised a hand to stop him. "Please excuse me now."

She left him at the table wearing a perplexed expression.

That night she again dreamed of Hayden and Jillian. She also relived the dream where she and Jonah were together on a warm day. Apple blossoms rained from the sky like huge flakes of feathery light snow.

She was in his arms, waiting for him to kiss her. She leaned into him and strained upward. Yearning.

He released her to turn away. "I can't kiss you."

"Of course you may." She wanted this kiss!

"You're a married woman, Meredith. We won't be seeing each other again."

She woke from that dream with tears slipping from her eyes to the pillow. Was that what she could expect her future to feel like? Would marriage to Ivan be painful because she had denied her heart and her dreams?

Ivan may not have spoken of love, but neither had Jonah.

She sat and wiped her face on her sleeve.

But she hadn't allowed herself to even consider love because she was so afraid of never having it—afraid of letting emotions rule her decisions.

She didn't love Ivan, of that much she was sure. She definitely had feelings for Jonah, and she loved the way he made her feel. She liked everything about him, actually.

Not only was he brave and resourceful, he'd been nothing but kind and generous to Hayden and Jillian. He'd put their safety above his own. He hadn't made promises he couldn't keep, but he'd done everything within his power to protect them and to provide for their future.

She thought of the way his cheeks creased when he smiled. She remembered his low-timbered laugh and the feel of his arms around her.

Meredith presented herself as headstrong and confident—fearless in the face of danger…but she was a coward. At the thought of being rejected or not matching up to his expectations, fear gripped her heart. Her greatest fear was that she didn't deserve more than the way her father treated her—that she was merely window dressing.

She didn't believe Jonah saw her that way, but did she mean anything beyond duty to him?

If she simply went to Ivan and agreed to marry him, she would never know.

If she risked her pride and went to Jonah, she might be hurt, but at least she'd be certain she'd given hope a chance.

She lay awake until the first embers of dawn crept between the drapes, and then she dressed, arranged her hair and left her room.

Jonah woke to the sounds of carriages on the street below. He'd had a message from Swope the night before. Judge Martin would hear their case that day.

He got up, washed and made shaving lather in cold water.

A tap on his door started him.

He set down the razor and picked up his .45 before crossing the room. "Yeah?"

"It's me, Meredith."

He opened the door. "Something wrong?"

She wore a dark green coat with a fur-lined hood. Her eyes were round and he had the impression she was frightened.

"What's the matter?"

"May I come in?"

He stepped back. "Yes, of course."

"I came to speak with you." She glanced at his bare chest, at the white lather on his face. "This isn't a good time."

"It's fine. Let me finish and put on a shirt." He gestured to a straight chair. "Have a seat."

She went directly to it, perched, then stood to remove her coat and hang it on an empty hook. Sitting again, she watched him.

Jonah raised the razor to his cheek and scraped whiskers with a loud rasp. He rinsed the blade and made another swipe.

"Oh, this is ridiculous." She stood and marched up beside him. "I'm sitting over there like we're strangers."

"Pretty unseemly for you to be in my room."

"We've slept together," she pointed out. "Shared more than one rather enjoyable kiss."

"That was a different circumstance." He tried not to let her words affect him so he wouldn't slice off his nose. He finished the job and wiped his face clean with a damp towel.

"So you place all the focus on our situation. In other words you would never have been drawn to me if you'd met me in a different place and time."

"Learned a lot about you that I wouldn't have in another place and time."

"Such as?" she asked.

"You here begging compliments?" He reached for his shirt.

She grabbed him arm and stopped him. "I'm not begging compliments. I'm just pointing out we're not strangers."

"Both of us are better off forgetting about that."

"I can't stop wondering if that's true," she said.

"It's true. You have a plan. Or should I call him a fiancé by now?"

"No. But he has proposed…technically, I suppose."

"What does that mean?"

"He made his points about why it would be wise for us to marry."

He used one hand to disengage her fingers from the other arm and picked up the shirt. "Did you agree?"

The muscles in his chest and shoulders flexed as he shrugged into the shirt.

"I haven't agreed because I can't stop thinking of you. I dream about you. You enter my every thought and conversation. You're stuck in my head. I couldn't move forward with my life until I made certain about something."

"What?"

"That you don't return those feelings for me." She looked into his eyes, and there was no avoiding her directness. "I think I've fallen in love with you. I'm prepared for you to laugh or turn me away. But I'm not prepared to live my life without taking a risk and asking."

The ache in Jonah's chest was unfamiliar. Almost pain, almost pleasure, it grew in intensity as he absorbed her words and the meaning behind them. "I'm not going to laugh, Meredith. And I could never turn you away."

He saw a glimmer of hope in her eyes…a glimmer that sent his heart soaring.

"But we're too different. You're from a prominent family and you're used to things money can buy. My father was a miner. We never had two sticks to rub together. I've spend the past fifteen years traveling, guarding gold shipments, chasing outlaws. I don't have a home."

"Do you want one?"

He changed his stance and looked aside, thinking. "Yeah, I want one."

"Jonah, you know me. At least I believe you do. My life is what's expected of me. I live here, I live there…I travel. I'm courted by a man who wants to be governor one day. No one ever asked me what I wanted."

Silence lapsed between them. A horse clomped by on the street below the window. "What do you want?"

Her expression softened…her chin trembled. "You."

He couldn't bear that she feared his rejection. He stepped close and placed a palm on either side of her lovely open face. "I want you, too. But I don't want you to give up anything. Don't want you to do this now and regret it later. I love everything about you. Your braveness, your honesty…the way you get riled when you think someone's talking down to you. I love your tenderness and your stubborn streak.

"Suspected I loved you already, but when you stood up to me, holdin' that cat, and gave me the ultimatum, I was convinced. You're more woman than I can handle, but I'd sacrifice anything to give it a try."

"Then kiss me."

He obliged her, pouring his feelings into the moment, hoping she felt how much he wanted her.

She leaned back enough to ask, "What about Hayden and Jillian?"

"A judge is hearing us today. We'll ask him to place them in our custody just as soon as we're married. If that's what you want."

"It's exactly what I want." She accepted another kiss. "Where will we live?"

"Anywhere you like. My traveling days are over. I turned in my badge yesterday. I sure don't want to be governor, but I'd like to try my hand at a ranch." He drew back to look at her. "Would you want to be a rancher's wife?"

"Thanks for asking." She spread her hands over his chest. "There's nothing I'd like better."

Jonah took a deep breath. "Maybe that judge will be up to marrying us this afternoon."

Meredith then laughed and kissed him again, until she thought of something. "I'll need a dress!"

It was his turn to laugh.

* * * * *

REQUEST YOUR FREE BOOKS!

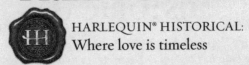

HARLEQUIN® HISTORICAL:
Where love is timeless

2 FREE NOVELS PLUS 2 **FREE GIFTS!**

YES! Please send me 2 FREE Harlequin® Historical novels and my 2 FREE gifts (gifts are worth about $10). After receiving them, if I don't wish to receive any more books, I can return the shipping statement marked "cancel." If I don't cancel, I will receive 6 brand-new novels every month and be billed just $5.19 per book in the U.S. or $5.74 per book in Canada. That's a savings of at least 17% off the cover price! It's quite a bargain! Shipping and handling is just 50¢ per book in the U.S. and 75¢ per book in Canada.* I understand that accepting the 2 free books and gifts places me under no obligation to buy anything. I can always return a shipment and cancel at any time. Even if I never buy another book, the two free books and gifts are mine to keep forever.

246/349 HDN FEQQ

Name _____ (PLEASE PRINT) _____

Address _____ Apt. #

City _____ State/Prov. _____ Zip/Postal Code

Signature (if under 18, a parent or guardian must sign)

Mail to the **Reader Service:**
IN U.S.A.: P.O. Box 1867, Buffalo, NY 14240-1867
IN CANADA: P.O. Box 609, Fort Erie, Ontario L2A 5X3
Not valid for current subscribers to Harlequin Historical books.

Want to try two free books from another line?
Call 1-800-873-8635 or visit www.ReaderService.com.

* Terms and prices subject to change without notice. Prices do not include applicable taxes. Sales tax applicable in N.Y. Canadian residents will be charged applicable taxes. Offer not valid in Quebec. This offer is limited to one order per household. All orders subject to credit approval. Credit or debit balances in a customer's account(s) may be offset by any other outstanding balance owed by or to the customer. Please allow 4 to 6 weeks for delivery. Offer available while quantities last.

Your Privacy—The Reader Service is committed to protecting your privacy. Our Privacy Policy is available online at www.ReaderService.com or upon request from the Reader Service.

We make a portion of our mailing list available to reputable third parties that offer products we believe may interest you. If you prefer that we not exchange your name with third parties, or if you wish to clarify or modify your communication preferences, please visit us at www.ReaderService.com/consumerschoice or write to us at Reader Service Preference Service, P.O. Box 9062, Buffalo, NY 14269. Include your complete name and address.

Harlequin® Special Edition® is thrilled to present a new installment in USA TODAY bestselling author RaeAnne Thayne's reader-favorite miniseries, THE COWBOYS OF COLD CREEK.

Join the excitement as we meet the Bowmans—four siblings who lost their parents but keep family ties alive in Pine Gulch. First up is Trace. Only two things get under this rugged lawman's skin: beautiful women and secrets. And in Rebecca Parsons, he finds both!

Read on for a sneak peek of CHRISTMAS IN COLD CREEK. Available November 2011 from Harlequin® Special Edition®.

On impulse, he unfolded himself from the bar stool. "Need a hand?"

"Thank you! I…" She lifted her gaze from the floor to his jeans and then raised her eyes. When she identified him her hazel eyes turned from grateful to unfriendly and cold, as if he'd somehow thrown the broken glasses at her head.

He also thought he saw a glimmer of panic in those interesting depths, which instantly stirred his curiosity like cream swirling through coffee.

"I've got it, Officer. Thank you." Her voice was several degrees colder than the whirl of sleet outside the windows.

Despite her protests, he knelt down beside her and began to pick up shards of broken glass. "No problem. Those trays can be slippery."

This close, he picked up the scent of her, something fresh and flowery that made him think of a mountain meadow on a July afternoon. She had a soft, lush mouth and for one brief, insane moment, he wanted to push aside that stray lock of hair slipping from her ponytail and taste her. Apparently he needed to spend a lot less time working and a great deal *more* time recreating with the opposite sex if he could have sudden random fantasies about a woman he wasn't even inclined to like, pretty or not.

"I'm Trace Bowman. You must be new in town."

She didn't answer immediately and he could almost see the wheels turning in her head. Why the hesitancy? And why that little hint of unease he could see clouding the edge of her gaze? His presence was obviously making her uncomfortable and Trace couldn't help wondering why.

"Yes. We've been here a few weeks."

"Well, I'm just up the road about four lots, in the white house with the cedar shake roof, if you or your daughter need anything." He smiled at her as he picked up the last shard of glass and set it on her tray.

Definitely a story there, he thought as she hurried away. He just might need to dig a little into her background to find out why someone with fine clothes and nice jewelry, and who so obviously didn't have experience as a waitress, would be here slinging hash at The Gulch. Was she running away from someone? A bad marriage?

So…Rebecca Parsons. Not Becky. An intriguing woman. It had been a long time since one of those had crossed his path here in Pine Gulch.

Trace won't rest until he finds out Rebecca's secret, but will he still have that same attraction to her once he does? Find out in CHRISTMAS IN COLD CREEK. Available November 2011 from Harlequin® Special Edition®.